The wager he had made bothered him.

And his conscience, that he'd thought long since dead, chose that moment to resurrect itself. Realizing the enormity of what he'd done, William was already regretting it. He had taken the wager to seduce a woman he found to be full of goodness, trusting and candid—a combination of wisdom and naïveté that was undeniably lovely. Miss Greenwood was above a mere dalliance. It was madness, and he hated himself with a virulence that nearly knocked the breath out of him.

For the first time in a long time he had met a woman without guile. Her young, innocent face passed before his mind's eye, a face of much seriousness, a ripe, opulent beauty that made his blood stir hotly. Never in his wildest dreams had he imagined anyone like Miss Greenwood. For some peculiar reason that was quite beyond him, it mattered what she thought of him.

* * *

A Scoundrel of Consequence
Harlequin® Historical #248—November 2008

HELEN DICKSON

was born and still lives in south Yorkshire, with her husband on a busy arable farm, where she combines writing with keeping a chaotic farmhouse. An incurable romantic, she writes for pleasure, owing much of her inspiration to the beauty of the surrounding countryside. She enjoys reading and music. History has always captivated her, and she likes travel and visiting ancient buildings.

A Scoundrel of Consequence

HELEN DICKSON

TORONTO • NEW YORK • LONDON
AMSTERDAM • PARIS • SYDNEY • HAMBURG
STOCKHOLM • ATHENS • TOKYO • MILAN • MADRID
PRAGUE • WARSAW • BUDAPEST • AUCKLAND

ISBN-13: 978-0-373-30557-5
ISBN-10:   0-373-30557-5

A SCOUNDREL OF CONSEQUENCE

Available from Harlequin® Historical and
HELEN DICKSON

Chapter One

1813

Thundering down the length of track in a deserted Green Park as dawn was breaking filled William Lampard with exhilaration. A stiff breeze was rolling away the early morning mist and the park stretched out in shades of green and brown and grey. Stabs of sunlight between the clouds edged the colours in bright gilding, and birds were waking in the foliage. For those few minutes as he raced along, there was just him and his horse—no duties, no expectations, just sheer abandon and forgetfulness of all the obligations that awaited him.

Slowing his horse to a more sedate trot, he left the track and directed it beneath some sheltering trees, thinking how good it felt to be back in London after three years as a soldier fighting the war in Spain. Suddenly, the serenity of the early summer morning was shattered by the explosion of a gunshot. A force hit him in the shoulder and the world hurtled in a slow tumble as he toppled out of the saddle on to the dew-soaked grass, where he sank into a black hole and everything ceased to exist.

Cassandra was travelling to her place of work earlier than usual and taking a short cut through the park when she heard the shot. Seeing a horse and rider leave the shelter of the trees and ride as if the devil himself was after him, she urged Clem to drive the carriage into the trees to investigate. On seeing the wounded man she immediately climbed out, believing he had been shot in a duel, since Green Park was often a venue for those sinister appointments in the dawn mist. Coming to her side, Clem bent and rolled the limp form over, nodding his head in relief as he took in the slow, shallow breathing.

'He isn't dead, thank the Lord.'

When sanity returned to William, somewhat hazily, it was to find a young woman in a dark grey coat kneeling beside him, and a short, stout man holding his frightened horse. There was a dull throbbing in his head, and an ache in his shoulder that pulsed in unison with it.

Cassandra gazed down into two crystal-clear orbs. There was a vibrant life and an intensity in those eyes, dark, brilliant blue, like the sea in a summer storm that no one could deny. 'I'm happy to see you are still with us,' the woman said in a soft, well-bred voice. She held her head gracefully, the brim of her bonnet casting a light shadow over her face. 'You have been shot. Let's hope your wound is not serious.'

William returned her smile with difficulty and tried to allay her fears by pushing himself up against a tree. He winced as pain—red hot and piercing—shot through his shoulder, then closed his eyes and rested his head back. Without more ado the woman briskly unfastened his bloodsoaked jacket, removed his crisp white cravat and opened his shirt, her expression schooled to a nun-like impassivity as she examined his wound. William's gaze flickered to the slender fingers pressing a wad of cloth against the torn flesh to staunch the flow of blood.

'You've done this before, I can see that,' he remarked, his voice deep and strong.

'I have, but usually my patients haven't been shot and they are much smaller than you.'

As she worked, Cassandra noted that the wounded man's clothes were of expensive elegance that could only have come from one of the *ton*'s foremost tailors. Having lost his hat in the fall, his hair, thick and dark brown, fell in disarray about his head, shading his wide brow and brushing his collar. About thirty years of age, his face was handsome, recklessly so, lean and hard. His nose was straight, his jaw uncompromisingly square. He had fine dark brows that curved neatly, and a firm but almost sensuous mouth. Everything about him was elegantly aristocratic, exuding power and a sense of force.

When the wad was secure she rested back on her heels and met his gaze. 'There. I think you'll live. Not much damage done—more to your pride I'd say. When will you gentlemen learn to settle your quarrels in a more civilised manner? Duelling is certainly not the answer.' Without giving William a chance to utter a reply in his defence, she got to her feet. 'Now come along. Try to stand. I think a doctor should take a look at that shoulder.'

'There's no need for that. If you'll get your man to bring my horse, I'll be on my way.'

'The bullet's still in there. It will have to be extracted and the wound dressed properly.' William uttered a protest, but it emerged as little more than a croak and when he tried to move, his limbs would not obey. Cassandra looked at him crossly. 'Please don't argue. You are in no position to object.' She turned to Clem. 'Come and help Mr…'

'Captain. I am Captain William Lampard,' he provided with difficulty as a fresh wave of pain swept through him.

'Oh!'

William saw an odd, awed expression cross her face as she scrutinised him, and in her eyes a momentary flash of a deeply rooted dislike. 'You've heard of me?'

'Yes, your name is familiar to me—although you are better known as Lord Lampard, the Earl of Carlow.'

Cassandra had heard all about Captain Lampard. He was

an arrogant lord who thought he could do as he pleased with whomever he pleased. For years, gossip had linked him with every beautiful female in London. His scandals were infamous. Whenever he was on respites from his military duties he was the talk of the town, and any sensible young woman mindful of her reputation kept well out of his way. The same could be said of his young cousin, Edward Lampard, who she had already decided possessed the same traits—for hadn't he tried to compromise her own sister, and the silly girl would have let him if she could have had her way?

'You've recently returned from foreign parts, I believe.' Her expression did not alter, but something in her eyes stirred and hardened and she compressed her lips.

'Spain.'

'Yes, well, I'd have thought you would have had enough of fighting in the Peninsula,' she remarked haughtily.

William had to stifle the urge to smile at her tart reprimand. 'I have, more than enough. By your reaction to my identity, I strongly suspect my reputation has gone before me, but let me tell you that it is much a matter of gossip and wishful dreaming.'

'If you say so, Captain Lampard, but it really is none of my business.'

'Would you think it forward of me if I were to ask you your name?'

'Not at all. I am Cassandra Greenwood.'

'Miss Greenwood, I am most pleased to meet you, and I'm thankful you came along when you did.'

Cassandra slowly arched a brow and her smile was bland. 'So you should be. Now come along and I'll get Dr Brookes to take a look at you.'

'Dr Brookes?'

'He's a doctor at St Bartholomew's Hospital. He comes to help out when I need him at the institute. I'm expecting him first thing, which is why you find me out and about so early.

Don't worry. I have every faith in his ability as a doctor. He'll soon have you fixed up.'

Observing the stubborn thrust of her chin and the glint of determination in her eye, William raised a brow in amusement. 'I see you have no intention of relenting.'

'Quite right, sir. When Dr Brookes has finished with you, Clem will take you home to Grosvenor Square in the carriage.'

William gave her a quizzical look. 'You know where I live?'

'Oh, yes, Captain Lampard, I do know that much about you—and some more,' she uttered softly, which brought a puzzled frown to William's brow, 'but we won't go into that just now. It would be inadvisable for you to ride after sustaining a wound that rendered you unconscious. There is every possibility that you would fall off your horse and incur a more severe injury, which would incapacitate you for some time.'

'Perish the thought,' William said wryly.

'Quite,' Cassandra replied. 'After awaiting your return from Spain for so long, no doubt the entire female population in London would go into a decline. Now come along. See if you can stand.' She would have liked nothing more than to help him on to his horse and send him on his way, but that would be a cowardly thing to do simply because he had a poor reputation.

Impressed by her efficiency and naturally authoritative tone, William tried to get up, but fell back as a fresh haziness swept over him.

Without more ado, Clem took the wounded man's arm over his broad shoulders and hoisted him unceremoniously into the carriage. After securing the Captain's horse to the back, he set off towards Soho, where they drew up outside a grim-looking building among streets where poverty and disease ran side by side. A score or more of undernourished children dressed in rags, their legs bowed and eyes enormous in pinched faces, were hanging about. William was helped out of the carriage and Clem again took his arm. With Cassandra leading the way, Clem half-carried the wounded man inside and into a room, where he lowered him on to a narrow bed, obviously not made for a man as tall as the Captain.

Taking deep breaths in an attempt to remain conscious, William was aware of dim forms moving about the room. Turning his head on the pillow, he saw a child lying in the bed next to him. Whimpering in his sleep and no more than seven years old, his stick-thin legs were poking out from beneath a blanket. Both his feet were bandaged. His face was an unhealthy grey, his skin ingrained with dirt, and his knees scraped raw.

Dragging his gaze away from the pitiful sight of the child, he took stock of the room, which looked like a small infirmary. It was quite large with five bunks and sparse, stark furnishings. With small windows and a stone-flagged floor, it was scrubbed clean. There was a stone sink in which a trim, white-aproned young woman was washing utensils and a fire burned in the hearth. The air was tinged with the aroma of food cooking—not unappetising—plain, mutton stew, he guessed. Suddenly a cup was pressed to his lips.

'Drink,' Miss Greenwood commanded.

Doing as he was told, William gulped the water down gratefully, letting his head fall back on the pillow when replete. 'Where in damnation am I?' he breathed, his curiosity aroused.

'Please don't swear,' Cassandra chided, having discarded her outdoor clothes and fastened an apron about her slender waist. 'I'll have no obscene language spoken here. You are not in damnation, but a small infirmary in a house that is a place of refuge for destitute children.'

William's lips twitched with a suppressed smile. 'I stand rebuked. I did not mean to be disrespectful.'

'Yes—well, keep a close rein on your tongue, Captain Lampard, lest the children overhear—although sadly some of them use a few choice words themselves and might be able to teach even you a thing or two. Ah, here is Dr Brookes.' She stood back to allow a good-looking man in his mid-forties enough room to make his examination.

'Good day, Captain Lampard.' Dr Brookes proceeded brusquely and cheerily as was his custom. 'It's not every day I get a distinguished patient to attend—especially one who's been shot.'

Cassandra brought a tray of salves and implements, placing them on a small table at the side of the bed.

Dr Brookes wrinkled his nose as he glanced at the injury. 'That looks to be a nasty wound. Right, we'd better get to work before you bleed to death. I don't think the shot's too far in so it shouldn't be especially difficult getting it out. There'll be a bit of digging around to do though. Can you stand it?'

'Captain Lampard has recently returned from the war in the Peninsula, Dr Brookes,' Cassandra provided. 'I'm sure he's had to endure worse.'

'Spain, eh?' Dr Brookes remarked, impressed. 'Would have gone myself—had I been years younger.'

'Miss Greenwood speaks the truth. I have seen and endured many things during the war, but this is the first time I've been shot—so get on with it, Dr Brookes.' William looked at the young woman who had taken a stance beside him, a wicked twinkle in his bold, appraising eyes. 'Are you to stay and hold my hand, Miss Greenwood?'

'No,' she replied primly. 'I shall stay to assist Dr Brookes.'

'Pity. Here is my last scrap of dignity. Enjoy it while you can, but I would advise you to step back, Miss Greenwood,' he said, eyeing with trepidation the probe Dr Brookes was holding. 'My temper is about to take a decided turn for the worse.'

Cassandra spoke no word, but stood aside while Dr Brookes began his work.

William gritted his teeth against the white shards of pain that were shooting through his shoulder as Dr Brookes probed the wound. Mercifully, within a matter of minutes the shot was located and removed.

'There—all done,' Dr Brookes said with a satisfied smile,

showing his patient the round ball. 'The wound's clean so it should heal nicely—though you should keep it rested for a time.'

'Thank you for all that you've done. You won't go unrewarded, I shall see to that.'

Dr Brookes nodded, and there was a gleam in his eye when he glanced at Cassandra. 'A small donation to the institute wouldn't go amiss, is that not so, Cassandra? Have your own physician keep an eye on the wound—and perhaps take some laudanum if the pain becomes severe. Now excuse me if I leave you in Miss Greenwood's capable hands. I must fly—patients to see at the hospital.' Hesitating by the young boy's bed as he began to mumble and mutter, to twist and turn, he placed a hand to the child's forehead. Shaking his head, he turned to go. 'I'll be in tomorrow to take another look the boy.' He paused a moment longer before enquiring haltingly, 'Will—your mother be at the institute?'

Cassandra lowered her head to hide a knowing smile. She had long suspected that it was her mother, as well as his concern for the children, that drew Dr Brookes to the institute. 'Yes, she should be—around midday, I think.'

Looking pleased, Dr Brookes nodded and hurried out.

Cassandra turned back to Captain Lampard to dress his wound, amazed that he had endured the whole procedure without a murmur.

'What happened to the boy?' William asked. 'How did he come to be in that state?'

'That's Archie,' she answered, her expression softening when her gaze rested on the child's face. 'His mother sold him to a sweep for a few shillings, poor mite.'

'How old is he?'

'Six years. Climbing boys don't stand a chance, any of them. So many die of consumption and they are never washed except by the rain. No one knows the cruelty that they undergo. Bullied and beaten by their masters, they rub their poor elbows and knees raw climbing the dark flues. Their flesh must be hardened. This is done by rubbing it with the strongest brine. But often their skin—if they survive—doesn't harden for years.'

'And Archie's feet?'

'Burnt by the fires—which aren't always completely out.'

If William was disturbed by this, apart from a tightening of his features he made no comment. Though her voice was without expression, before Miss Greenwood turned her face away, he was startled to see tears in her eyes mingled with compassion for the child.

'He doesn't complain, but I know he's in constant pain. It is my intention to find him a situation—but it will be weeks before he is fully recovered. One thing is for certain, it will not be with the sweeps—although it will be hard to place him. Your coat is ruined, I'm afraid,' Cassandra said, picking it up and placing it at the bottom of the bed with his equally ruined shirt.

'I'll get another.'

'Yes, I suppose you will,' she said, smiling then and forcing her eyes from the bronzed, dark, fur-matted muscular chest. The shoulder muscles jerked as she proceeded to dress his wound. This close he smelled of shaving soap and sandalwood. Overwhelmed by every scandalous tale she had ever heard about him, she willed herself to ignore the strength of the lean, hard body stretched out on the bed beneath her, to complete her task and send him on his way.

William caught his breath at her unexpected glowing smile and started in amazement when he felt a peculiar, inner tingle from her touch. Light fell on her face only inches away from his own. She really was the most glorious creature, even in her sombre dark grey dress buttoned up to her throat. Her softly scented skin glowed like silk, and her mouth was a soft coral pink. Her hair was honey gold, pulled up to a chignon, but from which endearing rebellious tendrils escaped. Her blue-green eyes gleamed as she smiled.

'Do you work here all the time?' he asked.

'No, not all the time. I do have a life away from here.'

'I'm glad to hear it. It would be a crime for you to spend your entire life in this dreary place. There are better areas of London to focus your energies on. I would have thought young ladies could find more interesting and exciting ways of passing their time.'

Giving her a long, leisurely look, there was a twist of humour around his attractively moulded lips. The smile building about his mouth softened the hardness of his jaw and made him appear in that moment the most handsome man in the world to Cassandra. Then, suddenly, his direct, masculine assurance disconcerted her. She was acutely conscious of his close proximity to her and she felt a mad, unfamiliar rush of blood singing through her veins.

Instantly she felt resentful towards him. He had made too much of an impact on her and she was afraid that if he looked at her much longer he would read her thoughts with those brilliant clever eyes of his—which he did when her cheeks pinked, bringing a darkening to his eyes and an amused, satisfied smile to his lips.

'I am sure you're right, Captain Lampard, but not nearly as rewarding or as worthwhile. What I do here is more than a pastime for me and I am content with the way things are. The institute was brought into being by my father with the intention of providing aid and provision for destitute children—a place of Christian charity. He died three years ago. Like Dr Brookes, he was a surgeon at St Bartholomew's hospital. It's quiet just now, but it gets busier towards supper time. My mother is keen to carry on what my father began and devotes many hours to the institute. We also have volunteers who come to help for what they can do, not for what they can get. The institute really couldn't manage without them—or the benefactors, who help fund it. We feed the children, provide them with articles of clothing, which are donated to us, and if they are sick or injured we patch them up as best we can.'

'Even though some of them are criminals, uncivilised and riddled with vermin and diseases they might pass on to you?' William asked, raising himself up so she could pass the bandage over his shoulder.

'Yes, and since that is exactly the kind of children who come here, we have all the more reason to try and make their young lives more bearable. The place might not look much, but times are hard just now. However, we do have plans and raise funds in many ways to enable us to find larger premises and hopefully found an orphanage.'

'And are you successful in your fund raising?'

'Sometimes. You see, I make it my business to know the names of wealthy people I can approach for monetary contributions.' She smiled when she saw his eyes register surprise. 'You must think me terribly mercenary to go around trying to extract money from people like I do, but it's because I care for the children.'

'You are so hungry for their money?'

'Oh, yes—and I am not ashamed to say so.'

'Just remember that greed is a terrible thing, Miss Greenwood.'

Cassandra started at his statement, her gaze darting to his enigmatic dark blue eyes. 'Please don't look at me like that, Captain Lampard. I'm not greedy—at least not for myself. Only for the children. Money means nothing to me, but you have to agree that it is a useful commodity, and a few pennies can be the means of life or death to a starving child.'

'Maybe so, but for a young lady to tout for money by herself is highly irregular I would have thought. It is also a dangerous game you play.'

'Nothing is only a game, Captain Lampard.' The sparkle was gone, leaving only a frosted blue in Cassandra Greenwood's eyes. 'To many people, the notion of becoming allied with a woman in such a way is so extraordinary as to be laugh-able—and distasteful when they realise I am indeed serious.'

'Do you not think you should take what God sends you and be thankful?'

His words were so glib and offhand that Cassandra gave him a rueful stare. 'Try telling that to the children. You look surprised by what I do, Captain.'

'Surprised, yes—and appalled to a certain extent. You are an attractive young woman, and why your family has allowed you to become involved in this unusual and somewhat dangerous enterprise, I cannot imagine.'

'My work at the institute is often hard and intense and keeps me away from home for long periods, but I take pride in what my father began and in my work and what I achieve—that the children who come here go away with full bellies and, if they're lucky, a pair of boots, even though I know that in all probability they will sell them for a few pennies when they are back on the streets. A great many of them are orphans, others are unwanted, having been turned out by parents who have too many mouths to feed already, and others have been sold to chimneysweeps and the like for a few shillings. The children who come to us have nothing—and very little hope. Someone has to watch over them.'

'And you think you can make a difference to their lives?'

'A few of them, yes.'

'There are always the workhouses—and the charity schools—and the hospital for those who are injured.'

'The workhouses are appalling places, but better than living on the streets, I do agree, but they don't house all the children and the hospitals exclude children under the age of seven—except for those who require amputations.' Her lips curved in a wry smile. 'How sad is that? Are you aware that out of all the people in London who die, almost half of them are children?'

'No, I was not aware of that,' William replied stiffly, never having thought of it since this was the first time he'd had contact with anything to do with destitute children. He scowled. Cassandra Greenwood had an irritating tendency to prick his conscience and to make him feel inadequate in some way, which he was beginning to find most unpleasant.

Having finished her task, Cassandra looked him straight in the eye. 'I'm not proud, sir, just determined to carry out what my father started, and if you can find fault with that then I am sorry for you.'

'No, Miss Greenwood, I can find no fault with that. You speak brave words. Such sentiments are highly commendable and admirable to say the least.' Swinging his long legs on to the floor and standing up, he was relieved that the last vestiges of haziness had left his mind.

Cassandra's breath caught in her throat, for the lean frame unfolded until the man stood a full head and shoulders taller than herself. Assisting him into his ruined jacket, collecting the soiled dressing and instruments Dr Brookes had used, she moved away from him.

As she busied herself with the task at hand, William watched her, his eyes roving approvingly over her lithe figure, stopping at the swelling breasts beneath the restricting fabric, then straying back to the shock of honey-gold hair. His fingers ached to release it from its strictures, to run them through the luxuriant softness and kiss the shaded hollow in her throat where a small brooch was pinned to the neck of her dress. He studied her stance and the language of her slender form. Despite his experience with the opposite sex, he wasn't familiar with women of her class. He'd made a point not to be, but this one made him curious.

All of a sudden warning bells sounded in his mind with such unexpected force that he knew he had to get out of that place, to dispel the unwelcome, unpleasant thoughts as he tried to understand what it was that made an attractive woman like Cassandra Greenwood want to waste her life in this sorry establishment for underprivileged children.

He was a shrewd and rational man, a man of breeding and style who understood his motivations and knew his goals. He prided himself on his good sense not to be swayed by emotion or flights of fancy, so it came as a shock that he wanted to know more about Miss Greenwood—and that was the moment he realised what was happening. He—the ruthless and heartless Lord William Lampard, Earl of Carlow in Hertfordshire, with a distinguished army career, who kept London alive with gossip and scandal when he was in town—was afraid of the effect that this place and Cassandra Greenwood was having on him.

'Tell me, is there no board of trustees you are answerable to?'

Cassandra stopped what she was doing and turned her blue-green eyes on his with a candid air. 'Trustees? Oh, yes. There are four on the board—Dr Brooks and a colleague of his at St Bartholomew's, my mother and me.'

'I see. I was beginning to think you were your own woman, Miss Greenwood.'

'I am, in every other way, answerable to no one. Very much so.'

'And there is no prospective husband in the offing?'

'No. I like my freedom and independence—which is something a husband isn't likely to give me.'

'That depends on the husband. No doubt, given time, things will change.'

When Cassandra met his gaze she experienced a shock of something between recognition and a kind of thrilling fear. Those eyes, deep blue and narrowed by a knowing, intrusive smile, seemed to look right past her face and into her self. For that split second she felt completely exposed and vulnerable—traits unfamiliar to her, traits she did not like.

'Not if I have my way, Captain Lampard. And I always do.'

'I can see that. However, I am not here because I want to be convinced of the merits of children's charities. I am here because I was shot and in no condition to object—although I do thank you for all you and Dr Brookes have done.'

'Don't you like children, Captain Lampard?' she asked suddenly.

'It's not a case of not liking them. I've never had anything to do with them.'

William became thoughtful and a heavy frown creased his brow. It was an expression those who knew him well would recognise, for it indicated his interest. His curiosity was aroused. Cassandra Greenwood was a woman who lived and breathed her cause and he did not know how he knew, but he knew he was looking at that rare individual who would tell the whole world to go to blazes should it get in her way.

As the initial shock of his assault by an unknown assailant began to wear off, an instinct, a built-in awareness that thrived inside the soldier in him and was essential if one was to survive, told him that here was the dedication, ambition, determination and a sense of purpose of one who meant to succeed. There was an air about her, in the set of her chin and the firmness of her lips, a resolve so obstinate and positive that he found it difficult to restrain himself from showing the same enthusiasm as she did.

Donning his hat, he turned from her, his gaze resting for a brief moment on the child. He seemed to hesitate before coming to a decision. Looking back at her, he said, 'The boy—Archie. When he is recovered, send him to my house in Grosvenor Square. I'll have a word with Thomas, my head groom. If the lad likes horses, Thomas might very well set him on in the stables. I'm sure we can find him something to do that will keep him off the streets. I shall also make sure you are repaid for your kindness.'

'Thank you,' she said, her expression registering surprise as he moved towards the door. 'It would be much appreciated,'—but he must not have heard her words, for he did not turn to look at her again. Unable to believe he had offered to provide Archie with work and a home, she stood staring at the door through which he had disappeared for several moments.

Just when she was beginning to believe that every scandalous thing she had heard about him was true, he had to do something nice.

It would appear Captain Lampard had hidden depths. By offering to provide Archie with work and a home, he had exposed one redeeming feature to her. Was it possible that the renowned rake had returned to England a reformed character?

As William sat in Miss Greenwood's carriage taking him to Grosvenor Square, his horse tethered to the back, he tried to define what had been so attractive about her. She certainly wasn't plain. Her real physical confidence was sensual and there had been an assured innocent vanity in her smile. He smiled to himself, remembering it, but then a more pressing matter entered his thoughts and he became preoccupied with discovering the identity of whoever it was who had tried to end his life. A cold, hard core of fury was growing inside him, shattering every other emotion he'd ever felt, leaving him incapable of feeling anything other than the need to find the person responsible.

Cassandra, her mother and her eighteen-year-old sister Emma lived in a house of modest proportions in Kensington compared with Aunt Elizabeth's grand residence in Mayfair. Cassandra's parents had been well matched in character, but they came from different backgrounds. The Greenwood family belonged to the entrepreneurial and professional classes. Her mother was of the landed gentry with aristocratic connections. What Cassandra's parents did have in common was that they came from the poorer branches of their respective families. Neither of them had a private fortune.

Deeply concerned with the sorry plight of the City's destitute children, James Greenwood had opened the small institute in Soho. Since his death three years earlier, Cassandra and her mother had struggled to keep it open. They were constantly short of funds. Dr Brookes, who had been Dr Greenwood's close friend and associate, generously gave up his time to tend the seriously ill or injured children who came to them, and raised funds on their behalf.

Bereft after the death of her beloved husband, Harriet Greenwood, not content to lead a quiet life, had become involved in the running of the institute and was willing to allow her eldest daughter to work alongside her, even though twenty-year-old Cassandra's break from convention shocked friends and acquaintances and brought severe disparagement. But Cassandra, undeterred, refused to allow a lot of small-minded, ignorant people to take from her all that she and her mother were trying to accomplish.

Harriet's cousin Lady Elizabeth Monkton, a widow, childless and a wealthy and extremely popular socialite, had taken both girls under her wing when James had died and done her utmost to guide them in the way she thought was best for them. Eager to give them each a Season, she had been disappointed when Cassandra, who had her own ideas and quietly despised the useless frivolity of the social scene, had declined her offer—although she was not opposed to using Lady Elizabeth's position to her advantage. In her own subtle and charming way, Cassandra was successful at coaxing money out of the well-to-do at the balls and parties she attended.

Tonight, Aunt Elizabeth—as she liked to be known to Harriet's girls—was to give a ball to mark her fiftieth birthday. Cassandra was to attend and, as a special concession, Emma, too, despite not having made her curtsy. They were at Monkton House, getting ready for the ball, and Emma was irritatingly out of sorts—one of the reasons being that she had earlier received a severe scolding from her mother for going riding in the rain and arriving back at the house soaked to the skin.

'It isn't fair,' Emma wailed, pouting petulantly, bemoaning the fact that Edward Lampard, the young man she was enamoured with, would not be at the ball. Ever since he had left London three weeks ago she had been restive and impatient for him to return. Flopping into a chair beside her sister seated at the dressing table as she put the finishing touches to her *toilette,* she scowled her displeasure.

'Please stop it, Emma. No good can come of your seeing that particular gentleman and I'm tired of discussing it. I've told you before that young man is a scoundrel in the making and will not be content until he's compromised you so completely that your reputation will be beyond redemption. Then no gentleman of worth will want you,' she finished severely.

Emma was stricken as she stared at the sister she loved and admired more than anyone else, whose strength and force of character were so much greater than her own. 'Scoundrel?' she protested heatedly, two high spots of colour burning on her cheeks. 'How can you possibly know that?'

'Because he happens to be the cousin of that renowned rake Captain William Lampard—a man with a string of broken hearts and shattered marital aspirations that would make any level-headed young woman steer well clear of him.'

'That's an awful thing to say, Cassy,' Emma retorted indignantly. 'Just because his cousin's a renowned libertine of the first order does not mean to say that Edward will follow suit. He is a decent, upright and honourable man—a gentleman.' There was a look of acute dismay in her eyes. She was bewildered by pain and confusion—anxious for Cassandra's approval and agonisingly aware that she did not understand her sister's antagonistic behaviour. 'He loves me and values what I think and feel—and raises me above all other considerations.'

'Well, with all these attributes he must be quite unique,' Cassandra said drily, unconvinced by her sister's defence of Edward Lampard. 'But he should not be saying these things to you, and to respond to a gentleman's attentions before his intentions are known is to risk the ridicule of others. I do wish you would behave with more propriety, Emma.'

'Really, Cassy, considering your limited experience, I need no instructions from you on how to behave in society.'

'It's not society that concerns me and you know it. I worry that this preoccupation you have with Edward Lampard will frighten away all the eligible young men before you come out—which Aunt Elizabeth seems set upon—although why she allows you to go out in company so much when you have not yet made your curtsy is quite beyond me.'

Emma stared at her. Their ability to communicate was truly broken down. 'Really, Cassy, what man could be more eligible than Edward?'

'I'm only trying to warn you of the dangers of you showing favour to any one man before your début, and you must not allow yourself to be alone with him.'

'Kindly keep your warnings to yourself. I am quite capable of taking care of myself.'

'How do you know he isn't merely toying with you, Emma?'

'Because he cares for me. Anyone would think you're jealous because you've failed to arouse any man's passions yourself,' Emma uttered petulantly.

'Passions? My dear Emma, I sincerely hope Edward Lampard keeps his passions under control when he is with you.'

'Cassy, will you please listen to me? I am in love. Really in love.'

'You think you are. Whatever the sentiments that young man has created, I have no doubt that in time the true nature of his character will be revealed. Now please go and get ready before Aunt Elizabeth comes looking for us.'

'You go to the ball, I don't feel like it,' Emma snapped petulantly.

Cassandra sighed and looked at her sister. Bold, open and loving, full of confidence and life, her green eyes set off by the lustrous gold of her hair, her nose pert and cute and her lips soft and full, at just eighteen years of age Emma had attended few social events. As a rule she looked forward to them and enjoyed them, always wearing her best gown and preening in front of the mirror like a bird of paradise determined on a grand display. Cassandra had thought tonight would be no exception, but she was wrong.

Emma had known Sir Edward Lampard for several weeks, meeting him at the odd soirée and the theatre, visiting neighbouring friends with Aunt Elizabeth in the mornings, and on outings in the park. Cassandra was not unaware that friendship of a certain kind was beginning to grow between them. At first she had considered it to be nothing more than youthful attraction, but Mr Lampard was persistent and always sought Emma's company, which, fearing he was intent on compromising her vulnerable and naïve sister, gave Cassandra cause for concern—particularly since he was closely related to the notorious scoundrel Captain Lampard—the man who had promised her a donation for the institute and had apparently reneged on his word. Now the thought of Emma having anything to do with that family did not sit easy.

'You're mean, Cassy.' Emma pouted. 'I don't know why you always have to say hateful things about Edward. You're spiteful.'

'No, I'm not. I'm just being realistic.'

Emma sulked for a moment longer, but, realising a fine pout would not sway her sister, she changed her tactics. 'Very well, I'll go and get ready. Perhaps his cousin, Captain Lampard, will tell me when Edward is to return.'

Cassandra swung round. 'Captain Lampard? He's coming here tonight?'

'I believe so. I know Aunt Elizabeth invited him.' Emma got up and, gathering up her skirts, flounced to the door. Ignoring her sister's perplexed frown, she rushed on. 'As well as being a magnificent combat officer, a man without fear and already a veteran of at least two campaigns— which Edward proudly told me about—he's extremely handsome, too, by all accounts. I've never seen him myself, but all the ladies positively drool over him.' She was the epitome of angelic goodness now her tirade was spent. With a delicious giggle she kicked the hem of her gown and opened the door.

'Emma, wait.' Getting up, Cassandra crossed to her sister. 'I want to be at the institute early tomorrow, so I don't intend being late to bed. I don't think you should be late, either.'

'I won't be, and I know you need your rest to pander to all those uncivilised children and to scrub the floors.' Perceiving that her thrust had hit its mark, Emma turned away.

Bruised by Emma's manner, the thoughtless insults cutting her to the quick, Cassandra drew a long breath, striving to get control of her temper. When she spoke again she was more composed and put her hand on her sister's arm.

'Please don't be angry, Emma. I'm sorry if I sounded harsh. Edward is handsome enough, I suppose, and I can understand why you are attracted to him. Such infatuations are common, but you are just eighteen and he is what—nineteen? You are an attractive and intelligent girl. Have you absolutely no idea of the harm this will do to your reputation? The way you have behaved with Edward Lampard is not a desirable mode of behaviour, and I know how much it upsets Mama.'

Cassandra's mention of their beloved mama made Emma look contrite. Their mother was a hard-working woman who doted on her daughters. 'I don't mean to upset her, truly. I know she desires me to be more like you—to take an interest in the institute that was so dear to Papa's heart—but I can't. It's just not in my nature.'

'I know, Emma, and it doesn't matter. I enjoy what I do; if I didn't, I couldn't do it, so I don't blame you. Only I do wish you'd listen to me when I attempt to advise you. I do have your best interests at heart, you know. Now go and get ready.'

On a sigh she watched Emma go out. She could only hope that, beneath her indignation, Emma had sufficient common sense to heed her words.

* * *

Escorted by Aunt Elizabeth, when Cassandra and Emma entered the large, mirrored ballroom with French windows leading out on to balconies, it was already congested with over two hundred of the *ton*'s most illustrious and sophisticated personages. Dancing was in progress, with ladies dipping and swaying, talking and laughing with their partners. Around the room were enormous bouquets of flowers and the immense chandeliers, dripping with sparkling crystals, reflected the dazzling kaleidoscope of colourful gowns and jewels.

Lady Monkton, a widow of ten years and one of society's most respected and influential ladies, was standing behind her charges like a protective mother hen, her chest puffed out, her back ramrod straight, her eyes proudly resting on her lovely girls.

There was little opportunity for the chaperons to relax and enjoy themselves at a ball, for they felt compelled to keep an eye on their charges at all times—to know who they were dancing with, and who they were dancing with too often.

Cassandra paused to casually overlook the throng to see who was present. Full purses would be plentiful. She never openly asked anyone for money—that would never do—but there were several here who were sympathetic to her cause and subscribed on a regular basis. She observed that Lord and Lady Ross were present. They were extremely wealthy, and Lady Faversham's husband was an influential London property owner who had frequently made generous donations to the institute in the past. Cassandra glanced at Emma when she gasped.

'Oh, look, Cassandra,' she remarked excitedly. 'It's Edward—over there. I had no idea he was back in London—and see, he's coming this way.'

Dismayed, Cassandra saw that the young man in question was indeed wending his way towards them, his blond hair falling attractively over his forehead and a smile on his lips.

She saw the pleasure that lit up his youthful face, warming him with astonishing intensity.

She sighed, defeated. 'So he is, Emma. I do so hope he is not going to be persistent and that you do not forget how to behave—and it is undignified, as well as unattractive, to stand with one's mouth open,' she chided, leaving her sister in Aunt Elizabeth's charge and strolling to the edge of the crowded dance floor to accost and charm anyone she thought would benefit her cause.

Alluring, fiery, and with an unshakeable sense of her own worth, Cassandra was bright and unpredictable—often playful and engaging, just as often frostily aloof. She drew men to her side almost without benefit of conscious effort. But those who fell victim to her potent magnetism soon learned to their cost that the fascinating Miss Cassandra Greenwood, while accepting their masculine admiration as both her right and her pleasure, kept herself beyond their reach.

An uncertain future loomed ahead of her, this she knew, but she was going to meet it squarely in the eye. She would not be looked over like ripe fruit on a costermonger's stall. There would be no inept youth with groping hands and wet kisses for her but a man, someone to love her with all the masculine authority at his command—experienced, bold and dashing— like Captain Lampard perhaps? She was shocked and instantly ashamed of the way her mind was working. Captain Lampard was totally unsuitable in every way and it was a ridiculous thought which she dismissed at once—but she could not deny it.

Chapter Two

Since his return to London and conscious that someone was trying to kill him—the reason why still eluded him—William had lost interest in society events. When the invitation to Lady Monkton's birthday ball had arrived he'd given it a cursory glance and was tempted to instruct his secretary to send a polite refusal, despite any social occasion at Monkton House reputed as being exceptional. It was Edward, having returned to London from visiting friends in the country, who'd persuaded him to attend. In fact, young Edward seemed to be in an exuberant mood of late and William was curious as to the reason for it—a young lady, perhaps?

Arriving at Monkton House, he entered the ballroom, impatient to get the evening over with; since he had no desire to strike up a conversation with any of the people who seemed eager to talk to him, in particular the ladies who were delighted to see him back in London after so long an absence, he stepped into the shadows at the back of the room and lifted his champagne glass to his lips.

With one shoulder nonchalantly propped against a pillar, from his vantage point he idly watched the crowd. A smile curved his lips when Edward waltzed a small, exceedingly pretty and engaging young thing around the dance floor.

She was dressed in a white silk gown with a blue sash tied at one side in two small bows. The look of complete absorption on both their faces as they gazed into each other's eyes told him that here was the cause of Edward's recent preoccupation.

Not best pleased, a troubled frown furrowed his brow. Anyone with eyes in their head could not fail to notice that almost invisible aura with which two young people in love seemed to surround themselves. William had certainly seen it, and because of Edward's young age and William's expectations for his cousin to enter his own regiment, he had strong objections to his cousin forming a match with any woman just then. Influenced by his hopes and fears, he would observe his cousin's behaviour attentively and discourage any entanglement.

His eyes did a slow sweep of the room and came to rest on a young woman on the edge of the dance floor. He looked away, but his gaze was drawn back to her, for there was something about her that kindled his interest—something familiar—her stance, the tilt of her head. Recognition flowed across his face and pleasure lit his eyes, followed by pure masculine admiration as his gaze drifted over Miss Greenwood. The effect of seeing her surprised him.

Instead of the stiff and aloof young woman he remembered in an unflattering drab grey dress, she was now draped in the palest off-white gown, the satin clinging to her, hugging her waist and accentuating her rounded bosom. With regal poise, Miss Greenwood, a proud, striking young woman with large luminous eyes beneath thick dark lashes and exotically winged brows, moved serenely from group to group, untouched by the noise and bustle all around her.

Observing her with the impartiality of a connoisseur, looking for flaws that others would miss, he found only perfection. Her colouring was more vivid in this glamorous setting, William thought. Her hair was the same vibrant honey-gold glistening with innumerable shades beneath the light of the chandeliers. A delicate necklace of diamonds lay against her throat in perfect complement to the gown.

She belonged in beautiful gowns and glittering jewels, he decided. They suited her far better than the sombre grey. But who was she really and what was she doing among the cream of London society? He continued to stand in the shadows, admiring the alluringly beautiful woman, but far more intrigued by the indefinable but unmistakable presence that made her stand out so clearly from the rest.

'So, William, I trust you will enlighten me as to what your thoughts are as you look at the thoroughly enchanting and delectable Miss Cassandra Greenwood with that possessive gleam in your eyes. Damned engrossed you are.'

William turned and regarded Sir Charles Grisham, decked out in rich peacock-bright satins and velvets—obviously chosen to create an eyecatching display—with a bland expression. His manner was so indolent that he always gave the impression of being half-asleep.

'My thoughts are my own affair, Charles—though favourable,' he added with a cynical curl to his lips and an appreciative gleam in his eyes.

'Singled her out for yourself, have you?' Charles said in a bored drawl, raising his jewelled quizzing glass the better to study the lady under discussion, the rings on his fingers glinting in the light from the chandeliers. 'Can't say that I blame you, and if you are contemplating making her one of your amusing bed warmers, then you are going to be disappointed. Many have tried and all have failed. There are certain things you should know about that adorable creature, since you've been absent from the *ton* pursuing those damned Frenchies in the Peninsula for the past few years.'

'Go on,' William said, lifting his arrogant brows and waiting, his look both suspicious and intrigued. His curiosity was piqued, but he'd be damned if he let Charles see it. Well acquainted with Charles Grisham, who in spite of his affectations was one of the most intelligent and erudite of the Corinthians, William knew perfectly well that the man was one of the most influential members of the *ton*. At twenty-eight, fair haired, of a slender athletic build and fastidiously tailored, he was much envied for his ability to tie a neckcloth into perfect folds. He had an acid wit that accepted no boundaries and was able to shred a reputation in minutes, when he chose a human target. William deduced from his remarks about Miss Greenwood that he had made her just that.

After helping himself to a pinch of snuff, Charles went on to regale William with Miss Greenwood's attributes and shortcomings, much to William's irritation. If Charles were to be believed, the lady was as cold as an iceberg and set with wilful thorns—one of nature's disagreeable blunders, in fact.

'As a result she has been dubbed the Ice Maiden. And the unkind—though appropriate, some would say—sobriquet has stuck. It's unfortunate since the filly has spirit. She should prove highly entertaining in a chase. Miss Greenwood is one of those rare eccentrics who attend society events and rarely dances except to please herself—which makes her something of a challenge to the likes of me. In fact, she doesn't go out in society at all unless it's to tout for funds for that wretched institute of hers—you know about that?'

William nodded, languidly listening, turning his sardonic gaze back to Miss Greenwood at the same moment as she bestowed a melting smile on a smitten elderly gentleman who was handing her a glass of champagne.

'Lady Monkton—her aunt—takes an understanding view on the matter. Some might think it admirable—personally, I consider it a damn waste of both time and a beautiful woman. Her mama and Lady Monkton let her do exactly as she likes with relative impunity, the result being she has become an object of ridicule.'

William's brows lifted imperturbably. 'Which in your opinion she rightly deserves.'

'Exactly.'

William looked at Miss Greenwood with renewed interest. 'She is Lady Monkton's niece, you say?'

'Not quite. Her mother and Lady Monkton are cousins, but she has taken on the role of aunt to the two Misses Greenwood. The grand lady took both Cassandra and her sister under her wing when their father died. Intending to give both girls a Season, she was disappointed when the older girl declined—being of the unconventional type, if you see what I mean. It's hard to believe that any man's hands have ever touched that delectably soft skin of hers—and I doubt she knows what it feels like to be kissed.'

Though he would dearly like to silence Charles, from William's own dealings with Miss Greenwood it was obvious that what he was saying was mostly true.

'Any unattached bachelor who is foolish enough to show an interest in her, she sends packing.'

'Including you, Charles, which is why you are so ready to point out her faults to me.'

Sir Charles Grisham lifted his arrogant brows, drawling, 'Including me.' He admitted, chuckling softly, 'Indeed, I confess to having been afflicted with a touch of frostbite. Being a notorious rake, I naturally assumed I could seduce her—to initiate her into the art of love. It did nothing for my self-esteem when she added me to her string of rejections. Now you are back in town I can see that I and every other male smitten with the charming Miss Cassandra Greenwood will have to look to our laurels. With your breeding and looks—not to mention your wealth—your potent attraction to women has always been a topic of much scintillating feminine gossip. You do seem to have an extraordinary effect on them, William, but I very much doubt even you will melt that particular iceberg.'

Mild cynicism marred the lean handsomeness of William's features as he refused to be drawn on what his thoughts might be concerning the young woman who had in all probability saved his life.

'By the by,' Grisham went on. 'I saw Mark in town recently—upholding the family name while you've been chasing the Frenchies. I have to say he doesn't improve with age—still the same old bore he was at Cambridge. With so much starch in his veins, it's a miracle the man can sit down. It's difficult to believe he's your cousin. Is it true that he jumps to the tune of his wife?'

William smiled mildly, knowing of Grisham's intense dislike of Mark—in fact, Mark's austere, intolerant attitude did seem to put most people's backs up. There were certain things about Mark that irritated even him—and the same could be said of his acerbic wife, Lydia. But being possessed of a fierceness to protect any member of his family, which had sadly dwindled to just Mark and Edward during the past five years, with the demise of both his parents and older brother in a riding accident, William would not therefore, speak against his cousin.

'If he does, then it is entirely their own affair. I couldn't have left my affairs in better hands, Charles. My cousin is a man of steadfast character and unimpeachable honour, and I would be grateful if you did not cast aspersions.'

'I applaud your loyalty—though in my opinion he doesn't deserve it. Loyalty is a rare virtue in either sex these days.'

'Besides, Mark is next in line to the title and the estate— unless I marry and produce an heir.'

'And is there a possibility of that on the horizon?' Charles enquired, his eyes lighting with obvious interest, for with this devilishly handsome lord off the social scene, the likes of himself and his associates would stand in better favour with the ladies.

William's eyes suddenly glinted with amusement. 'Marriage is not high on my list of things to do just now. When I feel inclined to pledge my hand in order to produce an heir,' he replied with grim humour, 'I'm sure you will be one of the first to know.'

'I shall be journeying to Hertfordshire tomorrow—I'm to stay with my aunt for a few days. I've neglected her disgracefully of late,' Charles confessed. 'I'm quite fond of the old dear.'

'And her money,' William uttered pointedly.

'I admit it does hold some attraction,' he said without shame. 'I shall be close to Carlow Park and I've arranged to ride over to see Mark—though I intend the visit to be of short duration.'

'Then, feeling as you do, why do you visit him at all?'

'Two rather splendid horses you have in the stables—saw them on the hunting field in January and I was impressed. A chestnut full of quality took my fancy, although the grey was damned fine, too. I heard Mark's selling them, so I approached him with an interest to buying one. He invited me to Carlow Park to look them over.'

William's expression was bland when he turned and fixed him with a quizzical stare. 'And these are Mark's horses to sell?'

'Damned if I know—although I don't suppose they are, seeing as they're stabled at Carlow Park.'

'Their names?'

'Monarch and Franciscan.'

William's expression hardened. On learning of his brother's death, from Spain he had asked Mark to keep an eye on the estate until his return. He hadn't given him *carte blanche* to do as he pleased and he felt a faint stirring of antagonism over Mark's having usurped his position by selling off his horses—in particular Franciscan, his brother's horse. Although, on second thought, perhaps it had more to do with Lydia than Mark.

'The horses are not for sale.'

Not to be outdone, Charles's eyes narrowed and a calculating gleam shone in their depths as he moved close to William so that what he was about to say would not be overheard. 'A wager I will make, William.'

Apart from one sleek dark brow cocked in question, William's features remained impassive. 'A wager? I wonder what you're intending to propose, Charles. I'm listening.'

'A wager that you fail to seduce the delectable Miss Greenwood before the Season ends in June.'

'And why should I want to seduce her?'

Charles shrugged. 'To prove that you can—that you haven't lost your touch.'

The challenge was thrown lightly and William teetered on the brink of accepting when caution reared its head. Seducing virgins wasn't his forte—never had been—but the lovely Miss Cassandra Greenwood had captured his attention and the challenge was intriguing. He was a man who must conquer, must win, whatever the odds stacked against him. Whenever he set his mind on having something, he was not easily dissuaded.

'And if I don't?'

'Then one or the other of those splendid beasts in your stable will be mine.'

'And what's in it for me—besides the delectable Miss Greenwood, of course?'

'A thousand guineas if you succeed.'

William rose to the challenge with a confident smile. 'That's unfortunate for you. If there's one thing I dislike, it's seeing my opponent lose.'

'So do I. Think on it, William. To seduce a woman famous for her strict morals—a virgin, I have no doubt, and as yet untouched by world's cynicism—a lovely rose, just waiting to be plucked. What could be more prestigious?'

'What more, indeed?'

'A wager it is then. No need to put it in writing. A gentleman's agreement will do.'

When a well-satisfied Sir Charles Grisham had moved on, William watched Miss Greenwood move about the room with renewed interest. So, she was untouchable. Suddenly she had become an exciting enigma, a mystery, which had multiplied tenfold. Gentlemen of the *haut ton* hesitated to go near her, to take liberties with her. Suddenly she had become a challenge he could not resist.

William watched her pause to speak to this person and that, careful to be as charming and polite as her nature allowed, for it did not do to antagonise. She was well versed in taking hold of a situation and bringing it round to her advantage, since the future of the institute might depend on people such as these. Sharp and witty, she sparkled, encompassing them all with her brilliant smiles and laughter—a light and joyous sound that caressed him, enticed him—and animated chatter, all serving to project the persona of a confident and capable young woman. These people were like children, thrilled and flattered to the core to be noticed by this gorgeous woman. It didn't matter if she schemed to capture their attention. She had it.

Miss Greenwood was quite exquisite, William decided, with an air of fragility about her, but she reminded him of a rapier blade, a sliver of silver made of steel. He wanted to laugh out loud. So this was how she extracted donations for her precious institute.

Moving out of the shadows, completely impervious to the stir he was creating, since it was the first society event he'd attended since returning to London, William advanced towards her, the crowd parting as if he had ordered it.

Cassandra was in the process of deciding who to approach next when she saw him moving in her direction. He was tall, with an authoritative air of breeding and command and an unconscious swagger of arrogance, which spoke of generations of influence and superiority and advantage. With wide shoulders and a hard, stern face and iron jaw, his bright blue eyes beneath fine dark brows were disconcertingly amused as they gazed into hers. When he was close a strange, unfathomable smile tugged at the corner of his mouth, and he slowly inclined his head towards her.

'Hello, Miss Greenwood,' he said, in a deep, resonant and incredibly seductive voice.

His very nearness had her stiffening. The sensation unnerved her. His towering figure left her no avenue of escape. She wished she were nearly a foot taller so she could meet him eye to eye. He was too attractive and had too much charm for his own good. Some people were born like that. It was as if they had a magnet inside them.

'Why, Captain Lampard. This is a surprise.'

A crooked smile accompanied his reply. 'For me rather more than it is for you, Miss Greenwood. You look ravishing, by the way. That colour is far more flattering to your colouring than the diabolical grey dress you were wearing on the day we met.'

Resentment coursed through Cassandra's veins. It dawned on her as his gaze dropped to her breasts in a leisurely perusal that he was far more interested in what was beneath the gown than the gown itself. He raised his eyes to her face where they captured hers and held them prisoner until she felt a warmth suffuse her cheeks.

'What are you doing here, Captain Lampard?' she asked, her smile deliberately cold and ungracious.

'Your aunt invited me.'

'So, you are aware that Lady Monkton is my aunt. Really she is my mother's cousin, but she has always been known as aunt to me and my sister. How long have you known?'

'About ten minutes.' If she had suspected his presence at her aunt's ball had been staged with her specifically in mind, then she was mistaken—disappointed, too, he hoped. 'I grew bored watching the world go by in my town house so I came to see if the sights were any better here at Monkton House.' He spoke with slow deliberation and the corners of his lips twitched with amusement. His eyes gleamed into hers as he added softly, 'I am happy to report they far exceed my expectations and I'm glad I came.'

Cassandra turned aside, tossing him a cool glance

askance. 'Have you nothing better to do than ogle the ladies, Captain Lampard?'

'It might look like that, but in truth I was watching just one.'

Cassandra ignored the remark, but she could not ignore the seductive lowering of his eyelids or the quickening of her heart. 'The gaming tables seem to attract a good many gentlemen. Why don't you try that?'

'Because I find talking to you more enjoyable than anything else I could come up with.'

'Your shoulder is healing well, I trust?'

'Apart from the occasional twinge it is almost back to normal. Your Dr Brookes did a fine job. I am in your debt, Miss Greenwood.'

'Yes, you are, Captain Lampard,' she replied coldly, not having forgiven him for not having sent her the promised donation.

As though reading her mind, he said, 'You received the bank draft I sent to the institute?'

'I cannot recall having done so.'

William frowned, averting his eyes in angry disgust. He would have a few choice words to say to his secretary. Damn the man and his incompetence. 'Then I can only assume there has been a mix up somewhere. I gave it to my secretary to deliver in person. I apologise most sincerely that you have not received it. Rest assured that I shall look into the matter first thing in the morning.'

'Thank you. It will be appreciated,' she said coolly. 'Following that unfortunate experience, perhaps you will think twice before you fight a duel to settle a score—be it a difference of opinion, cheating at cards, or a case of adultery—which, if what I have heard about you is to be believed, was more than likely the reason that took you to Green Park that day.'

'You are mistaken, and it is clear to me that you know nothing about the rules of duelling.'

'I don't?'

'No. For one thing, the normal practice when a duel is arranged is for witnesses—seconds—to be in attendance, and possibly a physician. Do you recall seeing any?'

'Why—I—no, I do not.'

'And for another, I do not hold with the practice. Perhaps you would care to take a walk outside in Lady Monkton's exquisite gardens and allow me to enlighten you on the finer points of the art of duelling.'

Cassandra drew back. 'Certainly not. I refuse to go anywhere with you, sir.'

A mildly tolerant smile touched his handsome visage, but the glint in his blue eyes was as hard as steel. 'Very well, Miss Greenwood, but I would appreciate a word with you in private.' Placing his hand firmly on her elbow, he led her to a small recess and looked down at her, his expression hard. 'You are under a misconception as to what occurred when you came upon me in the park. There was no duel. I was there to enjoy the exercise and solitude of an early morning ride, nothing more sinister than that. In short, someone tried to kill me.'

Oddly enough, Cassandra's first fleeting thought was that he was joking, but, when she saw the firm set of his jaw, she was inclined to believe he was deadly serious. 'To kill you,' she repeated quietly, unable to entirely absorb such a macabre event taking place so close to herself, yet been unaware of it. 'But why would anyone want to kill you?'

'At the moment, the reason is unclear, but I will find out, that I promise you. Someone tried to bring my life to a premature end and I damned well intend finding out who and why. Did you happen to see anyone acting suspiciously that morning?'

'Why, yes. Now I come to think of it, a man rode out of the trees close to where we found you. I didn't see his face. He was wearing a hat pulled well down over his face, and a cloak.'

'His horse? What colour was it—brown, black, grey?' William demanded, sounding sharper than he intended, but he was impatient to discover any clue that would lead him to the culprit.

'Dark brown—but on hearing the shot, I was more concerned about what had occurred than to take note of what the man and his horse looked like.' She paused, becoming trapped in his blue gaze. 'Do you think whoever it was will try again?'

Expression grim, William nodded. 'When I'm in London, I frequently ride in the park at that time. He must have been waiting for me—he didn't try to rob me, so I can only assume he had murder in mind. There was no warning. Nothing. If he was prepared to try once, he'll not let it alone. The question is, when.'

'Then you will have to look to your safety and take all due care.'

'I intend to. I am not the sort who jumps at shadows, and nor do I run from threats. As a soldier on campaign I learned to watch my back—I didn't realise I would have to continue doing so in London.'

'It would seem you have an enemy, Captain Lampard, one who hates you enough to want you dead.'

'It looks like it.'

'So, you are the innocent party and didn't provoke a fight.'

His eyes glowed in the warm light as he gave her a lazy smile, his mood reverting back to what it had been a moment before. 'I cannot claim to be innocent, Miss Greenwood, but neither am I the black-hearted scoundrel I have been painted.'

'I would hardly expect you to admit it if you were,' Cassandra retorted crisply. 'However, I've heard stories to convince me that you are.'

The tantalising smile grew wider in the face of her derisive stare. Folding his arms, William leaned his back nonchalantly against a pillar. 'I am deeply curious about you, Miss Greenwood. Tell me, have you always rebelled against the fashionable world?'

'I suppose I have. I attend these affairs not because I enjoy them particularly, but because they are a means to bring about that which is closest to my heart.'

'I'm aware of that. When you told me how you collect donations for your cause, I was ready to question your methods, but now I can see that with a flash of your eyes and a few chosen words you have them reaching into their pockets.'

'That is my intention.'

He gazed at her for a long moment, his devilish, sensual mouth turning upward in the faintest of cynical smiles. 'You are an extremely forward, quite outrageous and outspoken young woman, Miss Greenwood.'

'If you got to know me, you would have to become used to my manner and the way in which I deal with people.' She met his gaze candidly. 'You don't approve of what I do, do you, Captain Lampard?'

'It is not for me to approve or disapprove of what you do, Miss Greenwood.'

'Nevertheless you're quick to voice your opinion.'

'That is in my nature—and my right.'

On a sigh and letting her expression slip to one of utter boredom. Cassandra looked around. 'I do so hate these occasions. I find little interest in society's entertainments. I wish I could leave right now. See all the mamas watching their offspring with eyes like hawks, Captain Lampard. Launched upon Society and made to parade for inspection like so many fillies at an auction. They will be sold to the highest bidder—to the largest title and the most wealthy.'

'I confess I haven't really thought about it,' William remarked, not really interested. He preferred looking at her. Her blue-green eyes, attentive, observing, carried a brilliance that held him transfixed. 'It must be horrendous for the young ladies.'

'Don't waste your pity. It's all they want from life—pretty gowns, jewels. They have no notion of anything else. Their mamas are obsessed with etiquette, fiercely concerned with morals and the approval of their friends and acquaintances, determined that their daughters do and say the right thing—not to dance more than two dances with any one gentleman, and so on. How tedious and tiresome it all is.'

'I have already decided that you are a very unconventional young woman, Miss Greenwood.'

'I am concerned with none of that. I do so detest all the restrictions of the social system that enslaves women.'

'Are you suggesting that you would care to redress the wrongs of our misguided society? Are you so uninhibited by the prejudice of class that you would break the mould of convention that has encased women for centuries?'

'I despise convention; as you will have gathered, I live very much as I please, but without causing offence to those I love and those who love me.

'And to add to all that, you rarely dance,' William said, pushing his long frame away from the pillar and moving close to her, his gaze capturing hers. 'Will you step out of your self-imposed restrictions and do me the honour of dancing with me?'

Cassandra stared up at him. Those glowing eyes burned into hers, suffusing her with a growing aura of warmth. 'I—I do not care to dance.'

'I insist. After all, this is a ball and that is what people do. You—do dance?'

Her smile was feral. 'Of course I do. I prefer not to.'

'You distress me, Miss Greenwood.' His mouth twisted in a lightly mocking grin. 'You give me no grounds to hope for better things.'

'Nor should I,' she returned pertly. 'I've told you, I do not like these occasions.'

He laughed briefly. 'You seem to take special delight in reminding me. But I am not convinced. There isn't a woman alive who doesn't like to dance—and I do not believe you are any different, Miss Greenwood.' William peered at her closely and took note of her uneasiness. 'I'm right, am I not?'

Cassandra tilted her slim nose upward as she turned it in profile to him. 'I meant what I said.'

'Tell me, Miss Greenwood. Why do you resent me? Can it be that it is because my secretary failed to deliver the donation—or is it more of a personal nature?'

Indignant colour stained Cassandra's cheeks. 'You're right, of course. I do resent you, but not for the reasons you state.'

'Then would you please enlighten me.'

She looked at him direct. 'It is to do with my sister.'

'Your sister?'

'And your cousin.'

'Edward?'

'Yes.' She turned towards the dance floor and observed Emma about to take to the floor in a lively country dance with Edward Lampard. Her annoyance was raised to new heights. 'It may have escaped your notice, Captain Lampard, but your cousin and my sister have danced two dances together and are about to embark on a third. My sister is just eighteen years old and her reputation is about to be ruined before she has been launched into society.'

Totally unprepared for the turn the conversation had taken, William's eyes sought out Edward, seeing him with the same young woman he had been dancing with earlier. 'That young lady is your sister?'

'Yes. Unfortunately, the two of them have developed a fondness for each other.'

'A fondness?'

'Exactly.'

'Edward is a sensible, sensitive young man. Speaking as his older cousin, I can only applaud your sister's taste.'

'He is neither sensible nor sensitive if he cannot see that he is in danger of ruining her reputation,' Cassandra argued. 'Because of the time they spend together, I believe my sister is about to be compromised by your cousin. Everywhere we go we bump into him—be it in the park, at a soirée or the theatre.

I am certain these meetings are not coincidence and are pre-arranged in some way known only to Emma and Edward.'

'Pardon me, Miss Greenwood, but you are contradicting your own words. Did you not imply that you find the rules and restrictions that govern polite society utterly ridiculous? If you feel that way, then why should your sister's reputation matter to you so much?'

Cassandra sent a cool glance skimming over him. Having her own words quoted back at her was disconcerting. 'What I said applies to me, Captain Lampard, not my sister. She is a different matter entirely. When I said what I did, I was giving an honest opinion.'

William's lips twitched with ill-suppressed amusement. 'Do you have an aversion to my cousin, Miss Greenwood? If so, I find any preconceived ideas you might have about him being a scoundrel insulting and deeply offensive. Perhaps you're afraid that scoundrels run in the Lampard family—and maybe you see him as some kind of threat?'

'I do not consider him as much a threat as an inconvenience.'

Laughter twinkled in his eyes. 'I can see how confused you must be. It is a wholly perplexing problem you have there.'

Cassandra's cheeks became flushed with indignation. 'Are you laughing at me, Captain Lampard?'

'Heaven forbid, I wouldn't dare. Now, shall we dance? I will even say please if that will persuade you.'

Cassandra did not want to be persuaded. She did not want to dance with him. She did not want to become better ac-quainted. Still, if it meant a large subscription to the institute, then she could at least be pleasant to him for a short while. Besides, if sufficiently provoked, he might be tempted to risk creating a fuss to gain what he sought.

When William saw her hesitate, he smiled. 'Come, Miss Greenwood. People are beginning to stare. Your reticence only heightens my determination. I will have this dance, oth-erwise I might very well change my mind about the size of my donation. The amount will be considerably smaller than it would be if you were to partner me on the floor. Should your colleagues at the institute find out, they would never forgive you.'

Quite unexpectedly she smiled pleasantly and William almost reeled under the impact. Her eyes seemed to contain sparkles of light and a soft rose tinted her cheeks. Her lips parted over even, white teeth that shone, and a small dimple in her cheek caught his eye. Her smile deepened, and so did the dimple. He was momentarily transported and utterly speechless.

'I suppose I could dance with you for the sake of civility.'

'And a generous donation,' he was quick to point out.

'Of course—but this sounds very much like blackmail to me, Captain Lampard.'

'*You* might say that,' he murmured softly. 'I would prefer to call it persuasion.'

'Very well. I am persuaded. I surrender.'

Decorously presenting her with his arm, he laughed. 'I was hoping you would,' he said quietly. 'If we continue in this fashion, Miss Greenwood, we might even become friends.'

Cassandra smiled thinly. 'I would advise you not to place any wagers on that, Captain Lampard.'

'I might be tempted,' he said, with more meaning than she realised, leading her forward on his arm as the musicians played a waltz. 'I am not averse to the odd gamble.'

A sudden hush settled over the guests as those present turned, anxious to appease their curiosity. What they saw amazed them. Cassandra Greenwood was taking to the floor with Lord Lampard—well, he always had been able to charm every female within sight—and it went to prove that the prim Miss Greenwood was no different from the rest after all. But the fact that she was to dance with Captain Lampard—his first dance since returning to London—caused other gentlemen she had declined to dance with in the past to consider their attraction. Aware of his reputation as a rake, they were admiringly speculative.

Taking Cassandra in his arms, William's hand slid slowly, possessively, about her trim waist, drawing her close. 'I sincerely hope you were telling the truth when you said you do know how to dance, Miss Greenwood, otherwise you will make a laughing stock of us both,' he murmured, his wicked, sensual mouth turning upward in the faintest of cynical smiles.

'Just because I don't usually dance, doesn't mean that I don't know how to, so lead the way, Captain, and I will follow.'

'My pleasure, Miss Greenwood. My pleasure. For this one dance, forget your institute, your children and your fund raising and be a young lady of the *ton,* intent on enjoying herself. Take it from me, it's more fun than trying to extract money from society's elite.'

So saying, William whirled her round the floor. His senses were alive with the elusive perfumed scent of her, to her supple young body. Getting to know Miss Greenwood could be very pleasurable indeed. Deliberately, he drew her closer so that his hips brushed hers and he felt a tremor pass down her spine. His imagination began to run riot and he dwelt on the thought of what it would be like to plunder those soft lips and make love to her. His blood stirred hotly and his body was beginning to react in such a way that he had to force the thoughts aside.

It would have surprised—and gratified—him to know that Cassandra's thoughts were not so very different from his own. Beneath her fingertips, his beautifully tailored claret jacket was without a crease. Smelling pleasantly of sandalwood and brandy, he moved with elegance and grace, but, light as his arms were, she could feel the steel beneath.

Her eyes were level with his broad, muscular shoulders. Every inch of his tall frame positively radiated raw power and leashed sensuality, causing her to remember every scandalous story she'd ever heard about him. Handsome, sinful—

strangely the thought excited her. How could she claim unin-
terest in the man when his mere presence could so effectually
stir her senses? Lifting her gaze to his ruggedly hewn features,
she met his knowing eyes, seeing something relentless and
challenging.

'You dance well, Captain Lampard.'

'Suddenly you're an expert?'

'I know the difference between good and bad. Tell me, do
you always get what you want?' Cassandra asked.

'Usually,' he replied. 'Perhaps because I'm totally selfish,
arrogant, inconsiderate and a complete scoundrel—or so I've
been told by those who know me. It's the way I was raised,
you see—having people pander to my smallest needs, to
gratify my every whim.'

Cassandra slanted him an arched glance. 'What you really
mean is that you were a spoilt child. Still,' she quipped,
'you're a male, so I would expect no less.'

The dance ended and he released her, but the warmth of
his touch lingered. He escorted her to where Lady Monkton
was seated beside other matrons who had gathered to
gossip and nibble on sweets. A tall woman, with the
family's fairness and a majestic bearing, Lady Monkton
looked up when they approached, pleasure lighting her
features.

'Cassandra, my dear, how nice it is to see you take to the
floor at long last—and with Captain Lampard. I had almost
given up on my niece,' she said not unkindly, although she
never stopped reiterating her disappointment that Cassandra
refused to let her arrange her début. 'You must excuse her. She
has no social graces—only social causes.'

'Which is to be admired, Lady Monkton.'

'I'm happy you think so, Captain Lampard. You know,
you are far too handsome for your own good. You are enjoying
yourself, I hope?'

'Indeed, Lady Monkton. Thank you for inviting me.'

William's smile and the way he bowed over the elderly lady's hand was the epitome of politeness and charm. 'May I say that you are more beautiful than ever.'

Lady Monkton laughed lightly, and Cassandra was certain her cheeks flushed beneath her rouge.

'Flatterer. I must say that I—and every lady present—are delighted by your reappearance in the *ton*. It's long overdue. London will be a far more exciting place with you in it. Thank goodness you have Bonaparte beat.'

The musicians were beginning to play another refrain. Not to be let off lightly, William turned to Cassandra.

'Miss Greenwood, may I have the pleasure of dancing one more waltz with you?'

Cassandra drew back, intending to decline. 'Why—I—'

'Of course you must, Cassandra,' Lady Monkton was quick to interrupt, relieved to see her niece taking an interest in the frivolous things other young ladies seemed to delight in. 'Two dances with the same partner is socially acceptable, so off you go now and enjoy yourself.'

Cassandra shot a look at her aunt, seeing the shrewd, uncannily knowing expression pass over her. Beaten, on a sigh she turned and moved away.

'I'm only asking for another dance—one more dance, Miss Greenwood,' William murmured, taking her arm and propelling her back towards the dance floor. 'Nothing more intimate than that.'

'It's a good thing, too, Captain Lampard. No matter how generous your donation, anything more intimate than a dance is definitely out of the question. I don't think I even like you.'

'Who said anything about liking?' he remarked, laughing lightly as he took her in his arms. 'It's the act that's pleasurable.'

'Captain Lampard,' she chided, feeling her cheeks flush rose-red as he whirled her round, 'you are embarrassing me. Kindly stop it or I shall be forced to leave you standing on the dance floor—which would never do.' Observing the humour in his eyes, she scowled, struggling to prevent her lips from smiling. 'Are you teasing me, by any chance?'

'Most assuredly.' He laughed, the sound low and so seductive that several people dancing close turned to look at them.

'Then please don't.'

His teeth flashed white in a lazy grin, but his gaze dipped lingeringly to her soft lips. 'I enjoy teasing you. I find it—intriguing and pleasurable.'

'And I don't like being teased. If you think I do, then you've taken leave of a major portion of your senses.' His smile widened and it was such a wonderful smile. Captain Lampard exuded provocative charm. He could probably charm the birds out of the trees, but this particular bird wasn't about to tumble for that silky voice. But she was not nearly as immune as she thought—as she wanted to be. He was a magnificent male, and she was human—flesh and blood—and his sexual magnetism was overwhelming, dislike him though she might.

'As soon as the dance ends I must circulate,' she told him. 'I must also have a stern word with my sister. In fact, I do believe your cousin is now escorting her into the buffet.'

William glanced across at Edward and the young woman, who was gazing up at him adoringly. Experiencing a sharp stab of unease, he frowned. 'You sister looks sweet and very young.'

'Don't let her looks deceive you. She has a romantic mind and your charming cousin has somehow managed to captivate my dear, gullible sister. They do say that love is blind, and it seems Emma has no sight when it comes to Edward. However, I will not let him take advantage of her and cast her off—which will most certainly get her banished from polite society before she has the chance to make her début. She's hellbent on holding on to him. I do expect Emma to behave with discretion and propriety, but unfortunately she is strong willed and the very opposite of biddable.'

William's brow lifted in amusement. 'Then perhaps she takes after her big sister.'

'She most certainly does not. She does not respect my opinion and she never listens to any edicts from me or Mama.'

'I can understand your anxiety, and, if it will put your mind at ease, I strongly disapprove of Edward forming any kind of liaison at this time.'

'You do? Then if we don't do something to discourage it at once, things could become complicated. Once Emma gets some maggot into her head, there's no stopping her.'

'What do you suggest I do?'

'Can't you order your cousin to avoid her, or failing that, send him away somewhere?'

'Your anxieties and fears may soon be at an end. Edward is shortly to enter the Military Academy as a cadet, with the hope of purchasing a commission. In the current climate it's inevitable that his regiment will see service overseas.'

Cassandra's relief was enormous. 'Oh—thank goodness. That would be the answer to everything. What you may do for me in the meantime is to speak to him, keep an eye on him. I don't relish the idea of having a Lampard as kin.'

A pair of cool blue eyes regarded her dispassionately. 'How extraordinary,' William mocked. 'All my life I have harboured the delusion that all young ladies yearn to snare wealthy husbands—and, despite having made his home with me on the demise of his parents, Edward is wealthy in his own right. I am amazed that you have objections to my family's suitability, for their breeding is unexceptionable and they are better connected than most.'

Cassandra was so carried away with making sure that he understood her concern, and that her sister's reputation must be protected at all costs, that she didn't heed the muscle that was beginning to tick in his tightly clenched jaw.

'I'm sure you're right, Captain Lampard,' she hurried on, her tone straightforward, not facetious, 'and that your family's credentials are impeccable, but wealth and an illustrious name does not give a man the right to do as he pleases and to do it with impunity. I am sorry to have to say this, but if Edward turns out to be anything like the hellion you are reputed to be—for I do understand that you have great experience in living—then he will make an exceedingly bad husband.'

William heard the insult in her smoothly worded statement, and any amusement that was left vanished from his expression. In one swift movement he whisked her off the dance floor and released her. He then looked down at her with hard, unforgiving eyes, a scowl drawing his brows together.

'Miss Greenwood,' he said in a voice dangerously low, 'if you imagine for one minute that I would approve of Edward marrying your sister, then you are living under an illusion. However, there is a whole procession of society matrons who are eager to lure me into marrying their daughters and who are perfectly willing to overlook my excesses in "living," as you so baldly put it. I'm beginning to realise that I do not rate highly in your estimation. As a rule I have never cared for anyone's opinion, and I most certainly would never let them influence my actions—and this includes you.'

Stung at being manhandled from the dance floor and offended by the tone of superiority with which he delivered this lecture, Cassandra gave him a lofty look, but on searching his shuttered features and taking judicious note of the taut set of his jaw, she realised that she had gone too far in voicing her disapproval of his character and was unable to retreat from a predicament into which she should never have put herself in the first place.

Biting her lip, suddenly feeling very small and very foolish, she said, 'I—apologise if I have offended you, but I only said what I thought out of concern for my sister.'

'You have said quite enough, Miss Greenwood,' he snapped, irrationally angry at her unprovoked attack on his character. 'If it is your intention to humble me, then you can forget it. Rest assured that my donation to your institute will be with you in the morning, and let that be an end to the matter. And now I bid you good night.'

William turned on his heel and strode purposefully from the ballroom, leaving Cassandra staring in his wake. Mortified, shocked and bewildered by his sudden departure, these emotions were banished in a blinding flash of fury. How dare he walk away from her like that? The man was rude beyond bearing, too full of himself, affecting pompous poses and delighting in turning the head of every female in the room.

As the music died she became aware of being stared at and noticed the whispered conferences as people gathered in groups, having witnessed the altercation that had taken place between Cassandra Greenwood and Captain Lampard. With as much dignity as she could muster, she lifted her head and returned to Aunt Elizabeth, and it wasn't long before she left the ball and went home without seeing anything more of the arrogant and pretentious Captain Lampard.

Then why, as she climbed into bed, did the thought of his smile and the remembered touch of his hand make her heart beat faster? Suddenly at a loss, she blew out the candle.

Chapter Three

Seated in his carriage taking him back to Grosvenor Square, the anger caused by Miss Greenwood's censure to his character continued to burn inside William. Normally he would have smiled and shrugged such comments off as being of no consequence, whereas this time the self-confident, invulnerable Lord Lampard, who always treated women with amused tolerance, had been driven to walk away from Miss Greenwood because she had artlessly spoken the truth.

The wager he had made with Charles against his better judgement bothered him, and his conscience that he thought long since dead chose that moment to resurrect itself. Realising the enormity of what he'd done, already he was regretting it. He had taken the wager to seduce and dishonour a woman he had found to be full of goodness, trusting and candid, with a combination of wisdom and naïveté and undeniably lovely. Miss Greenwood was above a mere dalliance. May God forgive him. It was madness, and he hated himself with a virulence that nearly knocked the breath out of him.

For the first time in a long time, he had met a woman without guile. Her young innocent face passed before his mind's eye, a face of much seriousness, a ripe, opulent beauty that made his blood stir hotly. Never in his wildest dreams had he imagined anyone like Miss Greenwood. What an enchanting creature she was, artlessly sophisticated, part-angel, part-spitfire. For some peculiar reason that was quite beyond him, it mattered to him what she thought of him.

By the time his carriage drew up outside his residence, his anger had abated and his stomach clenched at the unmannerly way in which he had left her. He had decided not to pursue Miss Greenwood. She would be in no danger from him. There was no room in his life for women like her—not even her blue-green eyes, her face of an angel and a body to rival that of Venus, would make him change his mind.

To hell with Grisham and his wager, he thought as he shoved open the carriage door and stepped down into the street. It was off. He could have the damned horse.

The following morning Cassandra left for Kensington, leaving Emma to spend the rest of the day with Aunt Elizabeth, who, according to Emma, was to indulge her young charge in her favourite pastime of shopping. Not having retired until the early hours, Aunt Elizabeth had not surfaced from her bed so Cassandra had to take Emma's word for this—although she had no reason to doubt what she said, for Emma spent a good deal of her time at Monkton House being pampered by Aunt Elizabeth.

When Cassandra bade her sister farewell, she thought how pale Emma looked. There was also a strange, vague look in her eyes that told Cassandra her mind was on other things. She did not pay any heed to it just then, but she would have reason to remember it later.

Cassandra and her mother had just finished their evening meal when a flustered and highly distraught Lady Monkton arrived.

'Oh, my dears, something quite dreadful has occurred—

something so dreadful I don't know how I am ever going to tell you.'

Concerned, Cassandra immediately went to her, anxiously studying the worried lines on her face. 'Dear Aunt Elizabeth,' she said, taking her hand, 'you are upset. Come and sit down.'

When her ample body was comfortably ensconced in a large winged chair, Lady Monkton snapped open her ivory fan and began to agitate the air close to her face. 'What I have to tell you will come as such a shock to you. I wonder how to break it.'

Instinct told Cassandra that her aunt's distressed state had something to do with Emma. 'It's Emma, isn't it? Tell us quickly, Aunt Elizabeth.'

'It's not good news, is it, Elizabeth?' Harriet whispered, her hand clutching the collar of her dress at her throat.

'She's—she's gone—run away—eloped—with Edward Lampard.'

'Run away?' Harriet recoiled, her voice incredulous. 'Oh, dear God.' She sat down, her colour gone, her eyes haunted.

Incensed, at first Cassandra couldn't form a coherent thought. Not until she looked up and saw her mother's pale face beneath her lace-and-ribbon cap did she collect her scattered wits.

Deeply shocked, reaching for Cassandra's hand, Harriet stared at her cousin. Her mother was a strong woman, renowned for her ability to maintain her composure even in times of stress, and through her work at the institute accustomed to hard work. Having dealt with the grief and heartache she had suffered on the death of her beloved James, she had thought she could deal with most things, but Emma's unpardonable, inconsiderate and shocking behaviour had come as a hard blow.

'Believe me when I tell you that I had no inclination she would do this,' Lady Monkton said in a broken voice, dabbing at her moist eyes with her handkerchief, 'and I am so sorry. I hold myself entirely responsible. Oh, I know she is fond of that young man—flattered by the attention he showers on her—what eighteen-year-old wouldn't be? He is handsome and exciting—first cousin to Lord William Lampard, whose lineage is impeccable. Their fathers were directly descended from one of England's oldest families, as was Lord Lampard's mother.'

'Yes—the ideal man for her to become acquainted with after she has made her début,' Harriet said quietly. 'But not at this time. I do so want her to meet other eligible young men before she settles down to marriage. Oh, the stupid girl. I knew Edward Lampard had drawn her attention, but I had no idea she had any partiality for him. Why could she not have waited? But patience never was one of Emma's good points. None of this is your fault, Elizabeth.'

'You are too kind, Harriet, but how could this have happened?' Lady Monkton wailed. 'All my hopes, all my plans—and then she elopes.' She shook her head dejectedly. 'I just can't believe it.'

'You have shown Emma nothing but kindness, doing all that could reasonably be expected of you—always steadfast and reliable. Since James died, you have been such a great comfort to me and made a real difference to all our lives—especially Emma's. For that I shall be eternally grateful. No, Elizabeth, I do not blame you—only my silly, wilful, Emma, and myself. I spend so much of my time at the institute that I failed to see what she was up to.'

'Ungrateful, foolish girl,' Cassandra retorted, seething, mentally berating her sister. 'I always said her forward behaviour would bring her grief. I knew how she felt about Edward Lampard and I tried talking to her, but where that young man is concerned she will not be reasoned with. Still, I never dreamt she would do something like this.'

'I truly believed Emma had returned home with you, Cassandra. It wasn't until one of the maids was tidying her room and came upon a note left on her dressing table that I became aware of what she had done.' Plunging her hand into her reticule, Lady Monkton produced the note.

Cassandra took it and scanned what was written in her sister's untidy handwriting. Her mind seized what Emma had done and her blood ran cold. 'She writes that she is leaving London, that she is running away with Edward Lampard. They are in love and cannot live without each other. They are to be married in Scotland.' The missive was signed with a flourishing, *Emma*.

'But where in Scotland can she have gone?' Harriet asked.

'Gretna Green, I would say,' her cousin answered, 'that is the first changing post over the border. The marriage of a minor without parental consent is illegal in England, but there is no such barrier in Scotland—and it does seem to be fashionable and romantic for young people to elope to Gretna Green at this time.'

'That young man must have arranged everything,' Harriet said. 'Emma wouldn't know how. Dear God in heaven, Cassandra! What are we to do? We must get her back before it's too late—before—before he…'

'There's only one thing we can do, Mama. I'll go and see Captain Lampard. If he knows about this, then he may already be halfway to Scotland in pursuit. My guess is that he doesn't. Edward wouldn't want him giving chase. If he decides to go after them, I'll go with him.'

Her mother was appalled. 'But—you can't go calling on a gentleman, Cassandra, and most certainly you cannot go all the way to Scotland. I forbid it.'

'Mama, this is no time to concern ourselves with such trivial matters. In this case I have no qualms about going against the rules of protocol. Emma's reputation is at stake so not a word of this must get out, otherwise she will never be able to show her face in society. Please don't worry. I'll bring her back.'

'I'll come with you,' Lady Monkton volunteered, trying to rise out of her chair. A pained expression crossed her features and her hand went to her chest. 'Oh, dear. My dyspepsia's beginning to trouble me again.'

'Please don't worry yourself,' Cassandra said, her jaw set as she stuffed Emma's note into her pocket. 'Stay and take care of Mama. I'll have a stomach powder and a glass of warm milk sent in.'

Harriet went to her daughter. 'Cassandra, when you see Captain Lampard, promise me you will watch that temper of yours. I know what you are like when roused.'

'I can't help it. I know what these hellraking lordlings can be like and I will not be patronised.'

Hurrying to her room, she quickly put some items of clothing she would need for a long journey—of short duration, she hoped—into a bag and within minutes she was in the carriage and heading for Grosvenor Square.

When Cassandra arrived outside Captain Lampard's London residence, she hardly noticed the grandeur of the house. Telling Clem to await further instructions, when she was admitted she couldn't fail to take in the breathtaking splendour.

William wasn't in the best of tempers and in no mood to be charitable or accommodating when Siddons flung open the door to the huge green-and-gold salon to announce a visitor. It was eight o'clock in the evening and Edward had been expected at the Military Academy at ten o'clock that morning, but the youth had mysteriously disappeared at nine o'clock and had not been seen since. William was at a side table, about to pour himself a calming glass of port when he was interrupted.

'I beg your pardon, my lord,' Siddons said, usually stiff and unflappable, but now looking extremely harassed, 'but this young lady insists on seeing you. I told her she would have to be announced, but she would not wait.'

With narrowed eyes, William looked beyond his butler into the stormy eyes of his uninvited visitor. 'Thank you, Siddons. It's all right. Miss Greenwood and I are acquainted, so you can leave us.'

'His lordship knows why I am here.'

'I do not recall inviting you.'

'I always was impetuous,' Cassandra retorted, striding purposefully past Siddons without taking her eyes off Captain Lampard, the man she considered to be the source of all her family's woes. His tall frame was clad in impeccably tailored light grey trousers and a white shirt and neckcloth at his throat. She didn't stop until she was just inches away.

William's eyes, glittering like hard metal, narrowed even more. At close range he saw the burning, spitting rage that fairly sizzled in her wide, clear eyes. 'Miss Greenwood,' he said when Siddons had closed the door, 'if you are here to collect the donation I promised, you are wasting your time. It was delivered to the institute first thing this morning.'

Thrown off track, Cassandra stared at him in stupefied amazement. 'Donation?' She moved a little closer. 'I did not come here for that. Do you think that's my only concern? Money?'

His lip curled derisively. 'What else? If it isn't money, then what is it that's got you all fired up and ready to explode?'

'My sister.'

'Blast your sister.'

'My sentiments entirely, Captain Lampard. She is the problem and I am having to deal with the consequences of what she and that conniving, smooth-talking cad of a cousin of yours have done.'

William could hardly believe his ears. 'What the hell are you talking about?'

'I am here to ask you why you did not heed my warning. Was it too much to ask that you take your cousin in hand and keep him away from my sister?'

Something unpleasant began to uncurl inside William. 'What are you saying?'

'Your precious cousin has run away with her. They have

eloped—gone to Scotland,' she informed him coldly, enunciating each word she uttered. 'More than likely to Gretna Green, where all young romantics flee to get married.'

William faltered. His surprise was genuine. He thought he could not have heard her correctly. 'Eloped?' His voice sharpened. 'Good God! Are you mad?'

'Mad? No, I am not mad, Captain Lampard. I am furious—as is my mother. She is quite beside herself with worry. Where is your lecherous cousin? Do you know?'

William shook his head. 'No, I confess I do not, and it is hardly my fault if your sister is too much for you to handle.' Surprise and fury made him brutal.

'Why, you conceited, unmitigated boor,' Cassandra fumed, her anger full bodied and fortifying. 'If I could stop her doing anything, I wouldn't be here.'

'And your mother, does she know you are here?'

'She knows I came here to speak to you. Since your cousin resides in your house, you are to a certain extent responsible for his actions.'

'And how do you know they have eloped? Have you proof of this?' William demanded.

'Emma left a note. Here.' She pulled the paper from her pocket and thrust it at him. 'Read it. See for yourself, and then tell me what you intend to do about it.'

Quickly William scanned the missive, which was concise and to the point, leaving him in no doubt that his cousin had indeed run off to Scotland to wed Emma Greenwood.

'The damned fool,' he growled, raking his hair back from his forehead. 'How long have they been gone?'

'Since nine o'clock this morning.'

'Eleven hours start. How are they travelling?'

'We don't know that.'

'Lady Monkton's carriage?'

'No.'

'Then they must have hired one. Knowing I would give

chase, to make good their escape, Edward will have hired a coach and four, which will mean a faster journey.'

'And frightfully expensive. No wonder only the very rich can afford to elope to Gretna Green,' Cassandra retorted drily. 'Are you going after them?'

'The young fools leave me with no choice.'

'Then you'll take me with you?'

William had turned to the door, ready to stride out to the stable yard to order his carriage to be made ready at once, but her voice halted him and he spoke quietly as he turned to answer her question. 'No. All you will be is a hindrance. I want neither you nor your company.'

Cassandra's face whitened, but she would not give way. She took a deliberate pace closer to him. 'Do you really think I will let you go alone? Do you think I would trust you to bring my sister back safely? Oh, no, I think not. For all any of us know she may have come to harm; should that be the case, then, when she is found she will have need of me.'

'I know you're upset,' William said, trying to moderate his tone to placate her, but there was a thrust to her jaw that told him she was ready to fight. She had an untamed quality running in dangerous undercurrents just beneath the surface that warned him to be wary. 'You have every right to be, but you are not going with me.'

Cassandra's chilled contempt met him face to face, and then, tossing her head, she turned from him and stalked towards the door. 'Very well. I certainly have no desire to accompany a man on a journey when he has no desire to have me along.'

William strode after her. 'Where, in heaven's name, are you going?'

'After them. I'll take Aunt Elizabeth's carriage.'

'I can appreciate your concern, but you cannot embark on this mad escapade alone.'

'Oh, no?'

His arm shot out, his fingers closing cruelly on her upper

arm, spinning her round to face him. 'You little idiot,' he seethed. 'Allow me to advise you to forget this foolish notion.'

'Advice? If I wanted advice, you would be the last person on earth I would ask,' Cassandra retorted, a flush of anger having spread over her cheeks and icy fire smouldering in the depths of her eyes. 'This is my business, as well as yours. How are you to stop me going after them? You must surely know by now that I do as I please. Now kindly release my arm before I scream the place down.'

William felt the situation slipping rapidly from his grasp. Whatever he threw at her she had an answer. Despite his intense anger—directed at her and his irresponsible cousin, and also at himself for not having heeded Miss Greenwood's warning—he did not have the mental capacity or the right to forbid her to journey to Scotland alone. Releasing her arm, he stepped back.

'You beast. How dare you lay your hands on me?' she fumed, glaring at him and rubbing her arm.

'Miss Greenwood, you are being quite unreasonable.'

'Unreasonable? Because I am worried about my sister? You, Captain Lampard, are the one who's being unreasonable.'

'If you go tearing off to Scotland, what about your institute? Are you not needed there?'

'I am always needed, but there are others to do the work in my absence.'

'Then consider the impropriety of travelling alone with me to Scotland. What will your mother have to say?'

'Mama is so upset about Emma absconding that she won't care as long as she is returned—unmarried.'

'I cannot believe that any parent in their right mind would let their daughter venture forth alone on the road to Scotland. Don't you care how much scandal it will cause?'

'My reputation is the last thing on my mind just now. I don't care that it's not the done thing for a young woman to go careering off with a single man unescorted. Nor do I care about the scandal that will be sure to ensue. Do you, Captain Lampard?'

Her question was thrown down as a challenge, one he could not ignore. For the first time he looked at what she was wearing. Attired in a sapphire-blue travelling costume and matching hat perched at a tantalising angle atop her coiffured hair, it occurred to him that she was dressed for travelling.

Cassandra watched him studying her as if seeing her for the first time. She held her breath expectantly, letting it out with relief when he put his hands up in surrender.

'Very well, we will go together. I'll order the carriage and perhaps you should call at your home to collect a few things you will need for the journey.'

'There's no need. I came prepared.'

William's eyes shot to the leather bag by the door and then back to her. For a moment he looked blank. He simply stared at her, then he shook his head as if trying to clear it. 'Why, you scheming minx!'

Planting her hands on her slim hips, calmly drumming her fingers, her smile was sublime. 'Aren't I just—I'm rebellious, too, in case you haven't noticed.'

'You knew I'd agree for you to accompany me.'

'Oh, yes, Captain Lampard. I was certain of it.'

Despite his fury, William experienced a mixture of disbelief, amusement and admiration as he gazed down at the exquisite young beauty who had skilfully managed to manipulate him into doing something he didn't want to do. He laughed out loud, the tension falling from him like a silken shroud.

'Miss Greenwood, you are incorrigible.'

'Yes, I know. Do you mind?'

He laughed some more. 'Not a bit. In fact, I suddenly find myself looking forward to our journey together. The company will be most welcome. It will be interesting to see which of us will have expired before the journey's end.'

'Oh, you never know, Captain Lampard—perhaps we'll be getting on so well by the time we reach Gretna Green, we too might recite our vows over the anvil.'

'I doubt it, Miss Greenwood. I really do.'

'So do I. Now, shall we go? I think enough time has been wasted.'

William's emotions veered from fury to mirth as he followed her out of the house, thinking Cassandra Greenwood to be the most provoking, insufferable female he had ever had the misfortune to meet. The idea of being bested by a twenty-year-old female in his own house was unthinkable and humiliating. In the course of twenty-four hours, she had gone out of her way to anger him and incur his displeasure with a rebellion and impertinence that both infuriated and exhilarated him.

She was also captivating and alluring, with the kind of face and body that stirred his blood. A reluctant smile curved his lips as his eyes focused on the impudent sway of her skirts. Despite his decision not to have anything more to do with her, her sudden appearance at his home had changed everything. She was a challenge, a challenge he couldn't resist, and the fact that she was determined to stand against him only spiced his interest.

Ensconced in Captain Lampard's sleek, well-sprung travelling coach drawn by four splendid bay horses and with two armed grooms in the driver's seat, they were soon heading up the Great North Road. Fortunately, the roads were dry and relatively quiet, so they should make good time.

'Make yourself comfortable,' William had said when he had assisted her into the spacious conveyance, the very height of luxury. 'Apart from the stops we make to change the horses, we'll travel throughout the night.'

She cast an apprehensive glance at him as he climbed in, but much to her relief he seated himself across from her. As he caught her gaze a slow smile touched his lips.

'It's safer if I sit here. I fear the nearness of you will destroy all my good intentions.'

'Then I can only hope that your good intentions will continue all the way to Scotland, Lord Lampard,' she replied archly.

Leaning back, they made themselves comfortable against the cushions. William stretched his long legs out in front of him, wondering how he was going to endure the journey. He wasn't made of stone, and the delectable young woman was so lovely she'd tempt any man who was alone with her for five minutes.

One of his legs almost touched Cassandra's own. Silently he dared his companion to object, watching her as one might observe a dew-laden flower, awed by its fragile beauty. Cassandra's dark lashes fluttered downward self-consciously as he continued to watch her, uneasy with his boldness and his close proximity in the confines of the coach. Too masculine, his potent virility made her feel entirely too vulnerable. Furtively she glanced at the offending lean and muscular limb, casually moving further into the corner to avoid contact.

Watching her from beneath lowered lids, William made no effort to move away, and grinned lazily when she spread a thick fur rug over her knees.

After they had travelled some distance in silence, the thought came to Cassandra that if she wanted to survive this journey with her sanity intact, they must have some conversation. It was dark outside and the lanterns' rays bathed the inside of the coach in a soft, golden light. She felt a sudden stillness envelope them. Vividly aware of the confined intimacy, she was overwhelmingly conscious of the man facing her.

She knew so little about Captain Lampard, only the unsavoury side to his character. As he stared intently out of the window at the starlit night, his granite face was in profile. There was indomitable pride and arrogance chiselled into his handsome face, along with intelligence and hard-bitten strength. His jaw was set in a hard line, his brow furrowed in angry preoccupation, and it suddenly occurred to her that this elopement was as much a shock to him as it was to her.

Taking a deep breath, she said, 'I'm sorry. I realise this is difficult for you, as well. I have been wondering where Emma and your cousin are just now. Do you think we will catch up with them, that we'll be in time to stop them marrying?'

Drawing the velvet curtain to shut out the night, William turned to look at her. 'Unless they meet with some mishap or decide to spend the night at a coaching inn, then I very much doubt it. Edward will know that your sister left a note telling her family what they intended, and will be afraid that I will have been made aware of that fact and will give chase—I am certain they'll go direct to Scotland.'

'Do you get on well with your cousin?'

He nodded. 'I do, but there'll be a reckoning when next we meet. I've always been too lenient with him. When his parents died it hit him hard. I don't know how he would have coped if he hadn't come to live at Carlow Park.'

'How old was he?'

'Just fourteen. Because I was away with the army a great deal, Robert, my older brother, saw to his well-being and education. Robert was killed in a riding accident two years ago.'

'I know. I'm sorry. What was he like—your brother? You—were close?'

'As close as brothers can be,' William said quietly.

Meeting his gaze, Cassandra saw the reflective, almost tender glimmer of light in his eyes.

'I was the lucky one,' he went on.

'Why do you say that?'

'Our parents loved us equally, but because Robert was the elder—the heir—he was singled out for special attention and made aware of his importance. It was hard for him. He wasn't allowed to climb trees, to take the boat out on to the lake without someone to watch over him, to realise his ambition and join the army as I did, which he would have loved to do. When our parents died and he came into his inheritance, I was away with my regiment.' The flexed muscles in his cheek gave evidence of his constrained grief. 'I was in Spain when I was notified of Robert's accident.'

'Did you come back?'

'No. I was in the thick of it at the time. I knew the estate was in good hands. Mark, my more-than-capable cousin, the son of my father's younger brother—there were three of them, Edward being the son of the youngest of the three—ran things until I resigned my commission and came back.'

He sighed, closing his eyes and resting his head back on the upholstery. 'I sometimes wonder if the very fabric of the Lampard family is not cursed. There is an unfortunate dark thread running through it, and who knows where the next tragedy will occur. My own life has been threatened, as well you know, Miss Greenwood. For what reason I still have no idea, but if whoever it was is intent on killing me, then perhaps the next time he attempts it he will succeed.'

'Please don't say that.'

He smiled a cynical smile, half opening his eyes and looking across at her. 'Why? Would you be sorry, Miss Greenwood?'

'I hate the thought of anyone being murdered—no matter who it is. You must be on your guard. Remember there are more ways to kill a man than by shooting him.'

William looked at her. 'I know.' After a moment's silence, to change the subject, he said, 'Are you and your sister close, Miss Greenwood?'

With surprise, Cassandra was conscious that he was now studying her with a different interest. 'Yes, I suppose we are—although Emma can be difficult at times. Family, especially sisters, can be complicated. Most of the time I think of Emma with exasperation. She's a trial. Papa was a quiet, hard-working, tolerant man, dedicated to his profession. When he died, Aunt Elizabeth, with no children of her own to spoil, stepped in and took us both under her wing. She is so looking forward to giving Emma a Season and will be extremely disappointed if she goes ahead with this foolish notion and weds your cousin. Both Mama and Aunt Elizabeth are devastated by their actions.'

'Then let us hope they see sense and have a change of heart.'

'In which case we should meet them on the road returning to London—although if this should get out, then the consequences for Emma will be dire indeed. In the eyes of polite society she has broken all the rules and will be shunned because of it. And then there is the delicate matter of—of…' She averted her eyes, feeling her face prickle with the heat of an intense blush. She was too embarrassed to voice what she had been about to say.

William knew exactly what was on her mind and that for her it was a delicate issue. 'Worry not, Miss Greenwood. Despite your opinion of him, my cousin has many fine attributes, one of them being that he is a gentleman. Deflowering gently reared virgins would violate Edward's code of behaviour.'

Cassandra flushed scarlet, embarrassed that he should phrase it so bluntly. 'Oh—I—I see. Then I am relieved to hear it.'

William found himself enjoying her discomfiture. 'My own code of honour is more relaxed—which you know all about.'

'Yes, so it would seem.' Looking at him, with his arms crossed imperturbably over his chest, his legs stretched out and his eyes glowing darkly in the dim light, there was something undeniably engaging about him. He made her feel alert and alive, and curiously stimulated. 'Now your military career is ended, will you take up your inheritance?'

He nodded. 'It's a pity, really. Mark would have been more suited to the inheritance than either Robert or me. He's very solemn—takes life seriously, has rigid ideas about behaviour and doesn't know how to enjoy life.'

'Does he approve of you, Captain Lampard?'

'Not a bit, but we've always rubbed along well enough. Unfortunately, he always gave credence to gossip and was too ready to believe what he heard.'

'Are you telling me you are not the libertine, the despoiler of women, you are portrayed as being?'

'No one is ever quite what they seem, Miss Greenwood. Not even you. You know,' he said, his gaze never leaving hers, 'you have a unique distinction.'

'What's that?'

'You have the distinction, apart from my mother, of being the only woman to have listed the failings of my character to my face.' His lips twitched with ill-suppressed amusement. 'When I left Lady Monkton's ball I felt wounded to the quick and deflated, as though I'd been pricked all over with thorns.'

'You have a hide thicker than an oxen's, Lord Lampard. I'm sure you'll heal.'

His amused laughter removed the sting from her words. 'Nevertheless I was curious as to how I had allowed such a feeling to come about. I find you an immense challenge.'

'You do?'

'Indeed. Aren't you afraid of being confined in this coach—alone with me all the way to Scotland?'

'Should I be?' Although she could feel her pulses racing, she somehow managed to maintain her calm expression.

He arched an eyebrow. 'No. However, considering my reputation as a scoundrel of the first order, don't you think you *should* be?'

'As you said yourself, Captain Lampard, no one is what they seem. Perhaps you are a scoundrel with a sudden urge to reform.'

A low chuckle preceded his reply. 'Heaven forbid. I confess that I find this unfortunate development a nuisance, but one good thing has come out of it.'

'Oh?'

'I get to spend time getting to know you better.'

'Why? Do you find my company pleasant?'

'When you're not being stubborn and temperamental.'

'I am never temperamental.'

'I disagree. There's no question about it.'

'Only if you drive me to it.'

'Tell me, Miss Greenwood, is there no young man in your life?'

'Of course not. I—have distinctive tastes.'

'Why of course not?' His eyes gleamed with devilish humour. 'A lovely young woman like you should be surrounded by doting swains.'

Cassandra was glad the light was so dim inside the coach that he couldn't see the blush that infused her cheeks and neck. 'I have my work at the institute, which is important to me. I will allow nothing to interfere with that.'

'Not even love,' he murmured softly, his gaze capturing hers.

'No.'

'Are you scared of love, Miss Greenwood?'

'No, I am not.'

'I don't believe you.'

'Believe what you like. It's true,' she retorted, feeling as if she were under attack.

'Then if you are not afraid of love, why do you hide behind your children and your institute?'

'I am not hiding and they are not my children. The institute is not mine, either.'

'Now you're prevaricating, Miss Greenwood. I think if you didn't have to mix with the *ton* in order to raise funds for your precious institute, you would be quite happy to make yourself invisible—to fade away into obscurity.' He smiled at her sudden look of indignation that his words had provoked. 'I apologise if my opinion is unkind—which is no more unkind than when you listed some of my shortcomings to me last night—but you must admit that it does have the ring of truth about it.'

'Whether it is true or not, I would not admit such a thing to you. I am not afraid of love, it's just that I have no experience of the kind of love you speak of and, at present, I am not interested in that sort of thing.'

'Then as a woman you are truly unique.'

Cassandra looked at him warily. 'You are not trying to seduce me, are you, Captain Lampard?'

'Would you allow me to seduce you, Miss Greenwood?'

In spite of the fact that his eyes were touching her like she had never been touched before, Cassandra gave him a defiant look. 'Now you're mocking me.'

'I wouldn't dream of doing that. You're far too adorable to mock.'

How could she be angry with him when he smiled that engaging smile? It was no longer possible. Her lips curved in a smile of her own. 'And you really are a complete rogue, Captain Lampard, arrogant and overbearing.'

He grinned. 'I am. I admit it. What I need is a lovely, patient and extremely tolerant young woman to take me in hand, to make me see the error of my ways and reform me.'

'Then I wish you luck. Intolerance and impatience have always been two of my failings, but there must be a female somewhere who will fall for a silken tongue and an accomplished womaniser, who will be willing to expend so much energy, time and effort on such an unenviable task.'

'Aye, but she will never be bored, I promise you that.'

Reaching up, Cassandra removed her hat and placed it on the seat beside her. 'How conceited you are, Captain Lampard. You rate yourself too highly. Now, if you don't mind, I'm going to shut my eyes and try to get some sleep.'

Resting her head against a cushion, she closed her eyes, thinking of the strange, easy conversation she had engaged in with her companion. Had she been too ready to judge, to believe the gossip she'd heard about him? Was he so different from what she had assumed? For the short time she had known him, she decided that none of it described him or did him justice. There was a powerful charisma about him that had nothing to do with his powerful physique or mocking smile.

There was something else, too, something behind that lazy smile and unbreachable wall of aloof strength, behind his piercing blue eyes, that told her that Captain William Lampard had done, seen and experienced all there was to do and see, that to know him properly would be exciting and dangerous, and therein lay his appeal—an appeal that frightened and unnerved her. She told herself that he was nothing to her, just a spectacularly handsome man who happened to be helping her solve a family crisis; as soon as this business with Emma was resolved, she decided that any association between her and this infamous captain would cease.

Eventually the gentle rocking motion of the coach, combined with the warmth, made her drowsy and she drifted into sleep. The night was hushed and still around them, the only sounds being the hoofbeats and the creaking of the coach as it progressed north.

William crossed his legs and looked over at the sleeping young woman. What a glorious creature she was. Her lips were moist and parted slightly, the thick crescent of her lashes sweeping her cheeks. He watched the slow rise and fall of her chest. Attired in her conservative travelling costume, the thought of all her soft, warm flesh beneath was causing his imagination to run wild.

Something in his heart moved and softened, then something stabbed him in the centre of his chest. What the hell was wrong with him? He had been angry and offended by her antagonistic manner at the ball, and at the same time overwhelmed by the realisation that if he didn't take care, she would come to mean something to him, and he wasn't ready for that. Miss Greenwood was an unusual female, intelligent, opinionated and full of surprises. She was also the epitome of stubborn, prideful woman. Yet for all her fire and spirit, there was no underlying viciousness. She was so very different from the sophisticated, worldly women he took to bed—experienced, sensual women, knowledgeable in the ways of love, women who knew how to please him.

No, Miss Greenwood was different, a phenomenon. She

had a touching belief in her cause. He sensed a goodness in her, something special, sensitive—something worth pursuing. There was also something untapped inside her that not even she was aware of—passion buried deep. What would happen if she allowed it all to come out? In sleep she looked like a child. He was dangerously fascinated by this vulnerable side to Miss Greenwood, he realised, and settled down to observe her sleeping profile. Nothing made sense, for nothing could explain why he was beginning to enjoy being alone with her.

Chapter Four

When Cassandra stirred and opened her eyes, dawn was breaking. Stretching her aching body and covering a yawn with the back of her hand, she glanced at her companion, who was now seated beside her. Apart from having removed his jacket and loosened his neckcloth, he looked exactly as he had when she had gone to sleep, watching her. Not all night, she hoped, and why had he changed his seat? There was a quiet alertness in his manner and his gaze was fixed warmly on her face. Self-consciously she tucked a stray silken lock of curling hair behind her ear.

'Do you feel rested? You've slept most of the night.'

Cassandra started at the sound of his deep voice. 'I do. Where are we?'

'Cambridgeshire.'

She sighed and made to move away from him, but his arm reached out and drew her to him and he smiled lazily.

'What are you doing?' she gasped, trying to pull away, but he held her firm against him. 'Have you been sitting there all night?'

He nodded with infuriating calm. 'You looked uncomfortable and your head was lolling about all over the place. You slept much better with it resting on my shoulder.'

A blush stained her cheeks, partly from indignation and partly from embarrassment. 'Oh, you really are quite insufferable. How dare you take liberties when I was asleep? Please remove your arm and allow me to sit up. I don't like being mauled.'

William's mouth curved in that faint, cynical smile of his and he kept his arm where it was. He liked the feel of her in his arms. 'Why are you so stubborn?' Tipping her chin up with his finger, he looked deep into her eyes. 'When a woman is willing to risk herself alone in my company, she has to expect certain consequences. I think it is time I adopted a different approach through the thick mire of our disagreement. It's time I tried a little persuasion of a different kind.' His eyes pinned hers and held them.

'Persuasion?' she asked, helplessly staring at him, heat running down her spine and her heart taking chaotic flight.

William noted the pulse beating in the long curve of her throat before his gaze settled on her lips. Placing his hands on her upper arms, he pulled her hard against his chest, his hands gentle and controlled, yet unyielding.

Cassandra had no time to protest before he lowered his mouth and took her lips with a gentle expertise that made her gasp. Stunned into silent quiescence, at first she froze at the initial shock of the contact, then a sense of wonder stirred within her subconscious mind, rousing her to a dazzling awareness of what he was doing to her. The assault on her senses was immediate and immense as she caught the clean, masculine scent of him, the feel of him, the taste of him. Often she had dreamed of such a kiss, but the experience of it made those insubstantial dreams seem like shadows.

Temporarily divested of the anger that had fortified her earlier, her body lost its resistance and relaxed. Sliding her hands up over his chest to his shoulders, feeling his body's heat and vibrancy through his clothes, she unwittingly moulded her melting body to his. He kissed her long and lingeringly, a compelling kiss, his lips moving back and forth, exploring with slow, searching intensity, gentling imperceptibly, and beneath the demanding persuasion was an insistence that she kiss him back that was almost beyond denial, and a promise that if she yielded it would become something quite different.

Any warning that her mind issued was stifled by the blood pounding in her ears and the shocking pleasure of being held in the arms of the man whom she had decided she would not allow to breach her self-control. His arm tightened, forcing her closer, while a large masculine hand curved round her nape, long fingers caressing and soothing her flesh.

William was both surprised and devastated by her response to his kiss, and when she began to kiss him back with more ardour than he had expected, her tongue became a flicking firebrand as his mouth consumed hers. With desire surging through him and pounding in his loins, he had to fight back the urge to lay her down on the seat and take there and then. Dragging his lips from hers, he gazed down at her upturned face. She was wide-eyed, vulnerable and trembling, her face flushed a glorious pink, and her lips moist and parted.

He lightly traced the curve of her cheek with his forefinger, admiring her freshness, her spirit, her innocence. She was everything he had known she would be, and much more. He was astounded to discover he wanted her with a fierceness that took his breath away, and he was impatient to waken all the passion in her lovely, untutored body.

'Do I see in your warming behaviour, in your response to my kiss, some glimmer of hope for a much more pleasurable understanding between us in the future? And do not deny what you feel, because I will not believe you.'

'It is possible,' Cassandra murmured, basking in the warmth of his smouldering gaze and the lazy smile that curved the firm sensual mouth, which had gently, then fiercely, explored hers. Unsteadily, she fixed her gaze on his mouth, not comprehending why he had broken off their kiss.

Tipping her chin up, he looked deeply into her eyes and quietly said, 'What do you think of my method of persuasion?'

Cassandra drew a long, steadying breath and slowly expelled it. She hesitated before answering, her magnificent eyes searching deeply into his. 'In truth, I do not trust my heart and mind to withstand the barrage of your persuasion.' Her feelings were nebulous, chaotic, yet one stood out clearly among all the others—desire. She had not wanted him to stop kissing her, and she was impatient for him to repeat the act. Something had happened to her while she had been in his arms, something quite splendid, daunting and exciting.

William glanced out of the window and released her. 'I'm happy to hear that, but we'll have to discontinue our amorous interlude. We're about to stop for breakfast.'

The coach was passing through the tall gates of a substantial coaching inn.

'I thought we'd stretch our legs and get some breakfast while the horses are being changed. However, time is precious. I don't want to waste one minute of it.'

Reaching for his jacket, he shrugged it on and solicitously helped her to alight from the coach. Aching in every limb and still in a state of shock about what had just happened, telling herself that she should have slapped his face, Cassandra disappeared to attend to her personal needs and to collect her scattered wits, while William stopped to issue instructions to the grooms.

Passing through a covered doorway, they entered the inn together. The general air was one of comfort and respectability. The stout landlord greeted them. Seeing the young couple were people of quality, he led them through the common room where several patrons were already eating breakfast, and ushered them into a low-beamed dining parlour, which provided a semblance of privacy.

The acrid odour of ale and the appetising aroma of hot food pervaded every corner and started Cassandra's mouth watering. Settling themselves at a table in a window recess, William stressed to the landlord their need for haste, and in no time at all, Annie, the landlord's plump and cheerful spouse in a starched cap and smelling of freshly baked bread, laid out a sumptuous breakfast in front of them.

Cassandra's stomach groaned for sustenance, and without wasting time she began to do the food justice.

'You're hungry,' William remarked, watching her with an amused gleam in his eyes as she munched on a piece of bacon.

'Ravenous, and this bacon is simply done to a turn. It's delicious,' she said, piercing a steamed mushroom. She paused just long enough to take a gulp of her coffee and glanced across at him to see that he was consuming his food more leisurely, savouring each taste fully. 'You really should eat plenty. Mama always says you should eat a hearty breakfast to start the day. She always says we do not eat to satisfy our appetite. Food is strength.'

'Wise woman, your mama.'

'So you must have something inside you to fortify you on the journey, Captain Lampard.'

'William.'

She stared at him. 'I'm sorry?'

'I would like you to call me William. I have left the army. My title is Lord Lampard—but I would like it if you would call me William.'

'I do not think that would be appropriate—in fact, it would be highly irregular—but Captain Lampard is such a mouthful.'

'There you are, then. You have my permission to call me William.'

'That is generous of you.'

'I have my good points.'

'I agree,' she said, laughing softly. 'Why—even scoundrels must have some somewhere.'

'Then I have managed to vindicate myself to you—just a little?'

'Yes—a little. Despite your earlier transgression—you know, kissing aside—so far you have been most courteous.'

'I do my best. And you will call me William?'

'Well, as you are already aware that I am the unconventional type, very well—William.'

A tremor ran through him when she spoke his name for the first time. 'That's better. Are you going to grant me permission in turn to use your Christian name?'

She shrugged. What did it matter what he called her since she had resolved never to see him again after this unpleasant business was done with—although his earlier assault on her lips almost made her wish he would do it again. 'I have a feeling that if I don't, you will use it anyway.'

'I take it that's a yes.'

She nodded, taking a bite out of her bread.

'Thank you—Cassandra. Now that is out of the way, enjoy your breakfast.'

'I intend to, even though you're thinking that I really ought to be worrying about getting to Scotland post haste and not stuffing myself with eggs and bacon.'

He smiled that slow smile of his, calmly slicing through his egg. 'Not at all. I'm glad you can live for the moment.'

'You mean I should not think of what will happen?' She sighed. 'Unfortunately, I do worry. Quite frankly, I find it depressing to contemplate all the fuss there will be when we do catch up with the runaways. If they are already married, then the scandal that will ensue when we all get back to London will be horrendous.'

'It can do no good worrying, so eat your breakfast.'

At that moment the landlord brought in a pot of fresh coffee and placed it on the table. 'Is everything to your liking?'

'It is. Thank you, landlord,' William answered.

'You and your lady wife are out and about early, sir,' the landlord said by way of conversation—as well as being inquisitive. 'Travelling far, are you?'

'Some considerable distance, yes. It's been a long night, landlord, and my *wife* and I would like to partake of this excellent breakfast and be on our way. Will you excuse us?'

'Of course, sir,' the landlord said in a flat tone, backing towards the door. 'Didn't mean to impose. Enjoy your breakfast.'

When he had closed the door, with a mischievous smile tugging at his lips and one eyebrow cocked, William looked at Cassandra, who was staring at him accusingly.

'You really are the limit,' she gasped, unable to believe what had just happened. 'I gave you freedom with my name, but now I think you are again taking liberties. You let that man think I am your wife.'

William shrugged indolently. 'Merely to quell the gossip. Consider the situation as it will look to him—a young woman travelling with a man unaccompanied. If you are not my wife, then in his eyes that makes you my mistress.'

Her eyes opened wide. 'Mistress? I will be no man's mistress.'

'Which is why I told him you are my wife—to avoid any embarrassing speculation, you understand.' He reached for the coffee pot. 'More coffee?' he offered with a lazy grin.

Meeting his clear blue eyes with their wicked sparkle, unable to keep a straight face Cassandra laughed and shoved her cup forward. 'I am quite overwhelmed by your consideration and, yes, thank you, I would like some more coffee.'

Eager to be on their way, with fresh horses harnessed to the coach, the two grooms replete after a hearty breakfast, William and Cassandra were about to leave the inn when a soberly dressed gentleman carrying a small brown leather bag came hurrying in, almost knocking Cassandra over in his haste. Immediately he reached out to steady her, apologising profusely for his clumsiness and hoping she was not harmed in any way. Cassandra laughed it off and assured him she was quite all right. At that moment the landlord appeared out of the common room and hurried over to the stranger, seeming relieved to see him. William took Cassandra's arm and they proceeded towards the door.

'Thank the Lord you're here, Dr Wade. I apologise for having to send for you, but the young lady's still very poorly. Her companion is beside himself. 'Tis to be hoped it's not infectious,' he said, shaking his head solemnly. 'Bad for business that would be.'

'I'll go straight up. Runaways, you say?'

'Aye, it appears so—not that they've said as much, but my Annie has a nose for these things. Arrived late last night.'

Having listened with little interest to the interchange between the landlord and Dr Wade, upon hearing the word 'runaways', William paused, suddenly alert, and turned back to them as they were about to climb the stairs.

'Wait!' he called, striding towards them.

The two men turned and looked down at him.

'There are a couple of runaways staying here?'

'Aye, there are,' the landlord replied. 'What of it?'

'What are their names?'

The landlord rubbed his chin. 'Well, now, I'm not sure—'

'It's all right landlord,' a quiet voice said from the top of the stairs. 'I'll speak to the gentleman.' The young man who suddenly appeared looked at Dr Wade. 'You must be the doctor. Please go and tend the young lady. She really is quite ill. I would be grateful if you could give her some medicine to make her feel better.'

As the doctor went to tend his patient with the landlord to show him the way, the man came slowly down the stairs. His attractive face was grey and drawn, his eyes shadowed with fatigue. Not until he stood in front of William did he speak.

'Hello, William. I knew you'd come.'

William's face darkened for an instant as he strove for control. 'Well, Edward,' he said, his voice coated with ice, 'what the hell do you think you're playing at?'

* * *

Noticing they were attracting curious glances from the other patrons, William requested a private room. The landlord immediately put one at their disposal.

When the door was closed, concern for her sister propelled Cassandra to Edward's side. 'Is it Emma who is ill?' she asked, deeply concerned that this was indeed so.

Edward nodded. 'She began feeling unwell shortly after we left London.'

'Then why on earth didn't you take her home? What could have possessed you to embark on this mad escapade when she was feeling unwell?'

'I wanted to go back, but Emma wouldn't hear of it. She said it was nothing more than a chill, that she would soon feel better and that we should go on to Scotland.'

Cassandra drew back angrily. 'Shame on you that you think to place all the blame on my sister. You knew perfectly well what you were doing when you arranged this elopement. The two of you have been alone together for twenty-four hours—spending the night with her in a sordid tavern room as if she were some common drab,' she fumed contemptuously. 'Are you like the rest of London's young rakes—play with women, make them fall in love with you, seduce them, and then tell them you have no need of them?'

Deeply offended, Edward's eyes flamed with anger. 'First, I am no rake, Miss Greenwood. I honour your sister and I would not lay one finger on her until she is my wife.'

'Wife? Ha! Any aspirations you might have to make her your wife you forfeited the moment you absconded with her.'

'Cassandra, enough,' William said quietly but firmly, taking her arm and drawing her to one side.

Furious, she shook her arm free. 'Enough, you say. That silly, impressionable girl, who is my sister, was so flattered by your cousin's attentions that she would foolishly allow him to talk her into anything. How do we know he hasn't seduced her already? His treatment of her has been abominable to say the least.'

'Stop it, Cassandra,' William said sharply. 'Calm down. I will listen to what Edward has to say while you go and see your sister.'

She glared at him. 'Since it is my sister he abducted, then I will stay to hear what he has to say. I shall go and see Emma when the doctor has examined her.'

William nodded. 'Very well, if you must, but please sit down and be quiet.'

As she perched on the edge of a chair, Cassandra's heart was beating in rhythmic thuds, but, difficult as it was to remain silent, she did as she was told and did not speak. William stood with his back to the fire, tall and impressive in his dark green cutaway coat and highly polished brown boots. He did not look like a man who had been travelling all night. His immaculate appearance made his cousin's dishevelled state more obvious. Edward's coat was unbuttoned, revealing a pale grey satin waistcoat. Though elegant, the clothes looked as though he had been wearing them a couple of days, and his white neckcloth was loose and rumpled.

As William's cold eyes flickered over him, Edward attempted to straighten his neck-linen. Knowing William's setdowns were lethal, he was filled with dread as he waited for his blistering tirade to begin, but all he could think of was his dear, sweet Emma lying ill in bed.

'I hope you'll pardon my appearance, William,' Edward said. 'With Emma being so unwell, I've been up all night.'

William nodded grimly. 'So have we, thanks to you. Well? What have you to say for yourself?'

Edward flinched before his cousin's controlled rage. He was ensnared in the web of his own folly, he knew that.

'You've been a fool, Edward, a stupid, self-indulgent bloody fool,' William went on furiously without giving Edward time to reply. 'I am disappointed in you—deeply disappointed. What in God's name made you do it? You have known Miss Greenwood—a well brought-up and guarded young girl—for such a short time.'

'Three months. I was drawn to her from the start, and in the time I have known her I have come to hold her in high esteem,' Edward said, doing his best to smile in an attempt to lighten the serious tones and harsh lines of his cousin's face. 'I did try to stay away from her, but fate intervened and kept throwing us together.'

William gave a brief, humourless snort. 'So, your ardour ran away with you and you began to woo her, beginning the pattern, the customs that a gentleman pursues with the lady of his choice, which eventually leads to marriage,' he rapped out, walking up and down the room in earnest frustration.

Edward swallowed hard and stepped back from the furious blast of those steely blue eyes. 'Yes—something like that.'

'What a load of mawkish rubbish. You must have been off your head. Did you not consider the young lady's age when you began trailing after her petticoats like some lovesick calf? For God's sake, Edward, she is just eighteen years old—seventeen when you first knew her—still a child in some people's thinking.'

'I know, but it made no difference to the way we felt about each other. We decided we wanted to be together, and, knowing both our families would be set against it—'

'Damned right we would,' William growled, his gaze relentless.

'We decided to elope—to bring forward what is inevitable.'

'And what about your army career? Did you not concern yourself with that when you were making declarations of love to Miss Greenwood and preparing to elope?'

Lowering his head in contrition, Edward said in a low voice, 'I didn't think it would matter if I put my career on hold for a while. I've done wrong, I know that, and I would like to put it right—so far as I can.' Raising his head, he directed his gaze at Cassandra. 'When we arrived at the tavern last night,

Emma was so sick and frightened, and there was nothing I could do to help her. I apologise most sincerely for any hurt I have caused you and your family, Miss Greenwood. For what satisfaction you may want of me later, I will bide by it. But I would ask you to let it wait until Emma is feeling well.'

Cassandra rose. 'Yes, you are right. Emma must be our main concern.'

'Wh-what is to be done, sir?' Edward asked his cousin haltingly.

'I have decided that you will leave for the army immediately when we return to London,' William informed him, turning his back and looking out of the window. 'It is where you should have been yesterday. There will be no further discussion on the subject. You will remain with your regiment until it is time for it to leave the country. To spare Miss Greenwood's reputation it is imperative that we avoid a scandal. I insist that we keep this unpleasant business between ourselves, and in this you will assist us by maintaining a discreet silence. You will have no further contact with Miss Greenwood. Is that understood?'

Edward stepped forward in alarm. 'But, William—you can't do this. I beg you to hear me out…'

William spun round. 'I can and I will, Edward. Until you are both of age and until her mother gives her consent, you will sever all ties. Finally, I expect your total cooperation. Do you agree?'

Edward capitulated before the seniority and the wrath of his cousin. 'Yes, sir.'

As he shoved his fair hair off his brow, Cassandra saw that his hand was trembling, his face set pale with deep emotion. Strangely, her heart welled with pity. He was crushed by the wave of events that had overtaken him. There was moisture in his eyes and he blinked rapidly, leaving her in no doubt of this young man's tender feelings and deep concern for Emma. The truth was, she had disparaged him because she did not want Emma to form an attachment to any man before she had made her début, and her sceptical attitude, once adopted, had stuck.

The anger that had consumed her from the moment she had learned of the elopement evaporated, along with her belief that Edward Lampard was anything like his cousin William, and nor would he be if he lived to be a hundred.

Cassandra was startled by Emma's condition. Nothing more than a severe chill, Dr Wade had said, and in his opinion it was safe to take her home. In Cassandra's opinion, she though her sister was extremely ill. Her cheeks were flushed, her skin beaded with perspiration. Resting against the pillows with her eyes closed, she looked so very young and vulnerable. Cassandra's heart went out to her.

Sitting on the bed, she took her hand. Emma opened her eyes. They were very bright and feverish, and there was a desperate look about her. Emma started when she saw her sister.

'It's all right, Emma,' Cassandra was quick to reassure her. 'Please don't upset yourself.'

Tears formed in Emma's eyes. 'Are you very angry with me, Cassy?' she whispered with difficulty. 'I know I must have put you to so much trouble. I am so sorry.'

'I'm not angry, although you do seem to have got yourself into something of a pickle. What you and Edward have done is very foolish, but at this moment all I am concerned about is you.'

'Poor Edward. Is he all right?' No longer able to hold her tears at bay, she began to weep.

'Yes, though he's worried about you.'

'I—I've been at my wit's end all night and I feel so poorly. Please be kind to him, Cassy.'

'Shush, not now, Emma.' Cassandra held her sister's feverish hand until her sobs subsided and she slept.

Getting up, she quietly left the room. William was waiting for her at the bottom of the stairs. His face was strained, as if he had been waiting for her in wretched suspension.

'How is she?' he asked. His voice was surprisingly gentle.

'Very ill indeed.' Suddenly feeling tired, she bent her head, putting the back of her hand to her eyes. 'I'm sorry, but I am so worried about her.' William's eyes were warm with concern—not for her, she knew that, but for her sister.

'That is completely understandable in these circumstances. You are upset. What can I do to help?' His offer was made in a tone of gentle commiseration.

Cassandra lifted her head, her eyes searching his. 'She can't stay here. I have to get her home where she can be properly looked after. Can it be done?'

He nodded. 'I don't see why not. The landlord isn't happy about her being here. Doctor Wade has stressed she has nothing infectious, but the landlord thinks a sick woman on the premises will put travellers off staying here.'

'Poor Emma. She was terribly glad to see me. She was so upset that I hadn't the heart to berate her.'

William's brow arched and he smiled. 'You are a very understanding woman.'

Cassandra was warmed by his smile and his solicitude. 'My sister is often of a different opinion.'

'Siblings usually are. We shall leave right away. You and your sister must travel in my coach—you will be more comfortable. I will accompany Edward. Get her dressed. I'll settle the account with the landlord and make sure the coaches are made ready to leave.'

'Where's Edward?'

William's eyes went to the closed door to the private room. 'Shall I go and tell him how Emma is?'

'No. Leave him,' William said curtly. 'Our main concern is to get your sister into the coach and be on our way.'

'Will—will you come up in a few minutes? Emma is terribly weak and she may need helping down the stairs. I'd be most grateful.'

William nodded, his expression grim. Turning from her, he strode out of the inn.

* * *

When he knocked on the door to Emma's room fifteen minutes later and entered, it was to find Cassandra struggling to get her sister into her coat. The girl was sitting on the bed, swaying as she tried to keep awake.

Cassandra shot him a beseeching, apologetic look. 'We're almost ready.'

When Emma tried to stand, in her weakened state she flopped back on to the bed. All the life seemed to have drained out of her, leaving her like a mechanical toy.

'Here, let me.' Without more ado, William strode to the bed and lifted her into his arms—so easy and quick. The weight that Cassandra had scarcely been able to move was casually carried across the room. 'Bring her things. I'll carry her out to the coach.'

Hastily gathering together Emma's few possessions, Cassandra followed him out of the inn.

After easing his burden into the coach, William turned to Cassandra. 'I believe your sister will be more comfortable with the cushions placed round her. I would advise you to sit beside her to prevent her rolling around. The day's warm enough, but wrap her in the blankets. Have you got everything?'

'Yes—I think so. Oh, I do hope she's going to be all right. We have such a long way to travel.'

'Don't worry. We'll drive the horses into the ground if need be. She'll be home and tucked up in her own bed in no time. We'll be travelling behind, so if you have to stop we'll know.'

As she was about to climb inside the coach, Cassandra hesitated and looked to where Edward was standing, observing the proceedings. He was motionless save for the steady movements of his breathing. His ashen face was a solemn, sad mask, his heart in his anguished eyes as, shoulders slumped with dejection, he turned and climbed into the other coach.

William watched Cassandra shake out a rug and tuck it around her sister. 'Will you be all right?' She nodded and in her face he saw grim resolution. 'Good girl. Order the coach to stop if you must. We'll be close behind.'

The driver whipped up the horses and the carriage sped and rocked along the main highway, passing slower conveyances. Cassandra did as William had suggested and sat beside Emma and with infinite tenderness held her slender body, which trembled against her own steady one as Emma slept fitfully. Her concern for her sister deepened when Emma began to mumble incoherently, but after a while it was as if the effort of speaking weakened her and her head fell sideways and her voice suddenly disappeared. She began to tremble, which increased, and her teeth began chattering violently.

Tucking another rug about her, Cassandra knew Emma was getting worse. She felt a wave of desperation as she strove for control and to calm her mounting fears. Nevertheless, panic lashed at her; worried to death, she ordered the coach driver to stop. The accompanying groom jumped down and lowered the steps. William's coach halted behind.

Jumping to the ground William strode towards her, taking her hand and drawing her close, his handsome face set in anxious lines. 'What is it?'

'Emma is much worse. She's delirious and all of a-tremble. We really must get her into a bed—anywhere.' She sighed, trying to keep her voice level, but William heard the quiver in its depths. 'I'm sorry. You must think I'm mad worrying like this.' William smiled almost…affectionate, she thought.

'I think you're doing splendidly.' William gazed at her strained features and felt a resurgence of the peculiar tenderness she sometimes seemed to evoke in him. 'It's inevitable that the strain of the past twenty-four hours is beginning to get to you, but I am certain your sister will be fine.'

'Please, William, London is hours away. Do you think we could find somewhere?'

William drew in a breath, his eyes meeting hers. After a

moment of thoughtful silence, he nodded. 'I know the very place. We'll be there shortly.'

Glad of his strength and reassurance that everything would be fine, Cassandra seized on that and clung to it for all the comfort it offered. Returning to the carriage, she felt enormous relief from knowing William was close. She remembered the moment when he had taken her hand, as if he hadn't been aware that he had done so. Her gaze had been drawn to it. There was something so masculine in the strength of that hand and the long fingers that made her heartbeat quicken at the memory. She sighed, gazing out of the window as villages, scattered cottages and a patchwork of fields flew past, realising that there were times when William Lampard was far too attractive for her peace of mind.

After travelling a few more miles they turned off the main thoroughfare into narrower, twisting lanes. Cassandra had no idea where they were going and she didn't care. She could only hope, when she looked at Emma lolling in the corner of the coach, that they got there quickly.

As her eyes searched ahead she was disheartened. There was nothing but parkland with browsing deer that seemed to go on for ever. A long avenue lined with tall trees led away round a bend and crossed a humpbacked bridge. After passing through some high gilded gates, she saw it—a house, old and imposing and of honey-coloured brick, with many windows, long and gleaming, unlike any she had ever seen before.

When the coach drew up at the bottom of a flight of steps leading up to the front door, she was aware of people—servants, male and female—coming out of the house and throwing up their arms in alarm.

Standing in the drive, Cassandra was awestruck as she looked at William striding towards her. 'William—who does this house belong to?'

'Me. Welcome to Carlow Park. Now, let's get your sister inside.'

Seemingly indifferent to the panic taking place on the steps, immediately he took charge of Emma. Gathering her into his arms, he went up the steps and into the house. Cassandra was behind him, her whole being concentrated on her sister.

Striding past the thunderstruck servants, who were speechless with shock at the sight of their master with a drooping young lady in his arms, his eyes lighted on an officious-looking woman dressed in black.

'Mrs Henderson, is there a room prepared?'

'Welcome home, my lord—and yes, the green room is always made ready for the unexpected guest.' Totally unprepared, Mrs Henderson, the housekeeper, was not at all pleased with his lordship's unexpected arrival after two years' absence. Her eyes glanced curiously from the unconscious young woman in his arms, to the young woman looking on anxiously and back to Lord Lampard.

'Thank you. Get someone to fetch Dr Tomlinson at once. They are to tell him it's urgent.'

Effortlessly climbing the stairs and walking along thickly carpeted landings hung with family portraits, he eventually shoved a door open to what Cassandra assumed must be the green room, and went inside. With infinite care he laid his burden on the bed and stood back to let Cassandra take over.

'I'll get her undressed and into bed,' she said, beginning to unfasten Emma's coat.

'I'll send one of the maids in to give you a hand.' He strode to the door.

Cassandra paused and looked at him. 'William.' He turned. 'Thank you. I really am grateful to you for letting us come here.'

'My pleasure. It was fortunate that Carlow Park was so close. And don't worry. The doctor will be here shortly.'

Half an hour later, having got Emma undressed and into bed with the help of an obliging maid called Molly, Mrs Henderson ushered Dr Tomlinson into the room.

Doctor Tomlinson confirmed what Dr Wade had said, that Emma had a severe chill. When the crisis was past he was sure the chill would leave no ill effects. He departed, ensuring she had a cordial to drink and prescribing mustard plasters, rest and warmth.

Having spent the time he had been back at Carlow Park settling in and familiarising himself with the order of things, William went to see Cassandra later that evening and to enquire after her sister. He'd hoped Cassandra would have left Emma in the care of one of the maids and joined him and a subdued Edward for dinner, but she had declined and dined in her room.

When he knocked she opened the door. He hesitated and stared at her. Her face glowed pale in the dim light. Seeing her unbound, honey-gold hair falling in a gentle cascade over her shoulders, he drew in a quick breath. For the space of half a dozen heartbeats he didn't move. Then slowly he smiled.

'I've come to enquire after your sister,' he said softly. 'May I come in? I am aware of the impropriety of such a visit, but these are hardly normal circumstances. I thought you might like some company.' Cassandra returned his gaze, wide-eyed and uncertain, then, opening the door wider, she invited him inside. 'How is she?' His eyes were drawn to the young woman in bed, but they did not linger. They preferred to dwell on the older sister.

'She is easier—slips in and out of sleep, but she's cooler and no longer delirious. I think she's over the worst of it.'

'I'm glad to hear it. Have you everything you need?' he asked, moving away from the bed to the fire so as not to disturb Emma.

'Yes. Everyone has been most kind. I can't thank them enough.' Cassandra stared at him, standing with his back to the fire, and she experienced such a rush of excitement it caused her to become tongue-tied. She was affected strongly by the force of his presence and the memory of his kiss and, studying him, was all too aware of the strength of his attraction. Overcome by tiredness, she sat in the chair she had been occupying when she'd heard his knock.

William was standing over her, looking down at her with concern. There were dark shadows beneath her eyes and she was pale. She had become soft and quiet in her distress for her sister. It was hard to believe that this was the same rebellious spitfire who had confronted him so courageously at his London residence.

'How are you, Cassandra?' he asked quietly.

The gentleness and warmth in his tone brought the heat creeping into her cheeks. 'Me? I'm all right.' She smiled tiredly. 'It's been quite a day.'

'You really must try and get some rest. A room has been made ready. One of the maids can sit with your sister.'

She shook her head. 'No. I would not consider it. Emma is my responsibility. If I'd spent more time with her, watching over her, perhaps we wouldn't be in this mess.'

'You shouldn't blame yourself. None of this is your fault. You are not your sister's keeper, Cassandra. She does have your mother and Lady Monkton.'

'Since Papa died, Mama spends a good deal of her time at the institute. Emma spends most of her time at Monkton House, but even Aunt Elizabeth would never have expected her to do something so stupid as to elope.'

William nodded towards the inviting green-silk winged chair positioned across from her own. 'Do you mind?'

She shook her head. 'Not at all.' Resting against the back of the chair, she half-closed her eyes. 'Please sit down, William. You must be feeling as exhausted as I do.'

He sat down, stretching his long muscular legs out in front of him and crossing them at the ankles.

The atmosphere was relaxed between them. There was silence inhabited by the living presence of the fire. In spite of herself, Cassandra found her eyes captured and held by William's dark blue ones. With his brown hair curling softly into his neck, the same magnetism she had seen before was in his eyes. The room seemed to come to life with his presence, infusing it with his own energy and vigour.

'Are you glad to be home?' she asked.

'I am, but I've been away a long time. It takes some getting used to.' He smiled and there was a suggestion of mischief in his eyes. 'My untimely arrival with two lovely ladies has set the house in turmoil and certainly given the servants something to gossip about.' He laughed softly. 'No doubt my return to Carlow Park with two female companions will spread through Hertfordshire like a wind through a hayfield.'

Cassandra was suddenly alarmed. 'I sincerely hope not. Emma's reputation is already teetering on the edge. I was hoping we could return to London with no one any the wiser.'

'Then allow me to allay your fears. Sticking close to the truth, I have told Pearson, my butler, and Mrs Henderson that I encountered you and your sister on the road and that you were travelling to London. When your sister became ill you sought rooms at a coaching inn, but the landlord was reluctant to accommodate you. I offered you my assistance.' His eyes glowed in the warm light of the fire as he gave her a lazy smile. 'I only did what any self-respecting gentleman would have done in such circumstances.'

'Thank you. You seem to have thought of everything.'

Silence reigned once more as they stared intently into the glowing heart of the fire, and then they looked at each other. Drawn by the depths of her eyes looking into his and by the soft freshness of her lips, William contemplated her for a moment.

Cassandra sat, riveted by the warm gaze. She had a strange idea that if she moved or spoke the rare moment would be broken and something precious lost. In the end it was William who sighed and spoke first.

'Tell me about your father,' he said, reluctant to leave her just yet. 'He must have been a remarkable man.'

'Yes, he was. I always looked up to him and admired him greatly for all he achieved. His death came as a terrible blow to us all. The institute was very important to him—his ultimate dream was to open a hospital for children in London. Sadly, he didn't live long enough to realise it—but one day it will happen.'

'And you say your mother works there.'

Cassandra nodded. 'She works extremely hard—I wish she didn't,' she said quietly. 'When my father died, Mama went all to pieces and we were so worried about her for a time. The institute became her salvation—mine, too, in a way. Together we did all we possibly could to keep it open—raising funds was difficult and a worry. We desperately needed more benefactors—we still do.'

'Is Lady Monkton a benefactor? But I suppose she must be, being a relative and extremely wealthy.'

'As a matter of fact, she isn't—though she has offered to make a sizeable donation many times. Mama refuses to take a penny of her money for the institute. She's so grateful for everything she's done for all of us since Papa died that she insists it stops there. When I approached the wealthy for donations, at first I was painfully aware that I was a social outcast. The *ton* patronised me, were amused by what I do. Some treated me with outright scorn, and I was miserable—and then angry that I allowed those people and their comments to upset me. Realising I was about to fall at the first hurdle, I took firm hold of myself and set about trying to change their opinion of me.'

'And you succeeded.'

'Yes. I practised detachment, I learned how to laugh, how to read people, how to charm.'

'What you really mean is that you became a virtuoso of deceit.'

'Yes, I suppose so. I had to win them over. I harbour no grudge against them for their ignorance.' Afraid that William might feel sorry for her, she smiled and shook her head dismissively. 'They soon began to accept me and what I do— thanks to Aunt Elizabeth.'

William thought it more poignant than funny. At that moment he felt an inexplicable surge of anger at all those small-minded people who had ostracised her. Deep inside he felt a stirring of protection towards her that surprised and disturbed him, and he turned his face away to cover his own bewildering emotions.

'It's late. I shall leave you to get some rest. Tomorrow I will escort Edward to London. It's time that young man began his army career—a spot of discipline will do him good.'

'Poor Edward. I'm beginning to feel sorry for him. He is hurting so much—and he is in love. People do foolish things when they are in love—so they say.' She flushed and laughed softly. 'Of course, I wouldn't know. Don't be too hard on him—otherwise you'll probably drive him to desert the army.'

William shot her a look of mock offence. 'I resent that. I have been the very soul of patience with the youth. Besides— I seem to recall you accusing him of being a lecherous, conniving, smooth-talking cad.'

'That was unpardonable of me—it was also before I knew him and saw how genuinely fond he is of Emma.'

William's look was one of incredulity. 'Miss Greenwood, I do believe you are becoming soft.'

Her lips curved in a smile and the dimple in her cheek deepened. 'Do you know, Lord Lampard, I do believe I am.' Cassandra tilted her head to one side and her eyes quizzed him.

'What?' William asked, suddenly wary of her. 'What's going through that busy head of yours now, Miss Greenwood?'

'I am wondering if this quiet, almost retiring man sitting opposite me really can be the arrogant rake I've heard about.'

'Retiring?' His chuckle sounded low and deep. 'Heaven

forbid! Are you trying to ruin my image, Miss Greenwood? How have I allowed you to imagine I am any less dangerous than society has painted me?' On a more serious note, he said, 'I did a lot of growing up in the army. It teaches you things you can't possibly learn in ordinary life. And now I've returned to Carlow Park to settle down and take an interest in the estate—and maybe find myself a wife.'

There was a sudden sparkle in his eyes that Cassandra prudently ignored. 'Then I am sure you will enjoy being pursued by women who fancy the title of Lady Lampard, Countess of Carlow, and have a respect for this beautiful house. The pursuit will be hot and strong. But what kind of marriage will it be? I suspect that you would not allow marriage to impair your freedom. Will you pay attention to your wife and doing what you call your duty, and then be off to London to take pleasure with your mistress?'

'That depends on the woman I choose to wed. There isn't a scoundrel alive who can't be tamed by the right woman, and I firmly believe that one should constantly strive to improve oneself.' He raised one sleek, well-defined eyebrow, watching, waiting for her reaction. A faint half-smile now played on his lips as if he knew exactly what was going on in her mind.

'I have a distinct feeling you are trying to proposition me, Lord Lampard.'

'Ah, now there's a thought. Scoundrel I may be, but I am a fairly honest person. Shall I convince you of my merits?'

'You've already tried that,' she quipped, reminding him of his assault on her lips in the coach. 'I should have slapped your face for your impudence.'

'Why? You enjoyed kissing me just as much as I enjoyed kissing you.'

'Nevertheless, marriage à la mode would not be for me. I think what I do is preferable to an unhappy marriage.' Cassandra looked at him and felt a curious warmth for the man whose profligate reputation gave her every reason to despise him. She considered it rather odd that she didn't. A woman was always flattered to learn a man was attracted to her—as remarkable as it might be. She sensed William was completely sincere, and she wasn't at all displeased.

William heaved himself out of the chair and stretched his aching body. A slow roguish grin moved across his features. 'Then I feel I shall have to persuade you—and enjoy doing so. But for now I will bid you good night. I intend to be away early. I'll call on your mother and explain everything.'

'Thank you. I'd appreciate that. She'll be out of her mind with worry over Emma, and will be so relieved that we reached her before she got to Scotland. Of course, we won't impose on you for longer than is necessary.'

'You are not imposing. Hospitality is one of my strong points.'

'Nevertheless, we'll be going home just as soon as Emma is fit to travel—perhaps in a couple of days, so if you would be so kind as to ask Mama to send Clem with the carriage, I would be grateful.'

'There won't be any need for that. I shall see you get back to London myself.'

As he left her, William reluctantly faced the fact that Cassandra Greenwood was a far cry from the women he usually associated with. What an enchanting, intriguing creature she was. In reality, she was warm, caring, sensitive and intelligent, but she was also a natural temptress, captivating and enchanting, alluring and vibrant, with a ripe beauty that heated and stirred his blood—and she had the softest, most appealing mouth he had ever tasted, and the largest blue-green eyes.

Chapter Five

The dark of the night crept around the house and the moon shone like an orange globe. For Cassandra, the hours flowed together, and when Emma rested in the quieter state of fevered sleep, she curled up in a chair in front of the fire, sometimes dozing, sometimes just staring into the glowing embers, trying to understand the turbulent, consuming emotions William Lampard was able to arouse in her. When she was with him there was an element of danger, which only added to the excitement.

How carelessly and artfully he was beginning to weave his web about her. She had not intended to become so ensnared. She knew him for a practising philanderer, so why had she allowed herself to be attracted by him? Why had she let her emotions become involved? The fact was that she had, and she greatly feared that she could be overwhelmed by him.

Early the next morning, opening the door to a quiet knock, Cassandra wasn't really surprised to find Edward standing there.

'Pardon my intrusion, Miss Greenwood. I have come to enquire after Emma. I do so hope she is no worse.' His tormented eyes went beyond her to the young woman in the bed.

Cassandra smiled understandably and stood aside for him

to enter. 'No, she is no worse. You will be relieved to know my sister is a little better,' she said in a quiet, reassuring voice.

Edward moved slowly to the bed. Bending and leaning forward, his eyes soft with love, he whispered her name. Emma's eyes flickered open. When his features came into focus her face lit up with the flame of her love.

'Edward,' she whispered hoarsely. 'Oh, Edward—my love.' Then her eyelids fluttered and closed and she settled against the pillows.

Cassandra turned away from the beseeching urgency in his eyes, unable to look upon their hot brown sweetness when he looked at Emma.

Seeing that she slept, Edward straightened and crossed to Cassandra, his expression one of deep concern. 'William and I are to leave for London shortly. It may be some time before I am able to return, depending on where my regiment sends me. I know we did wrong, Miss Greenwood, but please believe me when I say that I care for Emma deeply and intended no harm to come to her.'

'I know.'

'Will—will you allow me to write to her?'

'Unfortunately I cannot do that. It's not my place. It is my mother you will have to approach for any future association with Emma. And I must warn you that, because of your unacceptable behaviour, she may very well refuse.' When she noted the dismay this caused him, she smiled. 'Emma is very young. If her feelings for you are unchanged when she has made her début, then who knows. My sister is wilful and headstrong, and usually gets her own way in most things. I ask you to be patient, to give this unfortunate business time to settle down.'

He nodded, trying his best to hide his pain. With one last look at Emma, he opened the door and glanced back at Cassandra. He smiled a shaky smile. 'Emma is indeed fortunate to have such a loyal and caring sister. Goodbye, Miss Greenwood, and thank you.' And so Edward took his leave of Emma sadly, but with hope in his heart.

The next day, after partaking of a light breakfast and pleased that Emma had managed to eat a little, Cassandra left her resting peacefully and with Molly to sit with her. She walked in the grounds, relieved, after her confinement, to stretch her legs.

Carlow Park, the ancestral estate of generations of Lampards, green and full of life, was comprised of hundreds of acres of game-filled woods and rolling parkland, fertile fields and sheep in the meadows. It was pleasantly warm and the sun shone forth with splendour. Cassandra caught her breath at the sight of it stretching far into the distance beyond the gardens. Descending a low flight of steps from the terrace, she leisurely followed a path around the immaculately clipped velvet lawns, admiring the borders gloriously abloom with late spring and early summer flowers.

Carlow Park was more beautiful than any place she ever imagined. In the distance, down a gentle slope, the gardens gave way to an enormous lake. Swans and water fowl drifted on the tranquil surface, and it was overlooked by an ornate stone summerhouse. She began walking towards it, enjoying the gentle breeze that came off the water, feeling it blow through her hair, which fell loose about her shoulders.

From the corner of her eye she glimpsed a movement. Halting her step and half turning, she saw William astride a magnificent chestnut horse riding towards her. Her heart gave a leap of surprise, consternation and she admitted, a certain excitement. He was one of the most striking looking men she had ever seen—a man of power who set himself above others, as accustomed to obedience from those about him as he was from his horse, which he sat as though he were part of it.

When he was close his broad smile gleamed with a startling whiteness against his lean, tanned features. Short heavy wisps of his dark hair curled slightly about his face. There was a health and vitality about him that was almost mesmerising.

'I'm happy to see you taking the air, Cassandra, which can only mean that your sister is recovering, since I cannot imagine you leaving her alone otherwise.' He dismounted, thinking how ravishing she looked with her face all rosy from the sun's warmth. Her hair fell in a cascade of waves, with thin strands teasing her cheeks. Its lustrous simplicity gave her the look of a young innocent—which was precisely what she was. He had been unable to put her face from his mind since he had first seen her. It was the most compelling face he had ever seen and full of contradictions—open, yet guarded, anxious, determined, and so very vulnerable.

He still couldn't believe how he had left Edward at the academy and raced back to Carlow Park like a besotted idiot in his eagerness to see Cassandra. Unfortunately, a disturbing incident had occurred on the road that had delayed him and by the time he'd arrived home it had been too late to call on her. For the time being he decided to keep what had happened to himself, but one thing he was sure of—it had been another attempt on his life.

When the shadowy figure of what they thought was a masked highwayman had appeared in the road in front of them brandishing a pistol, the driver had pulled the coach to a halt. The man then rode to the side of the vehicle, his pistol aimed at William. With his reflexes honed to perfection in Spain, where he had dealt with men seeking to kill him on a regular basis, William was prepared with his own gun. He fired before his assailant could do so. Unfortunately, the shot terrified the horses and they bolted, leaving his assailant clutching his arm and disappearing into the dark.

His mood on returning to Carlow Park had turned bleak. He had pondered the silent admission that he was helpless before whoever it was who was trying to kill him, that he knew neither where to find him nor how to stop him trying again.

'Emma is a little better,' Cassandra replied, ignorant of his thoughts. 'It's such a glorious day—I thought I might walk to the lake.'

'Then if you don't mind the company, if you will allow me, I will join you.'

'There is no need. I'm sure there are many things you have to do.'

'Nothing that can't wait—and not nearly as interesting.'

Meeting his gaze, Cassandra saw the reflective, almost tender, glimmer of a warm light in his eyes.

'I insist,' he said.

'How was your journey to Woolwich yesterday?' Cassandra asked, falling into step beside him.

'Well enough. It was late when I got back.'

'And how was Edward when you left him? Do you think he'll settle down to military life?'

'I hope so. Edward is patriotic, with a tremendous regard for loyalty and honour. He has the makings of a good soldier—although the boy's in love, enraptured by the lovely young creature who has slipped so effortlessly into his life. I can only hope it won't be a handicap.'

'So do I. Did you see Mama?'

'I did. When I arrived at the house, fearing the worst, her distress was great. However, she was most relieved when I told her we had apprehended the runaways—although she was most upset to learn of your sister's illness.'

'Poor Mama. I know how this will have affected her—and Aunt Elizabeth. Emma was staying with her when she disappeared, and she blames herself entirely.'

'I can understand that. Now the shock is over, your mother longs for your return—but in the light of your sister being unwell, she does not press for it.'

'Emma will be well enough to travel tomorrow. I—think we should go home.'

'Shouldn't you stay another day or so—just to make sure?

Won't you let me try and persuade you?' He cocked a brow, humour dancing in his eyes.

She gave him a wry smile. 'I am well acquainted with your powers of persuasion, my lord, and I would appreciate it if you would keep them on a tight rein. I think we've imposed on your hospitality long enough.'

'Very well, if you must. I offered to take you back to London myself, but your mother would not hear of it. Clem will be arriving with the carriage tomorrow—around midday.'

'And the elopement?'

'You may rest assured it has not been circulated and remains a private matter among ourselves.'

'I am relieved to hear it.'

Reaching the water's edge, from beneath the heavy boughs of an elm they stood looking across the lake. The water was dark and still, shining silver here and there where it caught the sun. Moorhens drifted by and a heron on its stilted legs pierced the water with its long beak in its search for food.

'This is so peaceful—perfect,' Cassandra murmured. 'You are so lucky having all this—to grow up in such wonderful surroundings and to know it's yours.' She turned her head and looked up at him, seeing at once that he'd fallen in with her mood. How remote he looked, how detached.

'The fortunes of birth,' he answered quietly. 'Thank you for the compliment to my estate. I'm glad you like it. I feel an aching nostalgia when I remember the years I lived here as a child. I only wish my brother could have lived a full life to enjoy his inheritance.'

'I'm sure you do. I—if you would rather not talk about him,' she said, sensitive to his changing mood, 'there is no need to.'

William knew he would, but he didn't want to examine the myriad feelings that were compelling him to do it. 'I feel the wrenching loss of my parents and my brother. The poignancy of being here after Robert's loss is difficult. He was several years older than me—quiet, serious, duty bound.' He smiled down at her as his mood lightened. 'Unlike me—fun loving, reckless—'

'Impossible and irresponsible, to boot,' Cassandra added, laughing lightly.

'And charming,' William finished with a confident, amused lift to his brow.

'But of course.'

'I was always very much Robert's younger brother, but he was always willing to let me tag along. The village over there is Carlow, and the church you see is where generations of Lampards are interred—Robert, too.'

'And that rather splendid house?' Cassandra asked, pointing to a stately manor house that stood on the outskirts of the village, its tall graceful chimneys rising like dark fingers into the sky.

'That's Littleton Manor. My cousin Mark and his wife Lydia live there. Lydia was to have married Robert. After the accident, when Robert was killed, she married Mark.'

'And—do you mind about that?'

He shook his head and smiled. 'No. I thought they were ill suited. Mark is more her type—although I do not think theirs is a happy marriage.'

'And what type is she?'

'If the two of you should meet, you'll know what I mean—although I have to say that I know very little about her. Mark is rigidly upright, extremely competent, sound headed and was just the man to keep order at Carlow Park while I was in Spain.'

'And now you're no longer a commissioned officer having to take orders from your superiors, how do you think you will settle down to being a country gentleman? I don't suppose you've had time to reacquaint yourself with the people who live and work on the estate.'

'Not yet.'

'Well, like your ancestors, you must watch over them—and lead by example,' she told him with a forceful laugh.

His expression was one of mock horror. 'You mean I will have to reform?'

'Will that be so very difficult?'

'Impossible—but I value your advice.'

'I believe you are actually extremely good at what you do, with your sharp mind and commercial sense. Are you going to stay at Carlow Park—or do you intend returning to London?'

'I'll stay here for now. There's much to do, and people to see. I never sought the title or the estate. It suited me well enough being a soldier, but I suppose I'll soon get used to all the hard work that has to be done.' He looked at her seriously. 'You'll know all about that with what you do at the institute. You've made quite a life for yourself in London.'

'I work very hard.'

'I admire that,' he said quietly.

She smiled nervously. 'You must think I'm dreadfully ill-bred.'

'I think,' he said softly, 'that you are magnificent.'

'You certainly know how to flatter a woman.'

'It isn't flattery, just an honest opinion.'

The husky sincerity in his deep voice and the way he was looking at her snatched her breath away. His well-tailored jacket and buff-coloured trousers accentuated the long lines of his body, and she noticed again how incredibly blue his eyes were in the brightness of the day. It was impossible not to be drawn and respond to this man. A curious sharp thrill ran through her as he looked down at her, his eyes alert above the faintly smiling mouth, and she promptly forgot everything.

And so they faced one another—the soldier and libertine, and the gently reared young woman—and, despite Cassandra's opposition, the attraction between them was almost palpable. He looked at her, the sun filtering through the boughs of the elm sending prisms of light dancing around them, flickering on William's thick dark hair, outlining his strong face.

Raising his hand, he gently brushed the backs of his fingers over her warm cheek, relieved that she didn't resist. 'Has anyone ever told you how lovely you are, Miss Greenwood?'

Cassandra felt a sudden stillness envelope them. Vividly aware of the heat of the sun, she was overwhelmingly conscious of him, of the way his gaze had dropped to her mouth. Confused, and feeling her heart begin to pound with helpless anticipation, she looked away, but he placed his finger beneath her chin and turned her face back to him.

'What's the matter? Don't you like being complimented?' His voice was low and husky.

She shook her head slowly, feeling a surge of irrepressible excitement rising in her. His eyes met hers in silent, half-challenging amusement, saying things she dare not think about. She struggled impotently to maintain her hold on her thin control, feeling it weaken under the strain as he studied her, unabashed.

Gently he pushed a stray strand of hair from her brow. She leaned her back against the great elm, grateful for its support. She was no more capable of telling him to stop than she was of sprouting wings to take flight. When he put his hand upon her waist she leaned into him, and when he lowered his head and touched his lips to her cheek, she sighed and softly spoke his name. And when he began to kiss her with sweet demand she clung to him, wishing with all her heart it would never end.

Suddenly his arms were around her, the strength of them shattering her calm, her senses erupting. He kissed her with slow ardour, his hands moulding her close, stirring the passion in her blood. The fragrance of his cologne and skin pervaded her senses. She could not free herself from those sultry kisses and nor did she desire to. Her body was caught in a web of enchantment.

The moment was shattered when a footman seemed to appear from nowhere. They were so absorbed in each other that neither of them had heard him approach. They drew apart.

'I'm sorry to intrude, my lord, but Mr Palmer has arrived.'

William nodded. 'Thank you, Myers. I'll be there directly.'

He looked at Cassandra as the footman headed back to the house. They smiled at one another, aware suddenly of an intensity of feeling between them. To Cassandra it was new and exciting, as though the future held a secret and a promise.

'Mr Palmer is my lawyer. It quite slipped my mind that I'd arranged for him to come this morning.'

'You go. I'll stay here for a while longer.'

Cassandra watched him mount his horse and ride off before turning back to the lake. So many conflicting emotions swirled inside her, fighting for ascendancy. For just a few brief days they had been together and he was becoming more attractive by the minute. She was finding it impossible to shake off the effect he was having on her. A few moments ago before he had kissed her she had felt alarmed, particularly as she realised that it was not so much of him that she was afraid, but of herself.

After a while she turned away and slowly made her way back. Seeing a rose arbour ahead of her and a wooden bench, which she thought would be a nice place to sit a while to absorb the ambience of the gardens, she headed towards it, enjoying the warm feel of the sun on her face.

Something moved among the greenery—she felt eyes on her suddenly, and her flesh tingled warily. A man appeared in front of her, come from nowhere, it seemed. Plainly dressed in black, which threw up the whiteness of his cravat, tall and thin, he looked to be in his early thirties. His chin was strong and there was a scornful curl to his lips that gave him a somewhat proud and insolent appearance. His skin was pale and so were the hard, grey eyes, seemingly half-asleep beneath heavy lids. He had about him an extraordinary air of quiet power.

Cassandra shuddered, feeling trapped like a fly in the web of his gaze as he stared at her with intense, unwavering—and perhaps resentful, she thought—curiosity. He came towards her, leaning on the gold-knobbed cane he held.

'Miss Greenwood.'

Cassandra nodded briefly, calmly, considering him. 'You have the advantage. That is more than I can say of you, sir.'

He inclined his head ever so slightly. 'Mark Lampard— Baron Lampard of Littleton Manor, which is situated on the outskirts of Carlow village. I am Lord Lampard's cousin.'

Cassandra thought he was not dissimilar to his cousin. Both wore the look of the well-bred of generations, and possessed the complex traits that thrive in the families of those who are born to govern. But there was a fastidious air of supercilious taciturnity about Mark Lampard that William did not possess.

'For the past two years,' he went on, 'since the demise of Lord Lampard's brother, I have been acting steward to his estate. There is very little I do not know about what goes on.' He spoke in a slow, deep voice, essentially undramatic, conveying the perfect measure of its owner's self-control. 'William told me of your distressing circumstances. I hope your sister is feeling better.'

'She is a little better, thank you, which is why you find me taking a walk. I felt a need for some air after being confined to the sick room—and I have to say Carlow Park is indeed a lovely place.'

'There is none finer in these parts.'

'You—have spoken to your cousin.'

'I have, indeed—yesterday, before he left for London with young Edward. He recounted to me in detail his elopement with your sister, and I have to say I was shocked to hear it— very shocked indeed. Tell me, Miss Greenwood, does your sister usually give your family so much trouble? I do realise that young ladies of her age are often difficult to manage.'

Cassandra's heart swelled with indignation. 'Emma is the most tractable of young ladies and has never given my mother cause to worry. I believe in this case she was much influenced by your cousin Edward, who, do not forget, almost ruined her reputation beyond redemption. Does he usually get into scrapes of this sort?'

The arrogant Mark Lampard was undaunted by her show of indignation or her slight directed at his young cousin. 'As a rule, no. It is a blessing and a profound relief that you caught up with them in time, thereby avoiding a catastrophe of immense proportions. Edward has a military career mapped out. Marriage at this stage of his life would not be appropriate.'

Roused to anger and resentment by his insult, Cassandra did her utmost to retain her composure when she spoke. 'And does that apply to my sister or to any young lady Edward might be drawn to? From what you say, Mr Lampard, you seem to have strong objections to Emma's suitability. Are you objecting to my father having been a professional man and not a titled gentleman? Do you consider us to be inferior?'

'Not at all. I have great admiration for your late father's profession, and indeed I am certain your sister is most charming. I am merely pointing out that it would have been a most imprudent marriage.'

Cassandra was not so sure she believed in his admiration of her father. 'Next you will be accusing her of tricking Edward into eloping so she could ingratiate herself into your family.'

'Not at all, and I beg your pardon if I have upset you, but it is all so unsatisfactory.'

'I could not agree more, Mr Lampard. Do you often decide on the propriety of your cousin's inclination, and determine the manner in which he is to be happy? He is about to embark on a military career, where he may be called upon to lay down his life for others, so is he not old enough to decide for himself how to conduct his private life?'

'Miss Greenwood, are you saying that you would not have objected to a marriage between them?'

'Had I not objected, I would not have gone chasing off to Scotland to prevent it. However, since nothing has come of it we can put it behind us. As soon as Emma is well enough to travel, we will return to London.'

'That would be best,' he said with haughty composure.

'Pardon me, sir, but I will be the judge of what is best for both my sister and myself. Now, if you will excuse me, I will return to the house.'

He stiffened, but appeared to accept his dismissal. His eyes met hers coldly. 'Of course. I will detain you no longer. Good day, Miss Greenwood. It was interesting meeting you.' With these words he went on his way.

Cassandra's mind was in turmoil. Feeling a weakening in her legs, she sat on the bench and reflected on her highly charged encounter with Mark Lampard. Normally in control of her emotions, she was simmering, seething with anger. The meeting had been sudden, surprising and antagonistic—although why Mark Lampard had such strong feelings on the elopement she could only put down to concern for his cousin Edward. But that did not excuse his insufferable rudeness. His manner had been insulting and unacceptable and she sincerely hoped she would not have the misfortune to come into contact with him again.

Feeling a sudden chill, as if a shadow had passed in front of the sun and robbed her of its warmth, she stood up and headed back to the house.

It was early evening when Cassandra opened the door to William's knock. He was standing with his shoulder propped casually against the door post and his arms crossed over his chest, looking at her with a lazy smile. With his hair still damp from his bath and dressed in an olive-green jacket and light grey trousers, he looked incredibly handsome and completely at ease. Trying to ignore the treacherous leap her heart gave at the sight of that captivating, intimate smile and warm gaze, she invited him inside.

'I came to enquire after your sister's progress.'

'Emma is much recovered—so much so that she's been out

of bed this afternoon.' She tilted her head to one side, her eyes enquiring and her lips smiling slightly. 'Is that the only reason why you came calling, William?'

'I've grown used to having you around—I was missing you.'

Mesmerised by his tone and the expression in the fathomless depths of his eyes, Cassandra's pulse tripped. 'I am immune to your flattery, Lord Lampard,' she said, not unkindly and with a teasing light in her eyes.

'Then I am sorry to hear that. I shall have to try a different tack if I am to succeed in getting you to change your opinion of me. I have come to invite you to dine with me. Mrs Henderson tells me you have not yet eaten?'

'I really don't think that would be a good idea. Besides, I haven't seen the inside of a bed for two nights.'

'Then I'll forgive you if you nod off during the soup course.' His eyes held a challenge and a provocative smile curved his lips. 'Are you afraid of being alone with me, Miss Greenwood? Nervous, perhaps?'

'Lord Lampard, for the past two days you have been saying and doing things that make me extremely nervous.'

'Cassandra,' he said in a smooth, deep voice that had a dangerous effect on her heart rate, 'I am only asking you to have dinner with me—nothing more intimate than that.' He smiled. 'I think it's the least you can do in return for your board and lodging.'

Seeing the wicked mischief alight in his eyes, Cassandra laughed softly. 'Then, since you put it like that, how can I possibly refuse without appearing rude.'

Amusement touched his lips. 'You can't,' he said, pushing himself away from the wall.

'Although, with only one change of clothes, you'll have to take me as I am.'

His look became positively seductive. 'It is not your clothes I'll be looking at. I'll expect you in the dining room in a few minutes.'

* * *

When Cassandra entered the dining room, William was waiting for her, looking disgustingly relaxed with a glass of wine in his hand. When she appeared in the doorway his eyes appraised her. Her face flushed warm.

'You look enchanting, Cassandra. Hungry?' Handing her a glass of wine, he gestured towards the table.

Hearing the husky intimacy in his voice, Cassandra's heart rate increased. 'I confess that I am.'

The dining room was very grand. The long dining table and the chairs of dark blue velvet, gilt-edged mirrors, white marble columns and patterned ceiling, did not induce a relaxed atmosphere, but within a circle of candle light, the servants having been dismissed after serving the food, with William seated at the head of the table and Cassandra close to him on his right, the atmosphere was comfortable and intimate.

It was when they were on the sweet course that Cassandra remembered her encounter with Mark Lampard.

'I—I met your other cousin today—Mark.'

William raised his brows and glanced across at her. 'And?'

'And what?'

'Did you—have a conversation?'

She nodded. 'You—are not alike.'

'If you mean he isn't a scoundrel of the first order, then you're right. We're as different as chalk and cheese, but we rub along well enough. Mark is my heir, a pillar of the community, and has never made any secret of his disapproval of my easygoing ways.'

'He is also very—direct,' Cassandra remarked. Aware that she was a guest in his house, good manners made her choose her words with care so as not to give offence.

He arched his brows in question. 'Direct? In what way?'

'He—he told me how relieved he is that we reached Edward before he married Emma. At first I believed he was shocked by the elopement, but he soon made his sentiments known to me. He was most—explicit.'

William frowned, suddenly thoughtful. 'Please don't mis-understand Mark.'

'I don't. I think I understand him perfectly. He harbours a mistaken belief that Emma's allurements, in a moment of in-fatuation and weakness, made Edward forget himself. The long and the short of it is that I believe he would never consider my sister a suitable match for Edward. We belong to the professional class, you see—no wealth, no title.'

'Did Mark upset you?'

'No. He was perfectly civil to me, but the substance of our conversation made me angry.'

Having finished his sweet course, William pushed the dish away from him. There was an odd expression on his handsome face. 'I'm sorry about that, Cassandra,' he said grimly, 'and I apologise for my cousin. I'll speak to him, and I promise I will set matters right.'

'Please don't—not on my account. The last thing I want is to cause a rift between you and your cousin. Emma and I will be gone tomorrow, so let that be an end to the matter.'

William said no more on the subject, but he was concerned about what Mark could have said to upset her, and he was de-termined to have a word with him.

'How is Archie, by the way?' he asked, remembering the young boy with the burnt feet he had seen at the institute. 'I've been meaning to ask, since he hasn't appeared at my London residence as yet.'

'Archie? Oh—his feet are much better. He's almost recov-ered. Doctor Brookes removed his dressings a week ago and he's walking with the aid of a crutch at the moment. As soon as he feels he can do without it he will be well enough to leave the institute.'

'Then don't forget to send him to Grosvenor Square. I've told Thomas, the head groom, to expect him.'

'Thank you. I do appreciate it. You've no idea how diffi-cult it is trying to find places for the children who pass through our doors. Archie's a quiet boy. He won't give you any trouble,' she said, spooning up the last of her fruit.

Cassandra looked lovely and vulnerable in her pale, high-necked muslin, her hair coiled softly about her head. William couldn't tear his eyes away from her. Moving his chair away from the table, he leant with his arm draped across the back, his foot propped casually atop the opposite knee, relaxed, indulgent and very attractive as he watched her dab her mouth with her napkin and place it on the table.

In thoughtful silence, Cassandra sipped her wine, while contemplating the man reclining close to her, completely at ease. Everything about him bespoke power. His shoulders were broad, his chest well muscled under his jacket, and the muscles in his legs were outlined beneath his trousers. Years of fighting and army life had toughened him and she suspected that he would prefer to be with his fellow soldiers on campaign than mixing in society.

'Will—will you miss the army?' she ventured hesitantly.

'I already do,' he replied, distracted by the myriad emotions playing in her expressive eyes.

His admission struck Cassandra's tender heart. 'I get the sense that you don't feel comfortable when you're out in society, and that you think all the nonsense that goes with it as pointless as I do.'

'Occasionally—although it does have its compensations.'

'Such as?'

'I get to meet lovely young ladies I would not meet otherwise—proper young ladies with active, clever minds, other than those who think no further than how they look, the next society event and snaring the right catch. It may surprise you to know how bored I am with all that.' He smiled. 'I seem to have grown more particular in my tastes with age. Here, have some more wine,' he added smoothly, reaching for the bottle and pouring some into her glass.

'Do go on. I'm all attention,' Cassandra said, taking a sip of her wine. 'Although I must warn you that you are the kind of man my common sense and Mama tells me to avoid at all costs.'

'And do you always listen to your mama?'

'Of course. Her advice is always sound—it is the kind of advice that applies to all well-bred ladies who have very definite ideas of the way they wish to be thought of and treated by gentlemen. By well-bred, I mean different from the sort of ladies you normally associate with.'

Suppressing a smile, William smoothed his expression into an admissible imitation of earnest gravity. 'And how does a well-bred young lady wish to be treated by a gentleman?'

'He must have eyes for no one but her, he must be devoted to her—and be of a romantic nature, otherwise you haven't a prayer of success.'

'Romantic! Now there's an interesting word.'

Cassandra saw humour lurking in his eyes. Her delicate brows drew together and amusement teased the corners of her generous mouth as she surveyed him. 'Can you say that applies to you, Lord Lampard?'

'Oh, I've had my moments.'

Aware of what she regarded as his deliberate, unprecedented efforts to charm and disarm her, Cassandra met his gaze direct. 'Are you trying to seduce me, by any chance?'

The laughter left his eyes and he stood up. 'You are a naïve, idealistic young woman, Cassandra Greenwood. However, you are not a child and neither am I. Do you want me to spell it out so there's no mistaking my motives?' Taking her hand, he drew her to her feet, watching a heated flush stain her cheeks.

'Motives? And these motives you speak of—are they noble?' His eyes raked her face with the leisure of a well-fed wolf. She felt a tremulous feeling stirring inside.

His long, strong fingers cupped her face. 'They are adult and perfectly natural, and it's a foregone conclusion that any moment now I am going to kiss you. You know, you are a mystery to me, Cassandra Greenwood.'

'I cannot think why,' she remarked, as she sought to forestall what her heart knew was inevitable.

'You're also very beautiful.'

Thrown completely off balance by this unexpected turn of events, alarm, hot and fierce, sped through Cassandra's mind. He was being so tender, so gentle, so persuasive, and his gaze was warm and sensual. 'Please, let me go, William. I—I think the wine must have gone to my head. I am not in the mood for any of this.'

'Then we'll have to do something about that.'

'I—I must go and see if Emma is all right. I've been gone so long,' she said, her voice quavering.

'She'll cope.' Running the tip of his finger down her cheek, he felt it was warm and soft, like satin.

'William—I am extremely tired and would like to go to bed.'

'So would I. With you.'

'Please…'

'Are you going to get angry—to reject my advances?' Her eyes were dark, full of indecision. He smiled seductively. 'Come, Cassandra, you have been dubbed the Ice Maiden by every rake you've spurned. Prove them wrong. Shall we continue from where we left off earlier?'

'And I'm supposed to melt into your arms and sigh simply to prove I have blood in my veins and not ice? Please, William, my patience is wearing very thin.' Her words were definite, but her voice sounded unconvincing.

He laughed softly, his hooded eyes full of sardonic amusement as his arms went round her and pulled her close, moulding her body to his. 'I've certainly given you provocation.'

'I agree.' In his arms he was more attractive than ever, and despite her protestations the urgency to be even closer to him was more vivid than before. She watched him, anticipating, entranced, hardly breathing.

Bending his head and nuzzling her neck beneath her ear, hearing her gasp, in his sublime male arrogance, William knew her resistance was beginning to crumble. 'I'm difficult and impossible, I know, but that's because I'm attracted to you. I want you, Cassandra.'

'Want? There's nothing wrong with wanting, but it is a sin to take what is not offered.'

He laughed low in his throat, 'I have been sinning all my life, so there is nothing new there. I'll do my penance later. I do want you. I have from the first moment I laid eyes on you.'

'And you're sure of that?'

'Absolutely,' he murmured, nibbling her ear. 'I am sincere.'

Feeling divine sensations shoot through her body, Cassandra closed her eyes. 'You haven't a sincere bone in your body.'

'But I have an overwhelming need for you.'

Feeling her legs tremble and the back of her knees ache, Cassandra leaned into him. He was as smooth as silk, an accomplished womaniser, but he was so appealing, and she was no longer a child. For the first time she felt the deep pull of physical desire, and here was the danger. She no longer feared a man's touch—instead she feared her own weakness.

When he raised his head she was unable to look at anything other than his lips hovering close to her own. She was shocked by how much she wanted to feel those lips on hers once more. She breathed out slowly as excitement and longing almost overwhelmed her. The touch of his hands inflamed her. Lowering his head, he kissed her gently, his mouth beginning a slow, unbelievably erotic seduction, and Cassandra felt the power of him, real and tremendous, in his restraint.

There was pleasure at the feel and taste of his lips. It was exhilarating, thrilling, agonising, all at the same time, and she was lost in a sea of sensation. Excitement gripped her and there was terror of the unknown. His arms went round her, drawing her close, his hand sliding slowly down her spine as he moulded her to his body. As his lips moved on hers, those lips and his touch unlocked something within her, releasing all the repressions and restraints she had imposed on herself for so long. Cassandra's breathing quickened and her body began to speak a language new to her, a language William understood perfectly.

When she melted against him, sliding her hands slowly up his chest and around his neck as she returned his kiss, William experienced a burgeoning pleasure and incredible joy that was almost past bearing. Minutes later he finally forced himself to lift his head and gaze down into her eyes, feeling them pulling him inexorably into their depths. He saw something there that reflected what he was feeling—desire. It was the way she stood—still, poised, willing him to kiss her again. Tenderness began to unfold within him—a sensation that had been as foreign to him as the voice of his conscience until he'd met this truly remarkable person and he asked himself how it was possible that this one woman could make him lose his mind.

'Have you any idea how lovely you are, Cassandra Green-wood—how incredibly desirable and how rare?'

Seduced by his mouth and caressing hands, the feel of his long legs pressed intimately to her own, Cassandra felt her body brought vibrantly to life. Drawing a shattered breath, she whispered, 'This is madness, utter madness.'

'I couldn't agree more,' he breathed, his mouth opening hungrily over hers once again.

As he continued to kiss her thoroughly, endlessly, producing a knot of pure sensation in the pit of Cassandra's stomach, the passion that ignited between them surpassed even William's imaginings—it surpassed anything he'd ever felt. Lust hit him with such unexpected force. His conscience stirred. Could this warm, incredibly beautiful and physically aroused creature be the Cassandra Greenwood the rakes of the *ton* had dubbed the 'Ice Maiden', and not a goddess by any means? But, by God, when she pressed herself against him and he felt her soft, ripe curves, she had the body of one. She was telling him silently, with her lips, her body, that she was definitely not made of ice.

When he finally released her lips he gazed down into her upturned face. Her eyes were liquid bright, and her lips, slightly parted, trembled and were moist from his kiss. 'So, the Ice Maiden melts. You want me. You can't deny it.'

'I suppose I am human after all. You've just proved that.'

'You're afraid.'

Disorientated and bewildered by what had just happened between them, Cassandra let her forehead fall against his chest. 'Yes.'

'You've nothing to fear from me.'

Raising her head, she looked at him, seeing no teasing light in his eyes. 'I hope not.'

'Cassandra, do you want to talk?'

She shook her head.

His lips quirked. 'I don't usually render a woman speechless when I kiss her.' He sighed, placing a gentle kiss on her lips. 'You are tired. Go to bed. We'll talk in the morning.'

Disengaging herself from his arms, she stepped back. 'Yes—I am tired. Please excuse me.'

Cassandra looked in on Emma before climbing into the bed in the room next door, but, as exhausted as she was and try as she might, she lay awake until the early hours, trying to understand the disturbing and consuming emotions William had aroused in her. How could she possibly understand this mindless, wicked weakness he seemed to inspire in her? Did skilled libertines make every woman feel that she was special? The wonderful memory of his kisses sent happiness spreading through her that was so intense she ached from it.

Was it possible to be so happy, to feel such joyous elation shimmering inside? At that moment she felt like the most beautiful woman in the world. She savoured again that feeling of exhilaration she had experienced in his arms, a sensation as heady and potent as good wine. She felt a melting sensation in her secret parts. Her thoughts began to travel beyond the kiss, and she felt the madness and the delight of secrecy at her forbidden thoughts. How she wished she could feel the strength of his arms around her now, loving her. She knew he was a man she could love, a man she could happily spend the rest of her life with.

She also knew William was a skilled rake and an accomplished flirt, but at that moment when she felt as if she was special to him, her heart rebelled against believing it. But she was no fool. Compared to him, she knew she was as naïve and unsophisticated as the proverbial newborn babe.

The following morning, William received Sir Charles Grisham in the library, his expression one of bland courtesy. 'What brings you to Carlow Park, Charles? Isn't it rather early in the day for a social call?'

'Dear Lord, William, have your wits become addled since you quit the army? Don't you listen? Why, only several days ago I told you I was to visit my aunt in Hertford.'

William's expression showed nothing more than mild surprise. Was it really only a few days since Lady Monkton's ball? It seemed a lifetime away. 'Yes, of course I remember. You told me Mark had invited you to call—something about a horse.'

'Two, actually, but that was before our wager concerning that paragon of virtue, the ravishing, sophisticated and highly desirable Miss Cassandra Greenwood.'

William's eyes narrowed, and there was no humour in his expression. 'Yes, isn't she.'

'Your interaction at the ball and the way you stalked off and left her standing has become the talk of the *ton*. They're still trying to figure it out. London's abuzz with rumours.'

'And no doubt they'll put two and two together and make five,' William remarked drily. 'The rumours will soon be forgotten when some new scandal comes along to take their interest.'

'When I left Monkton House for White's, I had a mind to record our bet, but on second thoughts I decided against it, since a horse and no money is involved—except for the thousand guineas I shall have to part with if you win. I decided to keep the wager a private matter between ourselves.'

'I'm relieved to hear it.' This was one wager William wanted kept out of the exclusive gentleman's club White's famous betting book, in which its distinguished members recorded wagers on virtually everything, not only sporting events, but political and all manner of happenings whose outcome was unknown.

'Well, old man,' Charles said, sprawling, rather than sitting on the chaise before the fireplace, 'may your expectations be fulfilled—and my own—but if you're going to seduce the gently reared, unsuspecting Miss Greenwood before the Season ends, you're hardly going to carry it off buried in the country. The lady lives in town.'

'As if I need reminding.' On no account must Charles know Cassandra and her sister were residing at this very moment beneath his roof. Charles had many admirable traits, but discretion wasn't one of them.

'It's doubtful she's going to develop a *tendre* for you anyway in such a short time. Best get back to London, eh—otherwise that splendid beast you have in your stable will be mine. I think it will be anyway—so nothing to worry about there. You may have unscrupulously flayed the reputations of more pretentiously proud females than you can recall, but I told you when we made the wager that Miss Greenwood is made of different stuff.'

'Women fall for the most unlikely men, Charles,' William drawled, wearing a mask of genteel imperturbability, while becoming more irritated by Grisham's presence by the minute.

'There's no accounting for taste, I suppose, but in this instance you will fail—unless, of course, you have a strategy, Lampard. If so, be a good chap and pour me a brandy—and a cigar wouldn't go amiss—and I will listen with interest while you tell me all about it.'

Chapter Six

A wager! A horse!

Cassandra stood like a pillar of stone behind the slightly open door, her mind numb, unable to remember why she had been so eager to see William, to seek him out and look upon his handsome features once more, for him to confirm that she hadn't dreamt what had happened between them last night.

The conversation she had overheard hung in the air like a bad smell. No one had insulted her as much as this and it was more than her pride could bear. Dazed and unable to form any coherent thought, she backed away from the library door, and turning walked towards the stairs, wanting nothing more than to seek the refuge of her room. As the full realisation of what she had heard sank in and renewed life began to surge through her, her magnificent eyes shone with humiliation and wrath. She was appalled and outraged; there was no excuse, no possible way to deny the awful truth.

The unspeakable cad! The lecherous libertine! The man would seduce a nun in a nunnery if he had a mind. And just when she was beginning to trust him, to respect him and believe he had been unfairly maligned, to think that there was little truth in all the disgusting and immoral things she had heard about him—all her tender feelings were demolished.

William Lampard was a heartless beast and she could not believe that she, sensible and intelligent Cassandra Greenwood, had let him kiss her—and shame on shame, that she had wantonly kissed him back. What a fool she had been, a gullible, stupid, naïve fool.

Her mistake was that from the moment they had been thrust together, his easy banter and relaxed charm had completely disarmed her. She knew that men took advantage of foolish, innocent girls, so how had she allowed herself to fall into that trap? She had enjoyed his company, had melted into his arms like some besotted idiot, and had felt gratitude for his immense generosity in bringing them to his home, when all the time he had been playing a game with her. She was his prey, and he was intent on seducing her, dishonouring her, and to win his bet nothing was going to deter him from trying.

He had made a wager with Sir Charles Grisham to seduce her before the Season ended; should he fail, Sir Charles would be so much richer by a horse.

A horse, for heaven's sake! It was more than her lacerated pride could withstand. Her face blazed with fury. Oh, the humiliation of it. And if he succeeded, what would her life be like, following a tainted liaison with a renowned rake? The discovery of his treachery had destroyed all her illusions. She'd never trust him again, ever. How could she? He would never redeem himself from this.

As she went back upstairs, all these thoughts marched through her tormented and rage-filled mind. She would never forget what she had heard—ever—nor did she want to. She wanted to remember it so that never again would she be taken in by the likes of William Lampard. Of course, if she wanted to avenge herself, she could play him at his own game and he would have no idea of it—but, no, she wasn't like that and she had no time to waste on such foolishness.

By the time she reached her room an icy numbness had taken over and she was surprised to find she was no longer in the throes of heartwrenching pain. Stiffening her spine, she decided not to let him know what she had overheard, but this had given her an advantage and she was determined that she would outmanoeuvre him. Immediately she began planning a way to thwart and foil and exasperate the plans of this infuriating lord. She was strong and resilient and would get over this. They would leave Carlow Park just as soon as Clem arrived.

Back in the library, William poured a couple of brandies and handed one to Charles. Raising his own, he proposed a toast to Monarch.

'The horse is yours.'

Charles was incredulous, and then a slow, disbelieving smile broke across his face. 'But the wager? Good Lord! Have I heard right? Have you lost all reason?'

'I have never been more sane in my life.'

'So I am to assume you've had a change of heart and no longer wish to seduce Miss Greenwood? That you're folding—as easy as that?'

'Absolutely.'

'Then you're the most peculiar player I've ever had the pleasure of opposing,' Charles remarked, sensing something crucial was going on here that he knew nothing about. 'Unfortunately, I enjoy a challenge and the pleasure is somewhat muted by the wager's outcome.'

'Then I am sorry to disappoint you. I have developed a deep regard for Miss Greenwood. I will not dishonour her. However, I have no intention of reneging on our wager. You can take the horse with you today if you wish, Monarch—I refuse to part with Franciscan. He was my brother's horse, so I'm sure you will understand my reluctance to part with him.'

When Cassandra went in to Emma, she found her up and dressed and sitting on the window seat, her knees drawn up to her chest. She was staring bleakly out over the gardens, her eyes, soft as velvet, looking at nothing. She looked pale and fragile, but, when she saw Cassandra, she managed a weak smile.

'How do you feel?' Cassandra asked, sitting beside her, facing her.

'I have felt better.'

Cassandra squeezed her hand affectionately. 'We're going home shortly. Clem will soon be here with the carriage. You'll start to feel stronger when you're home with Mama to take care of you.'

'Is she very angry with me, Cassy?'

'Mama has been extremely concerned, Emma. She loves you very much and is sorry you're ill.'

'But is she angry,' Emma persisted, 'because I eloped with Edward?'

'Naturally she is upset by the whole dreadful event. She wasn't best pleased when she found out—and poor Aunt Elizabeth blamed herself most wretchedly.'

'Where is Edward?'

'He went to Woolwich with Will. Lord Lampard.'

Emma looked stricken. 'He's—he's gone to the academy—to be a soldier?' Cassandra nodded. 'Oh, I see.' She bent her head. 'It isn't fair. I wanted to be his wife so much. I shall be lost without him. How can I possibly carry on?'

'You are stronger than you know. In two or three years this will seem a small thing when you look back. Don't let it hurt so much, Emma.'

'But it does and this is now.'

'If you truly love Edward, it will endure.'

'You would, Cassy, I know. I have not your endurance. I— I won't give him up. I know you think I'm young and silly and that I don't know my own mind, but I do love him.'

Emma's face had taken on such a look of agony and despair that Cassandra softened involuntarily. 'I know you do,' she said gently and sighed. 'I know you're grown up, Emma, but do you really think you're ready to be married?'

'Yes, of course. Eloping was all my idea. I persuaded Edward. You mustn't think badly of him.'

'I was wrong about Edward, I realise that now. I misjudged him completely and I apologise for ever doubting him. You are right. He is a fine young man.'

Emma lifted her head, relief and hope lighting her eyes. 'You do? Oh, Cassy, I can't tell you what it means to me to hear you say that.'

'He loves you—genuinely loves you. Despite this foolish indiscretion, I believe him to be a good person—destined to be wounded by those harder, more selfish and less sensitive than he. I'll tell you what I said to him—give it time. Leave it for a while. I am of the opinion that things should be temporarily held in abeyance. Only until after you have come out, you understand, and this unfortunate business is behind us. Perhaps then, if you both still feel the same, then Mama will have no objections.'

Cassandra wished she didn't have to face William before she left. She remained with Emma for the rest of the morning. When it was time to leave, with her head held high and her delicate chin stubbornly set, she accompanied her sister downstairs. William was waiting for her in the hall. Outwardly she was composed and very calm, but inside she was seething.

William came towards her, curious as to why she had not come down earlier to see him. He ached for her—to touch her, to gaze on her lovely face, to hear the sweet, soft sound of her voice. When he had held her, she had touched a tenderness and protectiveness within him he hadn't known existed. After she favoured one of the footmen with her broadest smile, William was taken aback by the courteous and impersonal smile she gave him.

He wasn't to know how all her senses were crying out for him, how she was slowly dying inside. He had callously set out to dishonour her, and yet it was all Cassandra could do not to humble herself at his feet. With tremendous will she knew she would have to be strong to withstand a man of his character. William Lampard had no claim to being a gentleman in her interpretation of the word, but she knew him to be a proud man, and she intended to trample his pride to pieces.

'Did you sleep well?'

'Like a babe,' she quipped, trying to sound cool and amused. 'Indeed, I slept so well I failed to wake until a couple of hours ago.' She was surprised that her voice didn't shake.

Her tone, her very posture, were cool and aloof. William peered down at her, trying to read her expression. He wasn't sure what he had expected. An acknowledgement of what had passed between them, he supposed. His gaze went to Emma, who was hovering several paces behind, unsure how to approach Edward's imperious cousin who must be furious at their elopement. He took pity on her and softened his expression. 'Your sister looks pale. I told you I would be delighted to have you stay a while longer until she is fully recovered. I would not have said it if I did not mean it.'

'I know—and thank you,' Cassandra answered, her manner brusque, causing a flicker of consternation to cross William's face, 'but I am anxious to get home.' Only once did her composure slip a notch, and that was when Mark Lampard and a woman emerged from the study and came to stand behind William. Her bright smile faded uncertainly.

William turned to acknowledge them. 'Mark, you have met Miss Greenwood.'

'I have had that pleasure,' he replied, his eyes never leaving hers.

His hard, direct gaze told Cassandra their encounter had given him as little pleasure as it had her. 'It's good to see you again, sir,' she said politely.

He turned to the dark-haired woman standing beside him. 'Allow me to present my wife, Lydia.'

'I'm pleased to meet you, Lady Lampard,' Cassandra responded.

'Likewise,' Lydia replied smoothly.

Cassandra could read no expression in the woman's clear, attractive features, and as she regarded her closely, she felt her thoughts probed by careful fingers. She suppressed a shudder. Tall and slender, her nose aquiline and her hair perfectly coiffed, Lydia was quite beautiful, as a statue is beautiful—remote and cool. Her features were finely moulded and her lips showed a bitter twist. There was an indefinable poise about her, a certainty, and she had power. One thing Cassandra ascertained when she met her cold grey eyes—the coldest she had ever seen—was that this woman did not like her.

'Please excuse us. My sister and I are just leaving. We hope to make London before dark.'

'Then I wish you a safe journey.'

'Thank you. I'm sure it will be. Please excuse us.'

Taking Emma's arm, she led her outside to the waiting coach. William held out his hand to assist her down the steps, but she turned away. He was certain she had seen his hand, and he frowned in puzzlement as he watched her walk away. After a moment he realised she had an obligation to attend her sister, who still looked poorly, and he felt slightly easier. When Emma was inside the coach and it looked as if Cassandra was about to climb in without saying anything more to him, his face darkened and he took her arm.

'Cassandra, a moment, please.' He drew her aside out of earshot. 'Why are you doing this? Why are you angry with me?'

Her wide-eyed look was one of complete innocence. 'Angry? I am not angry,' she replied with a brittle gaiety, trying to harden herself against him, to forget his kiss and the way he had held her.

'I thought after last night—'

'Last night should never have happened. It was a mistake. We both lost control.' She looked up at him, looked away and back again. 'I should have known better than to submit to the charms of a philanderer.'

'I'm sorry you feel that way, because I think you are the loveliest, most courageous young woman I have ever met.'

Cassandra felt as if her heart was breaking. His gaze was one of consuming intensity, his mouth all wilful sensuality. 'Please stop it. Your compliments smack of insincerity. What happened was nothing more than an amusing diversion. It was just a sophisticated flirtation—the rule being the one you, a skilled libertine, usually play by—that no one takes anything seriously.'

He frowned. 'Are you afraid of what happened between us?' he asked in a voice of taut calm, wondering why she was behaving like this.

'Afraid? No, of course not. Why should I be? It's just that I do not want you to be courtly or romantic. It's not you. Why—before I know where I am I might start falling for it and believe you truly care.'

'You cannot mean that.'

'Why not?' she said, struggling valiantly to sound flippant.

'It meant nothing to you?'

'Shall we leave out the dramatics?'

William's face hardened into an expressionless mask, but his eyes were probing hers like daggers, looking for answers, as if he couldn't really believe this was the same woman who had melted in his arms with such sweet, innocent passion and yielded her lips to his. His disappointment made him carelessly cruel. 'You would do well to remember how you responded to my kiss—willingly—and how you enjoyed kissing me.'

'That was last night. This is now—and I didn't enjoy kissing you,' she lied primly, doing her utmost to avoid his eyes as a change came over him. In all her life she had never encountered such controlled purposeful anger.

William stared at her. 'Forgive me if I appear dense, but you gave a fair imitation of it last night.'

She smiled. 'And no doubt after all your conquests, you're surprised to discover there's a female who finds you resistible.'

Reaching out, William gripped her upper arms and jerked her against him. When he spoke his voice was dangerously low. 'I would like to convince you that you can overcome that problem—to persuade you.'

'Try as hard as you like, but you will not succeed. I will not allow it.'

His features were as hard as rock, his eyes like ice. 'And I thought you were different from the rest—fool that I am,' he said with biting sarcasm that made Cassandra's heart squeeze in the most awful, inexplicable way. William was no longer able to find her either amusing or admirable. His eyes moved over her face as if he were memorising it. His hands slid down her arms and abruptly he released her as he stepped back.

'I will detain you no longer. You'd best get into the carriage. Your sister is waiting. Goodbye, Cassandra. I hope you have a safe journey.'

The regret in his voice touched her to the core of her being. She would have turned back, but she sharply reminded herself of what she had overheard. But as she settled herself beside Emma, she experienced a sharp tug of loss at the realisation that she might never see him again. Her heart ached with the desolation of it.

His face inscrutable, his eyes as dark and ominous as the Thames on a stormy day, William stood and watched the carriage disappear down the drive. Truly believing that he was the injured party, he turned and stalked into the house, determined to purge her from his mind—purging her from his heart would not be so easy.

During the days that followed, he gave himself up to adjusting to life at Carlow Park and the day-to-day running of the estate. Bailiffs were called to give an account of their management, accounts gone into, acres of land ridden over, meetings with his tenant farmers—when he was finally satisfied that everything was as it should be, his thoughts turned unwillingly to Cassandra.

Alone in his elegant house, he restlessly wandered from room to room, unable to escape the throbbing emptiness that was gnawing away at him with a pain that increased unbearably with each passing day. He missed his military life and his fellow soldiers, and now that he was home the absence of his family cut through him like a knife. But what surprised him most was how much he missed Cassandra. She had entered his life like a breath of spring, and had left it after just a short time like a violent winter storm. With each hour that passed, the more impatient he grew to see her again.

How had he allowed her to get that close? A faint smile touched his lips as he remembered how heartbreakingly young and lovely she had looked at Lady Monkton's ball as, with intelligent logic, she had charmingly touted for donations for her precious institute, donations that would bring a small degree of humanity to children's lives. She was courageous, spirited and incorrigible. Only Cassandra would have dared do such a thing at a society ball, and only Cassandra would have taken him to task over what she considered to be his licentious ways.

The truth was that neither time nor distance had blunted the feelings he had for Cassandra Greenwood. From the moment he had set eyes on her she had bewitched him, cast a spell on him from which he could not set himself free. She had come between him and everything that up to meeting her had formed his pleasant and harmonious life.

But he could not understand why she had melted into his arms one minute and then, for no comprehensible reason, had treated him as if he were contemptible, as if she were trying to teach him some well-deserved lesson. Unable to concentrate on his work and becoming more frustrated by the day, he knew he was losing the battle to forget her. And so, after notifying Mark of his departure, he left for London with the hope of seeing her, and to fill the gaping emptiness of his life.

Harriet made a huge fuss when Cassandra and Emma arrived home. Between severe castigation, concern for Emma's health and tears of relief that she had both daughters secure beneath her roof once more, Harriet ordered Emma—penitent, pale and tired—to bed. Harriet was a sensible woman, but she was soft where her younger daughter was concerned.

Later, seated in front of the fire, Cassandra talked quietly to her mother, giving her an account of all that had transpired. When she rose to go to bed, Harriet said, 'Don't go yet, Cassandra. There is another matter I wish to discuss with you.'

'Oh?' Cassandra sat down again. Ever since they had arrived home she had known something other than Emma was worrying her mother. 'It's about the institute, isn't it?'

'I'm afraid it is.'

Harriet's eldest daughter worried her greatly. Cassandra's single-mindedness, her sense of purpose, was so strong, so directed, it was frightening. Ever since her dear papa had died she had dedicated all her time and energy to the institute. What Harriet was about to tell her would wound her deeply.

'As you know, things have been difficult for a long time. Despite Lord Lampard's generous donation, the funds are rapidly drying up. If—if things don't improve, then I fear that we will have to close the institute.'

Cassandra stiffened. 'Lord Lampard? I knew he had made a donation, but I have no idea how much.'

'A hundred pounds.'

Cassandra's eyes opened wide. 'That is a generous sum indeed.'

Maybe, she thought wryly, it would not have been so generous were it not for the wager he had made with Sir

Charles Grisham. She was beginning to realise that William Lampard never did anything without a motive, and she strongly suspected that his generous donation was all part of his seduction.

But what was to be done about this other matter? She was willing to tout for funds, but apart from that she left the financial side to her mother. Things had been serious for a long time, but she had not known how serious. Suddenly, despite the warmth of the room, she felt chilled to the bone, numbed by the enormity of what this could mean. Her mother was a gentle lady, with an aura of unflustered serenity. Yet below that surface was a quiet steeliness. Everything about her was ruled by the love she had shared with her husband.

'I can't believe things are so bad. We can't close the institute, Mama. The children rely on us. All Papa's hopes and dreams are wrapped up in that place.'

'I know. It pains me, too. The institute is very important to me. I feel as if, while ever I carry on with your dear papa's work, I still have a part of him with me. I wish there was some other way.'

'What we do makes such a difference to the children's wretched lives. We must find a way to keep it open. What are we to do?'

'I don't know. We should be able to keep going for a month or so. In the meantime I'll try and think of something.'

'We need to redouble our efforts. First thing tomorrow I'll write to the benefactors—maybe they will be extra-generous and give more. Things will work out for us,' Cassandra promised unconvincingly. 'Have you not considered accepting Aunt Elizabeth's offer?'

'No. We agreed in the beginning never to ask Elizabeth to donate money—even though she would be willing to do so. I am grateful for all she's done for us as a family—for her to fund the institute is one step too far.'

'I do agree with you, Mama. It was but a thought. I'll see

if we can get some government funding—although Lord knows how hard I've tried and failed in the past—but—Mama, will you write and thank Lord Lampard for his donation?'

'Yes, yes I will. I intended to, but this shocking business of Emma's elopement wiped it clean from my mind. She has broken all the rules governing moral conduct. Let us hope that none of this comes out. If it does, in the eyes of the *ton,* she will be considered shameless and wanton—soiled—unfit company for unsullied young ladies, gullible heirs and polite society. In short, her reputation will be ruined. What happened to the young man—Edward Lampard?'

'Lord Lampard took his cousin to the Military Academy at Woolwich, where he hopes he will settle down to soldiering.'

'Do you think he will try to see Emma?'

'Not unless you grant him permission. I have to say, Mama, that I misjudged him. He's a serious-minded, personable young man. It is plain that he loves Emma—and she him.'

'Nevertheless, we cannot escape the unforgivable fact that he compromised Emma most disgracefully. And Lord Lampard?' Harriet asked after a moment's hesitation, peering at her daughter's face with curious concern. 'You must have spent some considerable time alone with him—and—I know he has a certain reputation with the ladies. I may spend a great deal of my time at the institute, but I've heard endless gossip about him—rumours—not altogether favourable.'

'Whether they are true or not, Mama, what difference does it make? We were thrown together out of mutual concern for our respective relatives, nothing more. He was polite and attentive towards me, when Emma took a turn for the worse, I was indeed grateful that he put his house at our disposal.'

'Then that is to his credit, and perhaps his character is not as black as it has been painted after all.'

Cassandra lowered her eyes. How could she say to her mother that men like William Lampard brought nothing but anguish to any woman foolish enough to fall for their attractive looks and silken tongue? He was devilishly appealing, yes, but dangerous and destructive.

Two weeks had passed since that conversation in which Cassandra and her mother had decided to write letters to all the institute's benefactors, as yet, they had not received a single reply. All those who had made donations in the past were no longer dedicated to their cause.

Cassandra threw herself into her work, going about her duties with a calm demeanour that belied the multitude of emotions raging inside. No matter how adamantly she tried not to think of William Lampard, he had ways of creeping into her mind.

It was time for Archie to leave the institute. A rule Cassandra had made when she had first become involved with the institute was not to become too attached to any of the children, but because of the severity of Archie's injuries, which had made his stay at the institute longer than most, she had become extremely fond of him and would be sorry to see him go.

A timid, quiet body, he'd been terrified that he'd have to go back to work for the sweep when his feet healed. When Cassandra told him she had found him a place working with horses in Lord Lampard's stables here in London, he was overwhelmed with a mixture of relief and delight. Cassandra went to great lengths to groom and dress him for the occasion. His fair hair was cut and he was dressed in some decent second-hand clothes. And so, proudly wearing a new pair of boots and with his young face shining with excitement, Cassandra took him to Grosvenor Square.

The day was a brilliant blue, with a fresh warm breeze that carried the scent of flowers from Green Park. Full of trepidation in the carriage, Cassandra hoped fervently that William was still at Carlow Park, although, even if he had returned to London, she was hardly likely to encounter him in the stables. On Cassandra's instruction, Clem did not stop in front of the house, but went round to the back. They were directed to the stables by a kitchen maid.

Crossing the stable yard, they gingerly entered the stable's dim interior, the smell of hay, horses, manure and leather strong, though not unpleasant. Cassandra observed several people at work. Her gaze became focused on a man instructing a young stable boy on how to groom a tall bay mare in one of the boxes.

Tall and thin, Thomas was in his late thirties, yet he had a boyish look about him. When he saw them standing in the doorway, there was an unmistakable look of admiration in his eyes as he left off what he was doing and strode towards them.

'My name is Miss Greenwood. Lord Lampard told me there is a place for Archie here in his stables.'

Thomas looked at the young boy, whose wide-eyed gaze was fixed on the many horses in wonder. He smiled. 'I was told to expect him; with so many horses, there's always a need for an extra pair of hands. Do you like horses, lad?'

'Oh, yes, sir,' Archie was quick to respond, his reply coming straight from the heart.

'That's good, because his lordship likes his mounts to be well taken care of.'

'And what splendid mounts they are,' Cassandra remarked.

Hearing the voice of the woman who had been occupying his thoughts for the past two weeks, the man in the next stall jerked erect and swung around.

From the corner of her eye Cassandra glimpsed a tall man in the box to the side of her, and an uncontrollable tremor of dread shot through her. She could have sworn she saw him stiffen with shock, but in that instant she was absolutely besieged with cowardice and kept her head averted, her face hidden behind the brim of her straw bonnet.

'Miss Greenwood!' William's voice rang out.

As she turned her head their eyes met instantly, and so abrupt was William's appearance that Cassandra started. A world of feelings flashed across his face—surprise, disbelief, admiration—but only for a moment. Astonished and confused, she looked away and back again.

'A pleasure seeing you again, Miss Greenwood,' William said with grim formality.

The scathing tone of his voice, and the fantasy of seeing him remorseful following their bitter parting at Carlow Park, collapsed the instant she saw his face—it was as hard and forbidding as a rock. When they had parted she had not expected to feel the awful lack of him in her life. For a short while he had filled every moment of it, with his often difficult, sometimes passionate and demanding self. He had angered and amused her, aroused her, made her feel and think... and hurt, shamed and humiliated her. She would never forgive him.

He stood with his arm resting negligently on the back of a horse without bothering to come forward, watching her through narrowed eyes. His white shirt hung loosely about his wide shoulders and his thick hair was tousled and almost black in the dim light. His face was one of arrogant handsomeness with its sculpted mouth and striking eyes, but there was cynicism in those eyes and a ruthless set of his jaw. Everything about him exuded brute strength, and as she searched his features there was no sign that he had actually held her and kissed her with seductive tenderness. She flinched at the coolness of his eyes as they raked over her.

'How is your sister?' he enquired.

Cassandra swallowed and was surprised that she managed to reply without her voice shaking. 'She is very well, thank you. A—and you?'

'As you can see, I have survived our last encounter without scars.'

Thomas, who had observed the exchange and noticed Miss Greenwood's nervousness, found the incident as odd as his lordship's coldness towards her. However, it wasn't for the likes of him to criticise or speculate on what was between the two of them. 'Miss Greenwood has brought the lad Archie that you spoke of, milord.'

Coming out of the box, William looked down at the boy he had last seen stretched in bed with his feet bandaged. 'So, you are Archie. And are you recovered?'

'Yes, sir—milord,' Archie said, in awe of the towering man and having a hard time keeping his eyes off him.

'Well, then, I am glad to hear it. Welcome to my home, Archie.'

Archie flushed gratefully.

'Thomas will teach you all you need to know. You'll soon settle in and learn all about horses.'

'Thank you, sir,' Archie said, unmistakable eagerness in his young voice.

Looking on, Cassandra knew that a word from Lord Lampard had made Archie his servant for ever. Grateful to him for putting Archie at his ease, all the bitter heartache of the last two weeks began to lose its biting edge.

William addressed Thomas. 'Have Tim show Archie where he will sleep.'

Observing Miss Greenwood's worried look, Thomas was quick to reassure her. 'Don't worry about him, Miss Greenwood. He'll be perfectly all right. He'll share a room with young Tim here,' he said, drawing the lad forward. 'As you can see, they're of an age and I'm sure will become friends in no time.'

To confirm Thomas's words, an amiable-looking Tim took Archie's hand, and, with a smiling look at Cassandra, Archie followed his new friend up some wooden steps to the quarters above.

Thanking Thomas, Cassandra left the stable with William hard on her heels. 'Thank you. By treating Archie with courtesy, you have engendered his respect and you can be assured of his life-long devotion.'

'Pity the same cannot be said of you.'

Cassandra ignored his remark and averted her gaze. 'I am grateful to you for giving him a place. I only wish I could place others so well.' She looked back at him, meeting his gaze directly. 'I didn't expect to find you here, otherwise I would have asked Clem to bring Archie.'

'And deprive me of the pleasure of seeing you again? Shame on you, Cassandra.' The humour in his voice was disguised by a disapproving frown.

'Have you been in London long?'

'No more than twenty-four hours.'

'I see.'

The words were commonplace, such as might have been exchanged by virtual strangers.

'Please excuse me,' Cassandra said, her manner brusque. 'I must go.' She began to walk across the cobbled yard. Suddenly William's tall figure appeared in front of her, barring her way to the gate and freedom.

'And where are you off to in such a hurry?' he asked, taking her arm and halting her in her stride.

The touch of his hand made her breath come faster. It had always been so. It was beyond her power to control—but conceal it she must. The magnetic attraction still remained beneath all the irritation—she both hated and wanted this detestable man.

'Please release my arm,' she said stiffly, the wager he had made with Sir Charles Grisham at the forefront of her mind. Her mind still burned with the memory of what she had overheard at Carlow Park that day and she wasn't ready to be forgiving. 'I have brought Archie and now there is nothing more to be said.'

William had no mind to let her off lightly. He laughed, and it was such a warm, throaty laugh that ended in a smile, the kind of smile that would melt any woman's heart if she didn't know him for the arrogant, heartless libertine he was. His grip on her arm did not slacken, but it was painless.

'You think not? It seems to me we have a great deal to say to one another. When you left Carlow Park I was quite put out that I had been rebuffed by you. I couldn't help thinking about you—a great deal, as a matter of fact. I haven't been able to get you out of my mind. And now—here you are.'

'You are very convincing and you have a flattering tongue,' Cassandra uttered scathingly. 'In fact, I could actually believe you are speaking the truth, but then you have undoubtedly had a great deal of practice.' He raised a handsome brow as he gave her a lengthy inspection. 'Has anyone ever told you how infuriating you are?'

His white teeth gleamed behind a lopsided grin. 'Thus far, my dear Cassandra, every female I've ever encountered. I'm quite nonchalant about these things. For some reason unbeknown to me, I believe you are somehow testing me.' His blue eyes glinted like hard metal. 'I think this may bear further investigation and we must discuss the matter.'

It dawned on Cassandra as his gaze fastened on her lips that he was remembering their kisses. For a man who had received such a crushing let-down when they had parted company, William Lampard seemed disgustingly at ease.

'I don't think so. Anything I have to say to you I said when I left Carlow Park—and go and fondle someone else,' she retorted, dragging her arm from his grasp, her eyes flaring with poorly suppressed ire. 'I'm sure the kind of woman you usually consort with would welcome your attentions.'

He laughed softly at her condemning tones. 'I'd rather be fondling you.'

'Why?' she scoffed. 'Because you want to add me to your long string of conquests?'

Her chilled contempt startled him, and his eyes narrowed. 'Conquest! Now there's a controversial word. You're mistaken, Cassandra. To conquer is to overpower, to take and force one's strength on another. I do not ask you to yield to me and nor do I take anything that is not freely given. I know how you reacted when you were in my arms—I felt your desire. You enjoyed kissing me.'

'No,' Cassandra whispered, shamed by the memory of her own response.

'Do not deny it. I know the truth.'

'No, you don't. You don't know me,' she said furiously. 'And I don't know you. I don't trust you.'

'But you do want me, Cassandra,' he told her with a knowing smile.

Despite the fact that she shook her head, she knew it was true, but she wouldn't give him the satisfaction of saying so.

His gaze dropped meaningfully to her lips. 'When I kissed you, you found me very desirable.'

Cassandra jerked her face away. 'Stop looking at me like that. It isn't seemly. The yard is full of stable boys and we are in full view of your neighbours,' she stated, glancing at the many windows of the surrounding stately houses that overlooked the stable yard.

William looked at her flushed, entrancing, rebellious face and a reluctant smile tugged at his lips. 'You have no idea what I would dare do to you,' he warned with a lazy, suggestive smile. 'And do you have any idea what will happen if I follow my inclinations and kiss you? For a start, we will be talked about and you will be off limits to every respectable male in London.'

Her eyes shot daggers at him. 'I'm off limits anyway—of my own volition, as well you know. Just leave me alone. I'm going now.' She backed away and put her hands up defensively to ward him off when he took a step towards her. 'And if you come near me I shall scream and tell your servants you are molesting me. Goodbye, William. I really don't think I want to see you again.'

As she climbed into the carriage and ordered Clem to take her home, she refused to look back, so she didn't see his expression of quiet determination as he stood and watched her go. She felt her eyes sting. She must cling to the thought that she was extremely fortunate to have found out about the disgusting wager before she had made a complete fool of herself, that she had realised the full extent of his profligacy, and that the original rumours, which had told her to avoid him, had been correct. But it was all so dreadful and painful beyond anything she could have imagined.

When Cassandra's carriage had disappeared, William continued standing there, deep in thought. He gave up trying to understand the reason for what he was about to do. He wanted Cassandra Greenwood and that was reason enough. She represented everything most desirable in a woman. When he had taken Charles's wager, she had merely been the tantalising object of his lustful thoughts and he'd thought of little else but possessing her, but after giving it careful thought he'd quickly changed his mind.

Seducing gently reared virgins was not his style—he preferred the women he made love to to be experienced, sophisticated and undemanding of himself and his time, but that did not lessen his obsession with Cassandra in the least. The effect she had had on him then had been as unsettling as it was now, and he was unable to analyse the raw heat that ran through his veins whenever she was near him.

Since he had dispensed with his military career and returned to the responsibility of his inheritance, it was his duty to marry and provide an heir, a responsibility of which he had been constantly reminded from the day he learned of Robert's death. And now, when he thought of Cassandra—lovely to look at, a temptress, enchanting and alluring—he wanted her badly. She had inflamed him and stirred his lust without intention. He smiled, for he could not blame her. Beauty, combined with charm and sweet innocence, would sway any man.

The fact that she had determinedly begun to oppose him— the reason for which remained a mystery to him—did not deter him. Had he not felt her body's reaction, her desire for him when he had held her and kissed her? He did not have the slightest doubt that he would be able to lure her back into his arms. His mind made up, he turned and strode briskly back into the stables. His decision to make her his wife was one that brooked no further debate.

When Cassandra left Grosvenor Square, firmly believing that her association with Lord William Lampard was well and truly over, she was unprepared for what happened next.

The secret of Emma's elopement with Edward Lampard was revealed and the public and very unsavoury scandal that ensued was enormous. Harriet and Elizabeth were devastated. All their hopes and carefully laid plans to give her a Season were dashed. Cassandra scanned what was printed in the newspapers, her stomach churning.

Her eyes wounded and glazed with shock, Emma was seated on the sofa, shattered by the weight of responsibility for her foolishness. 'I'm sorry,' she whispered helplessly, looking from her mama to Aunt Elizabeth, speaking through the tears of shame and sorrow choking her. 'I'm so very sorry. I didn't intend any of this.'

Peering from her mother's face to Emma's stricken one, Cassandra said, 'Don't worry, Emma. We'll stand together on this.'

'Thank you,' Emma said. 'At a time like this, loyalty counts for a lot.'

Harriet and Elizabeth exchanged sympathetic glances, and Cassandra headed for her sister, sinking down beside her. 'I'm sorry,' she murmured, wrapping her in a fierce hug. 'You're not the first female to lose her head over a handsome young man, and you certainly won't be the last.'

'It's more than that, Cassy. I told you how I feel for Edward. I haven't changed and I miss him dreadfully—especially now, with all this going on.'

'I know. I wish I knew how details of your elopement were leaked—who is spreading these stories.'

Emma shook her head dejectedly. 'I suppose social prejudices will exclude me from respectable *ton* events—but none of that seems to matter any more without Edward.'

'I can't condone what you and that young man did, Emma, behaving with such indiscretion,' her mother said gently, deeply worried by the change in her daughter. 'But from what Elizabeth has told me, elopements are fashionable—why, there have been several already this year.'

'And all the couples succeeded. If Edward and I had reached Scotland and married, I might have been hailed as a heroine—just as Henrietta Kirkbride was when she eloped and wed Viscount Swinburn. N-nothing untoward happened between us. You do believe that, don't you, Mama?' Emma sounded as meek and bewildered as a child who has been punished for something it didn't do.

'Of course I do.'

Cassandra sighed. 'Whether it did or not, I'm afraid you are ruined just the same.'

Cassandra was right. Lurid versions of the elopement were spreading like wild fire through the *ton*. More damning by far was the story circulating that the young lovers had spent a night alone at a coaching inn before an irate Lord Lampard and Emma's sister had caught up with them—which was another intriguing story that people were beginning to get their teeth into and chew. And so, deciding that Emma's character must be of the blackest nature, she was summarily dropped by the *ton* before she'd even made her curtsy.

Chapter Seven

William arrived at the institute when a motley assortment of street children were partaking of their one proper meal of the day. He pushed his way inside a communal room and stood looking round at the uneven walls, sagging ceiling and old pitted beams, and yet, despite the dilapidation of the place, everything was scrubbed to a high quality of cleanliness.

Two of Cassandra's helpers had their arms in a bucket of water at a large pot sink, washing crockery. Children lined up eagerly with their bowls, all eyes on the huge steaming pot from which a cheerful, middle-aged woman, wearing a mob-cap and a huge apron wrapped round her rotund middle, was ladling out an appetising stew. Snatching up a hunk of bread to go with it, the children went to sit at a long table where some were already bolting their food under the watchful eyes of Miss Greenwood.

William's attention was drawn to her. Her hair was pinned up, her face all rosy from the steam of the cooking, but it was tense, which told him she was under great strain. He was anxious to fathom her mood, but where he had known her before as a quick-tempered, provocative and passionate young woman, he now perceived an air of quiet seriousness about her. Perhaps the tribulations of the past week had stripped all humour from her. She bore no hint of the happy, charming Cassandra he had seen at Lady Monkton's ball, or the feisty young woman who had courageously told him their associa-tion was over. He braced himself, but could not shrug off a dismal frame of mind. The outlook seemed far from bright.

As if she sensed his presence, Cassandra looked towards the door. If she was surprised to see him there, she didn't show it. He expected defiance, hauteur, but there was neither. She moved towards him, her eyes broodingly sad.

Gazing up at him, noting his usual careless elegance, Cas-sandra thought he was so like she remembered that she expected to feel the familiar warmth flow from him, but his eyes were fathomless and gave nothing back.

'You've come at a busy time,' she said. 'As you can see, this is when we prepare a meal for the children. They're so hungry they'd eat anything. At least what we give them is wholesome and nourishing.'

'I called at your home, hoping to see your mother. When I was informed she had gone away I thought I'd seek you out. I hope you don't mind me coming here.'

'No, of course I don't—it wouldn't take much working out where I would be. Mama and Aunt Elizabeth have taken Emma to the country—to Netherton Hall, Aunt Elizabeth's house near Guildford. A time spent out of town at this time will be a relief—you understand.'

William nodded. 'I'm here to help. It's an appalling state of affairs. How are you coping?'

'Not very well.' Sighing with great weariness, she bent her head, putting the back of her hand to her eyes for a moment. 'It's all such a dreadful mess.' She had tried so hard not to let her worry over Emma get to her, and she had succeeded to a certain extent, but she was storing up a terrible burden of emotion.

William's eyes were warm with concern. She looked tired and worn out, and behind her calm exterior he sensed she endured a nauseating turmoil of distress. He stood with his hands in his pockets, his face carefully blank, while all the time he wanted to reach out and take her in his arms, kiss and soothe her and tell her he was going to make everything all right, and yet, remembering the deep division that stood between them, how could he?

'Can you get away?' he asked quietly. 'I've got my carriage outside. We should talk about this. I would be grateful if you would grant me a little of your time and listen to what I have to say.'

She gave a wry smile. 'Talk? How will talking solve anything? Whatever you have to say to me can be said while I am working.'

'I came to talk with you privately. Please, Cassandra, I am in earnest. I'm sure they can manage without you for half an hour while we take a walk in the park.'

Cassandra stared at him for a long, indecisive moment. Since she must discuss this unfortunate business with him because it involved his cousin, she must at least be civil. 'I suppose I could, but as you can see I am not dressed in any proper state for a walk in the park.'

'You could be wearing sackcloth and ashes for all I care. I assure you that dress beneath your apron is most appropriate,' he said with that gentleness that always surprised Cassandra at unexpected times. 'That colour blue suits you—it matches your eyes. I am sure your bonnet will complement the look.'

She glanced at him, the black wave of despondency that had engulfed her for the past week lifting a little. 'Since it's only an old straw bonnet that I wear with almost everything, it will be an odd combination, but one I am sure will make me the envy of all the other ladies in the park,' she remarked with wry humour.

Admiration swelled in William at how valiantly she was rallying.

'I'm just slipping out for a while, Agatha,' she informed the woman ladling out the stew. 'There's something I have to do. Will you be all right?'

Agatha smiled broadly and nodded, openly admiring of their handsome, elegantly attired guest. 'Aye, lass. We'll manage. You go on. A break will do you the world of good.'

'Agatha's a true gem,' Cassandra said as she removed her apron and donned the aforesaid bonnet. 'Having lost her husband in the Peninsula and with no children of her own, she devotes all her time to the institute. She cares deeply for all the children who come here, and gets through as much work as anyone in an easy and efficient fashion. I don't know what we'd do without her, although she's not the only one. Several women come to help out. They are good women, charitable and respectable.'

The two women at the sink turned to watch her leave with William, their mouths agape. Never had they seen such a handsome gentleman at the institute, and already they were speculating as to who he could be and how close his association was with Miss Greenwood.

William handed Cassandra into the carriage and climbed in after her, instructing the driver to make for Green Park. She sat beside him perfectly still, her hands folded in her lap, her face now pale but composed. Several people were strolling in the park, governesses with their young charges and nursemaids pushing perambulators. Acquaintances exchanged greetings and children bowled hoops along the paths. Sweet scents of early summer, of flowers and cut grass drifted on the light breeze.

Not until they were walking slowly along a path did Cassandra find her voice. 'How has this happened? How did everyone find out about the elopement? Who saw—who told?'

'I have no idea. These things have a way of leaking out. Other people's love lives are endlessly fascinating to others. The stories thrive under the complicit though theoretically unseeing eyes of servants.' His lips curved in a wry smile. 'The servants' hall at my house here in London is privy to more secrets than the Prime Minister's cabinet. But no matter how it came out, it is done and we must deal with it.'

Cassandra stopped and looked at him in an agony of exasperation. William saw her defences rise as she said, 'We? How are you affected? It is Emma who is affected. Emma who is ostracised. Her own foolishness and that of your cousin has endangered her future—as a man it will not affect Edward the same and you know it. It never does and it is so unfair. Emma is young—young and deeply hurt.'

'You're not exactly in your dotage, Cassandra,' William murmured gently.

'Emma is not as strong as I am. I can cope with most things. My heart is filled with rage against a society that could treat a young woman who has done no wrong so harshly. They are savages. Personally I wouldn't care less if I was cut. As if I care a snap for the *ton*'s approval—but I care that Emma minds. She is so sensitive. When she read the awful things that were written about her in the newspapers she went to her room and stayed there for two days, weeping inconsolably.'

'I am sorry to hear that,' William murmured, genuinely moved by Emma's distress. 'She deserves none of this.'

'Knowing people are talking about her, laughing at her— she can't stand it—it's destroying her. Her future is in ruins. No decent gentleman will associate with a young woman of questionable virtue. And she is missing Edward dreadfully, not knowing if she will ever see him again. Mama is devastated and doesn't know how she will endure it. Thank God Aunt Elizabeth took them to Netherton Hall to get away from London and the gossip.'

Seeing a bench away from the path and prying eyes, and doing a quick scan of the area to make sure no one was about to take another shot at him, William took her elbow and led her towards the seat. They sat down and half turned to face each other. Cassandra was twenty years old and still unmarried—no one had offered for her, though she was a better woman than any of the women he had known. Naturally enough this had engendered in her contempt for men's opinions—her manner told them she could do without them and their help. But she had a fierce pride, so what he had to suggest must be approached with caution.

He stared at her very seriously. 'Edward is also suffering most wretchedly—mainly because he knows how the scandal will be affecting your sister. I can see how it is affecting you, too, Cassandra.'

'I can't pretend that I don't mind Emma being the object of derision, and myself for that matter, but I have to get on with things. Unfortunately the institute is doing badly—it has been for some time—because of lack of funding, and since the scandal broke the money's dried up completely. It's only a matter of time before we will have to close it down.'

'I am genuinely sorry. I do understand the gravity of the situation.'

'It's a merciless world,' she murmured, shaking her head sadly. 'There are so many unwanted children sleeping anywhere they can. I have to think of the streets and hovels where they struggle in dirt and filth such as no human being should endure. It's a wonder any of them survive. I try not to be too emotional about it, but I cannot bear to look upon the face of a starving child while the rest of the world goes by. Mama always tells me not to get too emotional, but I can't help it.'

'What a sensitive soul you are, Cassandra Greenwood. One day you will get your orphanage and then you can fill it with as many destitute children as you like.'

She shook her head and smiled. 'No. It's just a dream. I'm sorry. I've been talking too much. I'm often criticised for being too outspoken.'

'Who criticises you?'

'Mama and Aunt Elizabeth, but when I feel strongly about something I can't help it.'

William moved a little closer to her and took her hands in his own, both surprised and relieved that she didn't object, noting her eyes richly lashed under excellently marked eyebrows. The way in which she was looking at him, she suddenly seemed very young and defenceless.

'This is how I regard it. What is the very worst that can happen? What do you fear most?'

She swallowed hard and tried to speak as calmly as he. 'That Emma's reputation is ruined beyond redemption and that she has no future—and that the institute will have to close and the children who have come to depend on us will have nowhere else to go.'

William smiled—it was so like her to think of others before herself.

'Why do you smile?' she asked.

'Because that's your woman's heart speaking. Speaking as a soldier, I can think of no worse fate than death. So be it. Now, what is the best thing that can happen? What do you most desire?'

'That the two things I have just mentioned will be resolved,' she whispered fervently.

'Both are likely, and nothing is beyond one's strength, if the need is great enough.'

Cassandra looked startled. 'How can I believe that? I think you speak more to comfort than from belief.'

'I've got a suggestion that might appeal to you and your mother.' His smile widened and his blue eyes sparkled. 'It will certainly appeal to Emma. There is a solution, you know.'

'There is?' Unconvinced, her voice sounded flat. 'Then please tell me what it is so we can all be put out of our misery.'

'Edward and Emma could get married.'

Cassandra stared at him in amazement. 'Married?' This was not what she had expected him to say.

'I am cautiously optimistic that we can turn this around. If I doubted it, I would not suggest it, and nothing will be as effective at tossing aside the *ton*'s reticence. I'll admit I haven't given a great deal of time to working out all the details, but allowing for the scandal hanging over our heads, there is no reason in the world why Emma can't be introduced into society as a married woman. It might even offer her a certain notoriety, with everyone falling over each other to invite the newly-weds to this and that.'

Cassandra studied him. This was a different William Lampard from the one she had seen before. His easygoing manner, his ready understanding, his quiet attitude, brought calm to her troubled mind. But why was he doing this when he could so easily turn his back on them all and walk away? Did he still hope to win his part of the wager he had made with Sir Charles Grisham and turn this unfortunate situation to his own advantage? If so, he was going to be disappointed—for she would not fall for the soft words of a seducer—but she would willingly accept any suggestion he could come up with if it would solve the crisis. Aware that he was still holding her hands, his touch awakening her senses from their blissful anaesthesia, she slowly extricated them from his grasp.

'Why are you doing this? It's only a short time ago that you would have done anything to prevent Emma marrying your cousin.'

'If I did, that had nothing to do with your sister. Edward was due to begin his military career. Marriage was out of the question. As a soldier he will most certainly be sent abroad at some point—it would be a lonely time for a young wife.'

'Which will happen anyway if the marriage goes ahead.'

'Then that will be something for them to work out. Plenty of young ladies marry at eighteen. It is not unusual. Edward and Emma may be young, but they are in love, and if it lasts they'll be happier than those whose marriages are arranged with sole regard to the increase of family fortunes and no mutual affection between them.'

'Why, Lord Lampard! I never took you for a romantic.' Despite her family's dire predicament, and deeply suspicious of his motives for helping her family, Cassandra gave a teasing smile.

A rogue twinkle sparked in his eyes. 'Oh, I have my moments, but I would be obliged if you would keep it to yourself. Should it come out, my male pride would be wounded to such an extent that it will be irretrievable and my reputation as one of the *ton*'s most disreputable rakes will be in ruins.'

'So you do admit it—that you are just as disreputable as society says you are.'

He laughed good humouredly, relieved that her distress had lifted and she could indulge in light banter. 'No human being is perfect, Miss Greenwood.'

'You are quite right. Have you discussed this with Edward?'

'No. No one. If Emma and Edward decide marriage is what they want, then, since Lady Monkton can no longer bring Emma out, let her arrange the wedding—a truly splendid affair that will certainly give the *ton* something to gossip about—providing your mother is in agreement, naturally.'

'I think she will be thankful to have the situation resolved amicably—and Emma won't take any persuading. Aunt Elizabeth will be delighted with the outcome.'

'I'll write to my grandmother, the Dowager Countess of Carlow, and ask her to come to London. She is a lady of tremendous consequence.'

'Do you think that's necessary?'

'Absolutely. The more weight we have behind our campaign, the greater the chance of success. Society will soon change its attitude when they see not one, but two of the most influential ladies in London are championing Emma.'

'Does you grandmother live at Carlow?'

He nodded. 'I wanted her to move back into Carlow Park where she spent many happy years with my grandfather— Lord knows it's big enough—but she won't hear of it. She has a house on the estate, a companion and housekeeper and servants to look after her. She is content to remain where she is and make room for another generation of Lampards.'

'She sounds intriguing.'

'She is. She doesn't often come to town, but she will if I ask her. In her day she was one of the golden girls of society and never out of the newspapers. She's a bit of an eccentric and was something of a rebel in her time. She leaned towards the unconventional, running close to the limit, and never failed to disappoint either her fans or her critics. Until a few years ago she shamelessly adored forcing society to bend to her will. No one will dare say a word against Emma in her presence.'

'Oh, dear. She sounds quite formidable.'

'She is—in fact, you'll probably get on remarkably well,' he said with a reassuring, meaningful smile.

Cassandra stared into his compelling eyes incredulously. 'You really have thought all this out, haven't you?'

William laughed shortly, his eyes glowing in the warm light. 'Don't underrate my genius for strategy and subtlety. Since we cannot stop the gossip, we will redirect it. I'll prove to you how easy it will be to manipulate the *ton,* and to honour the Lampard tradition, it will have to be a church wedding done on a grand scale, with a vast number of relatives, friends and acquaintances from both sides—about seven hundred, I should think, maybe more—so as not to offend and alienate the *ton.*'

'Emma is passionate about everything spectacular and will relish any opportunity to be the centre of attention, so she will approve of that. Have you given any thought to the wedding breakfast, by any chance?'

'The venue can be left to your mother and Lady Monkton—perhaps Monkton House or my home in Grosvenor Square. Either will be suitable for such a large gathering.'

'A wedding on such a grand scale cannot be planned in a hurry. There will be so many arrangements to make—gowns to be made, invitations to be written, sent out and acknowledged. Why, it will take months.'

'Weeks,' William stated irrevocably. 'It must take place before the end of the Season, when everyone retires to their country estates for the summer. I shall put my entire staff at your disposal and I am certain Lady Monkton will waste no time in seeing her niece wed.'

'She'll love every minute of it…but…won't people talk and wonder at the need for such haste? I—I mean…' A light embarrassed flush suffused her, but she could not resist the query.

Knowing exactly what she was getting at, William's eyes narrowed and he smiled devilishly. 'I do know what you mean and I have considered that. Should it be true that Emma is *enceinte,* I doubt that either Edward or Emma would want a grand wedding, but a quiet affair out of the public eye. In any case, those who suspect this might be the case will be proved wrong given time.'

'Yes—of course, you're right.' She sighed, standing up, reluctant to leave the park, but there was so much to do at the institute. 'I must be getting back. How is Archie, by the way? Has he settled down?'

'He has. He's taken to his work well and likes being with the horses. He's become a favourite with cook, who says he's far too thin and needs fattening up. He's already put on weight. You wouldn't believe he was that scrawny scrap of a lad I saw at the institute that day I was shot.'

'I'm glad. He deserves a chance in life and I thank you for giving it to him.'

When they reached the carriage William handed her inside. 'The walk has done you good,' he remarked, noting the blooming rose colour in her cheeks as he settled himself across from her.

'I do feel better.'

'Good. Cassandra, when last we met you told me you never wanted to see me again—or words to that effect,' he said on a more serious note. 'If Edward and Emma agree to wed, I'm afraid you are going to see a good deal more of me. Will that be a problem for you?'

Across the distance that separated them, their gazes met and held, the silence punctuated by traffic and the clopping of the horses' hooves on the cobbled road. As they had talked, for Cassandra it was like taking a great burden and placing it on his strong shoulders, and she could breathe again. She was beginning to regard him with a new respect—and he had insinuated himself into her heart in a way she had never sought. But she could not forgive him that dreadful, shameful wager he had made and never would, but she was not about to be churlish about it now.

'Not if that's the way it has to be. It's a terrifying possibility,' she said with a hint of humour, 'but I'll risk it. When will you speak to Mama?'

'When will she be back in town?'

'That depends on Emma—a week or more.'

'Then perhaps we should drive to Guildford. The sooner the wheels are put in motion, the better—although I must speak to Edward first. I'll travel to Woolwich tomorrow and talk to him, and, if you can manage it, we can go to Surrey the day after.'

After seeing Edward and obtaining his ecstatic agreement to the suggestion that he marry his darling Emma, the following morning found William and Cassandra travelling to Guildford. It was a lovely day, warm and with fleecy white clouds drifting overhead on a gentle breeze.

Settled into the plush interior of the chaise and happy to have left the bustle of London behind, feeling unusually at ease following the tribulations of the past days, Cassandra let her gaze stray across to her companion. Attired in a cream-silk shirt and olive-green jacket, his muscular legs clad in calf-coloured superfine and shiny brown boots, William Lampard was the image of casual, relaxed elegance. Even his expression was casual—too casual, she thought. He seemed larger in the close confines of the coach, his shoulders broader, his face one of leashed sensuality and arrogant handsomeness, and there was a cynical twist to his sculpted mouth. Everything about him was forceful and exuded brute strength, and was most unsettling to her virgin heart.

'It's a pleasant day for a drive to Guildford,' William commented at length. 'I hope Lady Monkton will not mind us arriving unannounced.'

'She will be surprised, to say the least, when we arrive together—and will no doubt lecture me most severely on my lack of protocol for travelling with a gentleman alone. I suppose I must thank you for all you are doing to help Emma.'

'That is not my prime reason for doing it,' William answered smoothly.

Cassandra did not miss the meaningful glint in his eyes watching her from beneath hooded lids and was prompted to ask warily, 'Then what is your prime purpose?'

A slow smile curved his lips. 'Why, to get to know you better.'

'I think you know me well enough, Lord Lampard,' she retorted sharply, suddenly irate since his statement confirmed he intended to win the wager he had made with Sir Charles Grisham. 'And do you have to watch me so closely?'

'I like watching you. You are a stubborn woman, Miss Greenwood.'

'That's right. I am.'

'Beautiful, too. You look radiant this morning, by the way. The dress you are wearing is quite becoming—peacock-blue, I'd say.'

'Thank you. Every woman loves being likened to a bird,' she said drily.

'I meant it as a compliment,' he assured her.

'That's what worries me.'

William's eyes burned hotly behind his dark lashes. 'You know, you tempt me sorely, Cassandra.'

His gaze sparked a quickness within her, and she averted her eyes. No one before William had ever had such a turbulent effect on her. What was there about this man that aroused her so? There had been other handsome men—dashing, daring, some she considered intelligent—but not one had touched her like this man did and just the memory of his kiss filled her with delicious excitement, leaving her hungering for the consuming heat of his passion.

Greatly disturbed by the path her mind was taking, she turned away and gazed at the passing scenery, but after a moment's contemplation, she found herself looking back at him and inquiring, 'Have you ever been in love—really in love, I mean?'

William cocked a wondering brow at her and a lazy smile tugged at the corners of his mouth. 'There have been times when I thought I was, but now I'm beginning to realise I was mistaken.'

'Be serious,' she rebuked. 'Either you have or you haven't. It's as simple as that.'

He shrugged slightly. 'Nothing is that simple. There was a woman in Spain once—but I realise now that what I felt for her was only infatuation.' He smiled and his voice grew soft with the memory, as though remembering gave him pleasure. 'She was a widow woman, with the blackest hair and the darkest eyes. She taught me much—but it was a long time ago and best forgot.'

'I suppose you were besotted. Was she pretty?'

'She was very beautiful,' he conceded. 'Well-rounded in all the right places—twenty-five—worldly…'

A light blush touched Cassandra's cheeks and she quickly turned away, not wanting to meet his close perusal. 'You needn't go on.'

William chuckled softly. 'You did ask.'

'And I regret doing so.'

William sighed, folding his arms and leaning into the corner of the seat, wondering what she would have to say if he told her that the thought of other women soured in his mind when he contemplated her. 'Why have you grown averse to me of late, Cassandra? I am curious as to the reason.'

'I do not wish to encourage you in your blatant disregard for my status as an independent woman. I meant everything I said that day I took Archie to work for you. Nothing has changed.'

He laughed briefly. 'And you seem to take special delight in reminding me. Are you aware that there is a rumour spreading through the *ton* that I am trying to draw you into my clutches?' he said, watching her from beneath lowered lids. 'Our association has raised a few eyebrows.'

'Really,' Cassandra replied drily. 'I hadn't realised our acquaintance would cause such speculation.'

'People are talking.'

'It's not uncommon. It's how they communicate,' she retorted flippantly in an attempt to hide her unease about the direction the conversation was going.

'They're talking about us.'

'And what are they saying?'

'That you are about to become my mistress—if you are not already.'

Cassandra's eyes sparked angrily. 'Indeed! It's all very well for you. Your reputation isn't at stake. Nobody cares if you go about seducing every woman in London. It's what men do. But it's different for me. If people think you have seduced me, then I am ruined.' The words tumbled out.

William cocked an eyebrow, his eyes dancing with amusement. 'Ah—and all of a sudden you care what people think, do you?'

'Yes—in this instance I do.'

'And you wouldn't if it were some other man doing the seducing?'

'Perhaps not.'

'Then you will be relieved and happy to know that there are some members of society who credit you with more sense than to be caught by me.'

'I'm glad to hear it. As if I haven't enough to contend with right now.'

'The fact that the two of us left London to prevent the

runaways from reaching Gretna Green has been classed as compromising circumstances. It was my fault. I knew what the rules were and broke them when I allowed you to accompany me and later took two unchaperoned young ladies to my home.' His grin was devilish. 'Imagine—if we found ourselves in the same situation as Emma and Edward.'

Cassandra gave him a dire look. 'I am—it is my worst nightmare and it won't happen.'

Cassandra was unconscious of the vision she presented with her skin aglow, her lively eyes and the material of her travelling dress straining over her breasts. Her delectable face fed William's gaze, and his eyes passed over her shapely figure with warm admiration, creating a sweet, hungering ache inside him. He couldn't think of anything more pleasurable at that moment than having her warm and willing in his arms, soft and yielding, as she had been when he had kissed her at Carlow Park. He burned with a consuming desire for her, and he would be satisfied with nothing less than her complete submission. His intense physical attraction to her continued to surprise him.

Gazing out of the window, Cassandra expressed to her companion the wish that he had selected to travel in an open carriage.

'You're right, of course.' His smile faded, and he grew serious. 'But there is need for caution. My life may depend on it.'

'Have you found out any more about the man who shot you that day?'

'Twice.'

She met his eyes with an unwavering gaze. 'Twice? You mean he has tried again?'

He nodded, his face grim. 'When I was returning to Carlow Park after taking Edward to Woolwich.'

'But—you never said anything.'

'There was no need.' He went on to recount what had occurred and she listened in horror. 'Ever since that first attempt I no longer ride out alone and I am constantly looking over my shoulder. I've employed someone who specialises in investigating matters such as this, a Mr Jardine. Hopefully he will come up with something before whoever it is trying to kill me succeeds.'

'Wouldn't you be safer at Carlow Park, in the country, where you will know if there is a stranger loitering about?'

'You forget that I have spent precious little time at Carlow Park these past few years. Nearly everyone is a stranger to me. Besides, it was in the country the last time my would-be assassin tried to dispose of me. I just wish I could think of a reason why someone is so desperate to have me dead.'

The look that appeared on his face gave Cassandra a chill, but it was briefly seen. 'Jealousy, hatred, greed…someone from your military past, perhaps—someone out for revenge,' she suggested.

'I've thought of that—gone over and over it in my mind. I admit I've made enemies in the past, but I can't think of one who would want to kill me.'

'Then the only other motive I can think of is for personal gain. You—told me your cousin Mark is next in line to inherit your estate.'

'He is.'

'Since he is your cousin and you are close, I know how you will react when you hear what I have to say, but…' She hesitated, afraid of the risk she took, but somehow she found the courage to ask him, 'Do you think it's Mark who is trying to kill you? After all, he has much to gain.'

The muscles in William's cheeks tensed and flexed as he met her eyes. 'No. Never. Is that what you think, Cassandra?'

'Well—I don't know, but I suppose it is a possibility.'

'No one who knows him would think so.'

'Perhaps you do not know him well enough.'

Anger darkened Williams eyes. 'I believe I do. Take it from me, it is not Mark.'

'Well, I think you should keep a close eye on him all the

same.' She had only met him briefly, but there was something about him that told her Mark Lampard was not entirely to be trusted.

Not wishing to pursue that particular line of enquiry, William sat in brooding silence for the next few minutes, but the mere fact that Cassandra had suggested his cousin in connection with the shootings gave him a feeling of unease. Unconsciously he massaged his shoulder, which ached when he was tense.

Cassandra noticed. 'Does your shoulder still pain you?'

He shook his head. 'No more than a slight discomfort.'

The tranquillity of the journey was shattered when they left the London Road and turned into a narrow lane. Cassandra's gaze was drawn across some fields to a wooded hill and there, on the skyline and where the trees parted, was a lone horseman. The sun caught and glinted on an object he was holding up to his face. She was sure it was a telescope and that it was focused on them. She gave a gasp and her head spun round to William. She could tell by the expression on his face that he, too, had seen the horseman.

'William,' she said in alarm, 'I think that horseman is watching us.'

'So do I. Unfortunately he's too far away for us to see his face.'

'Do you think it's the same man who's been trying to kill you?'

'We'll soon find out. If it is, he's damned persistent. He must have followed us.'

William urged Boulting, the driver, to go faster. The horseman disappeared into the trees and, as the chaise lurched on, William expected him to reappear at any second. He looked ahead and peered into the dense woods on either side of the lane, but his sight could not penetrate the dark interior. Coming to a tight corner, the horses took it fast. The chaise lurched, two of the wheels running on to the verge, one of them sliding into a deep rut obscured by long grass. Boulting hauled on the reins, the chaise tilted. The spokes of the wheel took the weight and snapped, and the wheel rim shattered.

Miraculously Cassandra managed to stay in her seat. Panic threatened, but she steeled herself against it. His taut features clouded with grave concern for her safety, after assuring himself that she was all right, William jumped down into the road to join Boulting. He had alighted and was staring at the broken wheel in dismay.

'Now what do we do, milord?' he said, scratching his head, his hat having come off when he'd been thrown to one side.

Steeling himself, William stood and looked around, his senses alert. He stared down the lane, listening. The wheel was shattered, the body of the chaise lurched to one side, and the horses, half out of the traces, were restive—and he was sure he could hear hoofbeats in the wood and he couldn't see a damned thing.

Drawing his pistol from a holster beneath his jacket, he dove down. 'Cassandra,' he snapped, 'stay inside and keep down. You, too, Boulting. I believe we are about to have a visitor.'

Now the sounds coming from the undergrowth were getting closer. Crouching low, William cocked the pistol and strained to see into the blackness beyond the lane from which emanated tangible danger and waited. Boulting did the same, but had decided to reach for his hat, which lay in the grass in front of William, when the shot rang out, filling the air with a deafening crack and causing roosting birds to take flight. He cried out and fell backwards, clutching his head. William fell to one knee beside the wounded man at the same time that Cassandra, her heart racing and assailed by a terrible concern that William had been shot, flung open the door and climbed out.

'William!' Her eyes were wide and fearful, though a great flood of relief and joy swept through her to see he looked unharmed.

His expression grim, he shot her a glance. Her face was ashen. 'I'm all right, but the same cannot be said of Boulting.

He's been shot.' His eyes met hers. 'We both know it was meant for me.'

Without wasting a second, he hauled Boulting towards the protection of the carriage and urged Cassandra to do likewise. Giving himself no time to deliberate his actions, in a running crouch he ran several yards down the lane before disappearing into the dark interior of the woods.

Trying not to panic, Cassandra looked down at the driver. He was unconscious but alive, thank goodness. She knelt to tend him. There was so much blood. It was a head wound and she knew they always bled a lot. Immediately she lifted her skirt. Ripping a length of cloth from her petticoat, she made a wad from part of it and pressed it over the wound to staunch the flow of blood, winding the rest round his head to secure it. She then knelt beside him to wait for William to come back.

With the stealth of an Indian, William moved through the riotous undergrowth, careful not to trip on trailing briars. The conifers gave out a sweet resinous smell. Their needles were soft underfoot, the straight trunks rising up all round him like a body guard. He watched carefully for any movement that would expose his quarry. And then there he was, a dark-garbed figure sitting atop a dark brown horse, watching and waiting, his eyes intent on a small circle of light showing through the trees.

'I believe you are looking for me,' William said, his voice like steel. 'What kind of niggardly coward is it that shoots a man in the back?'

The assailant had been aware of no sound or movement. Now he spun round to see the tall figure of his prey, his arm raised, and at its end a pistol stared back at him. He raised his own, prepared to fire. There was a flash and then another. The sounds rent the air and there was a half-screaming grunt as the horseman fell from his mount and smashed face down to the ground. The horse bolted with fright and went crashing through the undergrowth. Going to his assailant, William turned him over with his foot. The man was of heavy build, his face that of a man in his mid-thirties, a complete stranger—and unfortunately he was dead.

Cassandra kept her eyes fastened on the woods, her ears straining to the slightest sound. She'd heard the shots and her heart had taken up a frantic beating while she waited. Tiny shards of fear pricked her spine while a coldness congealed in the pit of her stomach when she heard someone moving through the undergrowth in her direction. Shaking with apprehension, she crouched beside Boulting, not daring to breathe. Her skin crawled on the nape of her neck. Perhaps it wasn't William. Perhaps he was lying wounded or dead in the woods.

When William suddenly appeared, she experienced a rush of mixed and complex emotions, and her relief was so great she almost expired.

'William?' His name came in a tentative question.

He moved quickly towards her. His face was grim, but he managed a smile in an attempt to allay her fears. 'There's no longer any need to be afraid.'

'Why, what—what has happened?'

'The man's dead. I'd rather he wasn't, so I could have asked him what all this has been about—but it was either him or me.'

'Dead?' she whispered. 'Did—did you recognise him?'

'No—but that doesn't surprise me. I have no doubt he was paid to kill me—by whom I have yet to find out. There was nothing on him to identify him—no name, nothing.'

'What will you do? You can't leave him in the woods.'

'I don't intend to. I'll ride into Guildford later and speak to the authorities. But first we must get Boulting to a physician before he bleeds to death. How far do you think we are from Netherton Hall?'

'About two miles, I would say.'

'We need help. I'll unhitch the horses. You'll have to ride for help.'

Cassandra stared at him and shook her head. 'Ride? But— I don't,' she confessed, suddenly feeling totally inadequate and wishing she'd learned. 'Unlike Emma, I never took to horses. I've never been on a horse in my life.'

William's face was incredulous. 'You haven't? Damn. And I thought there was nothing you couldn't do. I can't leave you here alone with Boulting.'

'There's no need,' Cassandra said, looking back down the lane with relief. 'I think I can hear someone coming.'

An open carriage with a driver and a single male occupant was heading towards them. When the driver saw the chaise blocking the road, he slowed down and stopped. The man climbed out and hurried to William, who had managed to quieten the horses. William introduced himself and gave the stranger a brief account of how the chaise had come to grief. The shooting of Boulting and the dead man in the woods he preferred to keep to himself, his explanation for Boulting's injury being that he had been thrown from the box when the chaise had swerved.

'Where are you heading?' the gentleman asked, who had introduced himself as Mr Loftus, a businessman from Guildford.

'Netherton Hall. Do you know it?'

Mr Loftus nodded and smiled broadly. 'Indeed I do, sir. I have the honour of being acquainted with Lady Monkton. Very fine lady. I'll take you there directly.'

'I would be most grateful.'

Together they managed to lift the now semi-conscious Boulting—thankfully a small man of light weight—into the carriage.

William turned to Cassandra. 'Go with Mr Loftus, Cassandra. I'll stay with the horses. Send someone as soon as you reach Netherton Hall.'

'But—what about—?'

He placed a warning finger to her lips to silence her before she said too much. 'We'll discuss that later. Don't worry,' he said quietly, for her ears alone. 'I've told you. The man's dead. He won't be coming back.'

She stared up at him. When she had heard the shot, for a terrible stabbing moment she had known a tightening of fear so strong it seemed to take the breath from her body. For a moment she was held in a space of frozen time, unable to drag her eyes from the ones that commanded her attention. Swallowing her fear, she whispered, 'I know, but I feel he is still a threat. You will keep your pistol at the ready, won't you?'

Meeting her gaze, William saw her concern for him in her eyes. His smile was gentle, his eyes warm. 'Are you trying to protect me, Miss Greenwood?'

'You do seem to need it from time to time. Please take care.'

Taking heart from the lack of a threat, Cassandra climbed into the carriage.

Chapter Eight

Cassandra's unexpected arrival at Netherton Hall—and the manner of it—put the house in turmoil with servants hurrying all over the place. Aunt Elizabeth and her mother came out of the drawing room to see what all the fuss was about. Seeing a dishevelled and soiled Cassandra snapping out orders to the servants, they stood and watched in amazed stupefaction.

Boulting was carried to a bed in the servants' quarters, the doctor sent for and two grooms despatched to mend the broken wheel and assist Lord Lampard. Mr Loftus, happy to have been of help, went on his way after paying his respects to Lady Monkton. Not until they were in the drawing room did Aunt Elizabeth demand a full explanation of what had happened.

'An accident, you say,' Harriet said, her voice filled with concern. 'And did I hear you mention Lord Lampard?'

'Yes. He had to stay with the horses.' Cassandra decided it would be best for William to tell them about the shooting.

'I must say this is all highly irregular, Cassandra—travelling all this way, alone with Lord Lampard, without informing us of what you intended.'

'I know, Mama, and I'm sorry, but there was no other way. Lord Lampard has something of importance to discuss with you and Aunt Elizabeth and it couldn't wait.'

'But—just look at you,' Aunt Elizabeth remarked in shocked tones and slight admonishment. 'Oh, my goodness! Is that blood on your skirt? And just look at your petticoat— why, it appears to be in tatters.'

Cassandra glanced down at the sorry state of her clothes, seeing the torn hem of her petticoat peaking out from beneath her dress. 'I know I must look a sight, but poor Boulting bled quite profusely. I had to bind his wound—'

'With your petticoat?' Lady Monkton regarded her sternly. 'Some of it.'

'Well—I am all amazement and cannot wait to hear what you have to say.'

'How is Emma?' Cassandra asked, directing her gaze at her mother seated beside her on the *chaise-longue*.

'Better now she is away from London and the gossips, but her spirits are shaken. She spends most of her time in her room.' Equally concerned for her elder daughter, Harriet took Cassandra's hand. 'But how are you, my dear? You look tired and quite agitated. You work too hard at the institute, Cassandra. You really should let Agatha do more, especially when I'm away. Were you hurt when the carriage lost its wheel?'

'No, Mama, I am perfectly all right,' Cassandra was quick to reassure her. Forced to curb her agitation and anxious for William to arrive, her eyes kept flitting to the window that overlooked the drive.

Cassandra continued to answer their questions, striving to be composed, but her thoughts were elsewhere. Blue eyes invaded her unwilling mind, and a warmth slowly spread through her. They stared down to the depths of her being, stirring unwelcome longings. She sighed and looked out of the window once more. What was to be done?

The sooner William put forward his suggestion regarding Emma and Edward and left for London, the happier she would be. She would stay in Surrey and travel to London with her family in a few days' time. The institute was in good hands—

Agatha was more than capable of running things. If Emma agreed to marry Edward, then hectic preparations would begin in earnest as soon as they returned home, so a few days' respite would not go amiss.

William and the doctor—Dr Shaw—arrived within minutes of each other, both of them going straight to Boulting. William thought wryly that his demands on the medical men of late were happening all too frequently and he sincerely hoped this would be the last.

Later, when the doctor had left and William came striding in, he went directly to Lady Monkton. Cassandra stole a glance at his chiselled profile, marvelling at the strength and pride carved into every feature on the starkly handsome face.

'It's a pleasure meeting you again, Lady Monkton—and you, too, Mrs Greenwood,' he said with polite formality. 'I apologise for disturbing you like this and for coming here un-announced, but there is a matter of importance I wish to discuss with you. As Miss Greenwood will have explained we met with a mishap two miles down the road.'

'Thank goodness neither of you is the worse for your ordeal. Please sit down, Lord Lampard. Cassandra, ring the bell for tea. I do hope your man Boulting's wound isn't serious.'

'Not as serious as I first thought,' William said, selecting a chair close to Cassandra and sitting down. 'You should know that my driver was shot, Lady Monkton.'

William went on to give them a brief account of what had happened. Lady Monkton and Harriet Greenwood stared as if they had been struck dumb. Harriet was both alarmed and dis-tressed at the very idea that her daughter could have been hurt.

'And your assailant is dead, you say?'

'Unfortunately, he is. I would have liked it to be otherwise so that I could have questioned him. He carried nothing on his person to identify him.'

'No doubt he was some unmitigated rogue intent on highway robbery.'

'Yes—that's the conclusion we reached.' In keeping with his intention to keep quiet about the earlier threats to his person, William gave Cassandra a warning look that insisted on her unquestioning cooperation.

'If you would be so kind as to provide me with a horse to ride into Guildford to meet with the authorities, I would be most grateful. I shall have to offer some explanation to today's débâcle.'

When William returned to Netherton Hall he was shown into the drawing room where the ladies were gathered before dinner—all except Emma, who remained in her room.

Cassandra looked at him, her senses suddenly heightened by his presence. 'You saw the magistrate?'

He nodded, his expression closed as he accepted Lady Monkton's offer of a fortifying brandy. 'Everything is being taken care of. How is Boulting?' he asked, taking a large draught of the fiery liquid.

'He was sleeping when I looked in on him. I understand that Dr Shaw left him a sleeping draught. It seems to be working.'

'I use Dr Shaw myself,' Lady Monkton told William. 'I have absolute confidence in him, so Boulting is in good hands.'

William sat in the chair he had occupied earlier. 'I am sure he is. The wound is superficial and Dr Shaw is convinced there will be no permanent damage, but he has advised against moving him for a few days.'

'Then we shall ensure he is made comfortable while he is here—and you are welcome to stay as long as you like, Lord Lampard,' Lady Monkton offered, smiling pleasantly, hoping he would.

Alarm exploded within Cassandra. 'Oh—but I think Lord Lampard will have to return to London, Aunt Elizabeth—is that not so, Lord Lampard?'

He cocked a lazy brow, his look challenging. 'I do?'

'Yes. I am sure one of your grooms could take him back to town, Aunt Elizabeth.'

'That is up to Lord Lampard, my dear.'

William's eyes met Cassandra's squarely. She waited for him to decline the invitation, but he did nothing of the sort. A man to take advantage of all opportunities presented to him, he seized upon the offer. A smile played just behind his features and he gave a slow nod of what appeared to be acceptance.

'Because of my concern for Boulting, I would be happy to remain a few days, Lady Monkton, and I thank you for your kind invitation.'

'Good—that's splendid.' The elderly lady beamed.

'But…but your clothes…your wardrobe…' Cassandra retorted.

A roguish grin twisted his mouth. 'My military training taught me to always be prepared for the unexpected.'

Cassandra could only stare at him, and when she saw the satisfied smile sweeping across his face, she felt like telling him she could not possibly endure his presence at Netherton Hall indefinitely. It was only with great effort that she curbed her tongue.

Leaning back in his chair, a booted foot propped upon the opposite knee, supremely assured in his arrogance that he had scored a victory, he smiled across the distance into the less-than-warm depths of her eyes. In his own, there was a kindling fire that touched her like a hot brand. She glared at him. How dare he look at her like that when they were in the presence of her mother and Aunt Elizabeth? Cassandra had noticed the sharp glances that had passed between them during her exchange with William.

'Then I hope your stay will be a pleasant one,' she said stiffly, her cheeks burning as she endured William's mocking gaze. She had known instinctively that Aunt Elizabeth's warm and congenial offer would guarantee his acceptance, yet his visit would pose definite problems for her. 'Aunt Elizabeth is famous for her hospitality, but won't you be bored with only a house full of females for company?'

'Not at all. I'm sure I shall find plenty to occupy my time. I will start by teaching you how to ride. You're the only female I know who doesn't.'

Cassandra was astounded by his effrontery. 'Oh, no, you will not. I told you I have never been on a horse in my life and I do not intend doing so.'

'Come, Cassandra,' he said teasingly. 'Be adventuresome.' His laughing eyes communicated with hers in silent challenge. 'Afraid?'

'Yes—no—I don't know.' Why was he doing this? she wondered infuriatingly. The man was insufferable. He was positively revelling in her discomfort. 'I have a strong aversion to horses when they come too close,' she confessed.

'Then I shall help you to master your aversion. You'll have them eating out of your hand in no time at all. You might be a little sore from the experience at first, but I can assure you you will soon get the hang of it and enjoy yourself.' He switched his gaze to Lady Monkton, who, like Harriet, was listening to their exchange in quiet amazement. 'Do you have a suitable mount for your niece to ride, Lady Monkton?'

'Why, yes—a beautiful, gentle little mare called Jade. Emma used to ride her until she became more proficient. She will be perfect.'

'There you are then. I will give you your first lesson tomorrow morning.'

'You take too much upon yourself, Lord Lampard,' Cassandra replied stiffly. 'I shall think about it.'

William chuckled softly. 'Your daughter has a very strong opinion of me, Mrs Greenwood—unfavourable for the most part. She is also an extremely stubborn young woman.'

'I have no opinion of you whatsoever, Lord Lampard,'

Cassandra retorted, trying to ignore her mama's questioning eyes as she looked with curiosity from one to the other.

Harriet caught the intense look that passed between Cassandra and Lord Lampard. His eyes held a measure of admiration for her daughter, which asked a question—what on earth did this mean? She gave Cassandra a quizzical look, having observed her impatient fidgetings while awaiting Lord Lampard's arrival. Harriet was not very well acquainted with Lord Lampard, only having met him the once when he had called to tell her that Emily and Cassandra were at Carlow Park and to collect some clothes for Cassandra, but he was the first gentleman ever to show an interest in her elder daughter, so what was she to make of that?

When he had greeted her earlier and looked into her eyes, she had been struck by his great personal attraction. There was warmth about him and a sense of humour in his smile, yet his mouth was firm, with a twist to it that said he was not a man to be trifled with. She liked him and hoped she would see more of him in the future, although she was somewhat concerned by his unfavourable reputation and hoped he would not trifle with her daughter's affections.

'Cassandra does not have the slightest concept of the importance of appropriate behaviour, Lord Lampard,' Lady Monkton informed him. 'If she had, she wouldn't have travelled to Netherton Hall alone with you.'

'Why ever not?' Cassandra argued on a lighter note, having gathered her senses. 'I don't recall you voicing any objections when we went after Emma when she eloped.'

'That was a different matter entirely,' Lady Monkton reproached.

'If you say so, Aunt Elizabeth,' Cassandra conceded with a suppressed smile.

'Now, what is this matter of importance you wish to discuss with us, Lord Lampard?'

'I wish to confer with Mrs Greenwood and yourself on the

best way of solving this unfortunate affair concerning Edward and Emma—to salvage something decent out of this folly. I am thinking of their best interests. Please don't think I am interfering, but since Edward is my cousin and has no parents to advise him, I am involved. I am here to try and make an intolerable situation better.'

Harriet shot him a grateful smile. 'I won't pretend this is not an anxious time for me, Lord Lampard. Restoring Emma to society's good graces is important, so anything you can suggest is welcome. Elizabeth and I are at our wits' end over what is to be done so that Emma can hold her head up in society.'

William's smile was sympathetic. 'Then, since it concerns Emma, would you like her to be present?'

'No,' Harriet said quietly. 'I think we should listen to what you have to say first. My daughter is a complete innocent and a victim of her own foolishness. She is suffering because of it. I have no wish to add to her suffering until I know what it is you have to propose.'

'As you wish.' Leaning back in his chair, William steepled his fingers and regarded his audience seriously for several moments before he went on to put forward his suggestion. They listened intently without interrupting, their eyes opening wide with incredulity when they realised he was suggesting that Emma and Edward should be allowed to wed. Not until he had finished speaking did Harriet and Elizabeth look at each other.

'What are your thoughts, Elizabeth?'

Elizabeth looked immensely pleased and was almost bubbling with excitement. 'Why, I think it's a splendid idea. It is both bold and cunning, but what a splendid plan it is.'

Harriet sighed. 'I would have liked it better had Emma the chance of having more contenders for her hand.'

Elizabeth shook her head. 'Unfortunately, there never will be now. Edward is the only contender and the only one she wants. What do you say, Harriet?'

With no feasible reason to object, Harriet nodded. 'Very well. We will send for Emma and see what she has to say.' She shook her head and sighed regretfully. 'I only wish I had the funds to give her the wedding I know she will want.'

'Poverty is no barrier to social success, provided there is some other distinction to offer—be it brains or beauty,' Elizabeth retorted, 'and both your daughters have been blessed with both. Why, even the Prince Regent changes the accepted order of things when it suits him.'

'I dare say, but I'm not the Prince Regent.'

'It doesn't matter. Emma will not be alone. I will be with her, do not forget, and no one will dare ostracise her in front of me. I have no control over wagging tongues, but she has spirit enough to endure what they might put her through initially, knowing that the outcome will be favourable. No doubt the *ton* will enjoy dining out on her reputation until the betrothal is announced.'

'Which I think should be immediate,' William suggested quietly.

'I agree absolutely. My entire life has been scrupulously dedicated to the precepts of convention, but there are times when one has to go against the rules of the *ton*. This is one of them and I am prepared to fly in the face of decorum and convention. When we return to London we will begin with drives out, evenings at the theatre, shopping and exhibitions and the like. Oh, and one more thing—which concerns her dowry. I have decided to settle on her a generous sum, so that will no longer be a problem,' Elizabeth announced, looking extremely pleased by the way things were turning out.

Overwhelmed by this unlooked-for generosity, Harriet stared at her. Tears of gratitude swam in her eyes and tenderness welled in her heart. 'I don't know what to say. We are putting you to so much trouble already—it's beyond being kind of you to do this. Emma doesn't deserve it.'

'Nonsense. You seem to have forgotten that you are my

dear cousin and I am devoted to both your girls. Besides, it is what my dear husband would have wanted. He was extremely fond of Cassandra and Emma, you know—indeed, is Cassandra not our goddaughter?—and it is my duty to take care of you—all of you. What you don't deserve is what the *ton* is doing to you. You are coping valiantly and it does you credit.

'You are too good, Elizabeth,' Harriet murmured, reaching out and gripping her hand affectionately.

'Now, Harriet, don't come over all emotional. You know it gives me pleasure to do this for Emma, so indulge me.'

William looked from one to the other of the ladies with something akin to admiration. 'Edward's parents left him extremely well off—and their family home in Richmond, which has been closed up since their deaths, can be reopened. It's a splendid residence overlooking the park. Emma will love it and will want for nothing. If she wants to be close to Edward while he is doing his army training, then there is no reason why they can't take lodgings in Woolwich.'

Emma came in, looking wan and lifeless. She looked at her sister and Lord Lampard nervously. 'Why are you here, Cassy?'

'Because of you, actually.' Taking Emma's hand, Cassandra drew her down beside her and their mama on the *chaise-longue*. 'Please listen to what Lord Lampard has to say, Emma.'

Emma sat perfectly still, her hands clenched in her lap, her face pale but composed. Cassandra's heart went out to her, but she sincerely believed that, when she had heard what William had to say, they would see the old Emma restored to them.

What Lord Lampard suggested seemed so unlikely, so inconceivable, that Emma couldn't believe it.

'You have got your wish, Emma. What do you say to my suggestion?' William asked gently. Emma smiled, a smile that warmed his heart and promised her full cooperation.

'What does Edward say?' Emma asked. 'You have spoken to him?'

William nodded. 'It is what he wants.' Standing up, he

took a letter from inside his coat and handed it to her. 'Everything he has to say is in his letter.'

Emma looked at it as if it were the most precious gift. Excusing herself, she fled the room to read it in private.

When William began conversing with her mother, Cassandra watched him. He was the image of relaxed elegance, looking not only casual, but supremely self-satisfied, his expression so bland and complacent that once again she felt there was more behind this than bringing Edward and Emma together. She asked herself the question—how did she feel about this man who she seemed unable to banish from her life? She searched her mind carefully, frowning as she looked away from him, trying to be completely honest with herself. He was capable of plucking at the strings of her heart and turning her bones to water by simply kissing her—she already knew that, but what else did she feel for him?

Of course, she was extremely grateful to him for all he was doing for Emma, although at the back of her mind she knew he wasn't really doing it for Emma, Edward, her mother or Aunt Elizabeth, but to remain close to her in order to win his wager before the Season ended, and, despite her determination to steer clear of him, she had to go along with it for Emma's sake. He held all the cards and he knew it, and she couldn't walk away, not until Emma and Edward were married. Though it gave her no pleasure knowing she was indebted to him, she realised the generosity was all on his side and that one day soon he might extract payment.

When the evening meal was over the ladies retired to the drawing room to discuss Emma's forthcoming nuptials. After a while Cassandra rose and wandered through the long French windows on to the grey stone terrace. The air was soft and languid; the sweet scent of roses and honeysuckle hung heavily. The night was drawing in and already myriad stars shimmered in the dark blue velvet sky. The moon was a great yellow orb in the east, and to the west the dying sun blazed in the sky in a brilliant and dramatic display of crimson, orange and yellow.

Stepping down from the terrace, she strolled through the garden and sighed, thinking it was a time for lovers, yet she was thinking of the children at the institute and what would happen to them if it were to close. She had no doubt they would become lost in the alleyways and courts of wretched places like St Giles.

Slowly she wandered through the abundant rose bowers, idly fingering the velvety blooms, their scent heavy and erotic. All of a sudden, as she rounded a corner, she saw William. He had disappeared after dinner and she thought he had gone to his room, but here he was, seated on an ornate wrought-iron bench facing the crimson sky. He had one knee crossed over the other, the snowy whiteness of his elegant cravat shining bright.

Cassandra was struck by his stern profile and for a moment she was able to see a kind of beauty in it, but as quickly dismissed the thought. Her breath was suddenly caught in her throat and her heart was beating painfully fast. Not wishing to intrude on his solitude, she took a step back and was about to turn and disappear into the rose bushes, but she realised she must have made a sound or he sensed her presence, because without warning he turned his gaze directly at her. She felt heat in her face—felt it spread at that naked, desirous look. It was a look that spoke of invitation and need.

William saw her radiant gold hair, her cream dress that shaped the perfect form of which he was so enamoured and he had no mind to let her escape. When he looked at her, his eyes were as calm as the sea on a fair day.

'Don't go. Come and sit with me a while,' he said quietly.

'I—I don't wish to intrude.'

'You're not.' He sighed deeply. 'I think that when you found your way here, I was thinking of you. How lovely you look. I was half-afraid you were not real, but a ghost of the night.'

'No, I assure you I am flesh and blood.'

He nodded, his face expressionless. 'So you are. Come and look at the sky. Is it not beautiful?'

He calmly contemplated her for a moment before looking back at the sky, which he seemed to find so fascinating. Cassandra was drawn towards him and slowly made her way to the bench, seating herself a little way from him. She, too, gazed at the beauty of the sky. It was an intimate moment and she had the strange idea that if she made a sound something rare and precious would be broken. The silence was disturbed by the occasional call of a bird.

In the end it was William who spoke.

'I would sit and gaze at the sunset for hours in Spain. It always brought a sort of peace.'

'The war must seem very far away now.'

'It is. I spent a long time there.'

'What was it like?' she asked, trying to envisage him as a soldier, thinking how handsome he would look in uniform.

'Hot for the most part—dusty, although the winters, especially in the mountains, could be freezing. Food was frequently in short supply because supplies failed to get through.'

'How long were you in Spain?'

'Two years—most of it spent in the saddle.'

Cassandra gazed at him. He continued to look at the sky. She thought how different he was, how remote, how detached. She was baffled, then at a loss for words, for he was not usually like this—at least not the William she had come to know. And why did he not play the part she had assigned to him, and become the seductive scoundrel?

William turned his head and looked at her, and into his eyes, dark now, came a look like a sudden flame; he smiled slowly, as if in secret. 'You have no idea how lovely you look. The moonlight suits you. It makes you look fragile and vulnerable and very pliable, yet I know you are strong and determined—and more than a little obstinate.'

There was a caressing note in his voice, which at any other time would have brought a brittle retort to her lips. Instead, perhaps because of the quiet, the warmth and the beauty of the sky, she merely looked at him a little inquiringly and smiled.

'You are too free with your flattery, William, and I think you are teasing me.' She expected him to reach out and touch her hand, which lay on the seat between them, but he didn't, and she felt both glad and disappointed at the same time.

'Am I? I suppose I could be accused of worse.'

His voice was grave, quiet and compelling—almost mesmeric. Once again Cassandra felt that little flame flicker within her, making it all the more difficult for her to regard him as her enemy.

William said no more, and she, too, was silent, and he smiled to himself. He looked ahead of him, thinking of the woman beside him. The recurring images of her in his arms, of the kisses they had shared, drifted through his mind, still confused and contradictory—Cassandra by the lake at Carlow Park, her arms around his neck, her lips moist and willing, eyes shining under lids like petals; Cassandra turning away from him, distant and angry.

What was to be done? he asked himself. For she had wanted him. There was no mistaking that it had been a totally mutual thing between them from the very beginning, from the day he had taken her in his arms in the coach as they had chased after Edward and Emma. He smiled at the recollection. He had fully expected her to protest at the time and slap his face, but instead she had melted into his arms as if she belonged there. And she did. All he needed to do was make her realise it.

'Did you see much fighting in Spain?' Cassandra asked, breaking the silence.

'A great deal, as a matter of fact.'

'And did you suffer any injuries?'

'Several—minor ones. I was lucky.'

He turned away. It was hard to talk rationally when he remembered so much. How could he tell a gently reared young woman born and bred in England what it had been like—the nastiness of war, the terrible waste and slaughter, the long marches over mountainous terrain in pursuit of the enemy, the battles, the bombardment, the blood, the flies feasting on dead bodies? Most of the soldiers fought in a style that did credit to their training, but a great many of them were battle shocked, with a blank, haunted staring in their eyes—young men who had been forced to be brave for too long. Some had quite literally run out of courage—some had been too weary to bury the dead.

In the small circle of light that they inhabited, the warm, scented air lapping around them like a comfort blanket, binding them in a strange reserve, Cassandra was strangely sensitive to his thoughts and understood. 'You don't have to talk about it, William. I have spoken to a lot of soldiers who have returned from the Peninsula, so I do have a picture in my mind of what it was like.'

'Unless you were there, at Albuera or Badajoz, you can never know, Cassandra, and it's as well that you don't. Thank God we've seen the last of it. But there were times when we saw the real Spain, and at times like those, when the sun set over the brooding mountains and crimson lit the sky—like it does now, in a way that belongs to the radiance of midsummer—we saw the beauty of the country and it felt good to be alive.'

Again they fell silent and Cassandra felt strangely reluctant to break this magic moment. This was how she had often dreamed, sometimes when she had sat at home alone in the long evenings when her mother had been at the institute and Emma had been staying at Monkton House, that a man would talk to her and she would listen. She realised there was so much she didn't know about William. Who would have thought that one of London's rakes *par excellence* would sit looking enraptured at a sunset?

'How are you liking being back at Carlow Park?' she asked at length, tentatively.

'Well enough. It's very different from how I remember it. The covers have been taken off the furniture and the vases are filled with flowers, but the house seems empty to me—like a tomb,' he said quietly, almost to himself.

'All empty houses often feel like that,' Cassandra remarked, knowing how deeply he missed his family.

'You may be right. Carlow Park was always a happy house, full of laughter. It needs fresh life injecting into it, which is down to me—something for the future. Coming back from Spain, after being a soldier for so long, it's as if I've become somebody else and I'm still trying to find the old me.'

There was no mistaking that he was in earnest. His voice was full of an emotion Cassandra did not understand. 'It's bound to take time. And are you happy?'

'I suppose I am content.'

'What's the difference?'

'Contentment is a state of mind—when mind and body are compatible with each other. Happiness is something that comes and goes and has different levels. Music makes one happy, as does personal achievement; also seeing happiness in others—the birth of a child—knowing you have done something for others that improves their lives, like your work at the institute, the good you do for the children.'

Cassandra thought for a moment. 'I've never considered it like that before, but what I feel when I see the children go away from the institute with full bellies is more a feeling of satisfaction than happiness.' She looked at him curiously. 'Is it happiness you feel for what you are doing for Emma and Edward?'

They looked at each other across the short distance that separated them and William's eyes held hers for a long instant, with a light in them like the crimson flame in the sky.

He shrugged. 'Happiness, contentment and satisfaction— because it means I will see much of you, Cassandra.'

'And is that your reason for concocting this ingenious scheme?'

'One of them,' he confessed unashamedly. He stood up and smiled, his teeth gleaming white in the gathering gloom. 'Now come, enough open hearts and philosophising for one night. I'll walk you back to the house. I would like to keep you here, talking to you, but you have a big day ahead of you tomorrow. It is important that you have a good night's sleep if you are going to learn to ride a horse.'

Later, when she was alone in her room, Cassandra reflected on her encounter with William. To say she wasn't affected by it was a huge understatement. It had left her confused and slightly shaken. Just now as they had talked or just sat in silence looking at the sunset, when she had looked into his eyes they had been filled with such an enigmatic expression.

The whole incident had been incredible for her. For a time she had totally forgotten the gulf that yawned between them and she had responded with a spontaneity to his quiet thoughtful mood—a mood she wanted to capture and remember, which amazed her. When she had sat beside him it had felt so absolutely right, so amazingly natural she could feel it even now, as she prepared for bed, a warmth, a smoothness of something sweet running through her veins like warm honey.

The following morning Cassandra stood in front of the cheval mirror and cast a critical eye over her riding habit. She had borrowed it from Emma since she didn't possess one of her own. It was a little tight across her breasts, but apart from that it was a good fit everywhere else and rather chic, she thought approvingly, doing a twirl. After straightening the matching hat that sat jauntily on her fair curls, she slipped her hands into her kid gloves. Picking up her riding crop, she left the room and made her way to the stables, apprehensive about her first riding lesson and wondering why she had let herself be talked into it, but William Lampard had set the challenge, and, goaded by the mocking amusement in his eyes, she had refused to give him satisfaction by declining.

The stables were close to the house, but hidden from view by a tall box hedge. Sixteen stalls were set around the stable yard, not all of them occupied. Grooms and stable boys were going about their daily chores. William was there ahead of her, talking and joking with lazy good humour with one of the grooms.

Cassandra paused across the yard, slanting a long considering look at her tormentor; when she recalled their encounter in the garden the previous night and how drawn to him she had been, she felt a sudden warmth in her heart. In his tan jacket and white silk neckcloth, buckskin riding breeches and gleaming brown leather boots, his dark hair ruffled by the slight breeze, he was devilishly attractive to look at. Her pulse raced; she was unsure as to the cause—her handsome riding instructor or her fear of mounting the beast he was leading towards her.

Cassandra felt her legs begin to shake and cold fear race down her spine; her pulse accelerated wildly. All her life she'd been nervous around horses—she felt it was not about to change.

'Good morning, Cassandra. I trust you slept well?'

'Yes, perfectly, thank you.'

'I enjoyed watching the sunset with you.' His tone was intimate, his gaze warm and meaningful. 'We'll have to do it again.'

'Yes,' she replied, looking nervously at the horse.

Noting her apprehension and the way her eyes darted from the horse to him, William was determined that by the time he had finished she would have conquered her fear of horses. Like the countryside itself she was dressed in green with touches of gold setting off the rich shade. When he was close, a slow, lazy smile swept across his face and Cassandra braced her trembling body for him to say something mocking, but his deep voice was filled with admiration. 'You look lovely. Are you ready for your first lesson?'

'I think I'd prefer pistols at twenty paces,' she remarked, eyeing the mare suspiciously when it shook its head and snorted loudly.

'Whoa—easy, now,' William murmured soothingly to the mare. He smiled at Cassandra encouragingly. 'Try not to be nervous. Don't let the horse see your fear. Horses need to be taught obedience by their rider. Once that has been established, a good horse will always recognise its master—or, in your case, mistress. Come and make friends with Jade. See, she's as docile as a lamb.' Taking something out of his pocket, he offered his hand to the horse. Jade snorted and moved towards it, taking the piece of sugar and crunching appreciatively. William placed another piece of sugar in Cassandra's gloved hand. 'Now you try.'

Gingerly she did as he had done and was tempted to withdraw her hand at the last minute, but didn't, and her lips broke into a wondering smile when Jade nuzzled her hand and took the sugar.

'There, see how easy that was? Time and a lot of friendship can make anything happen.' William casually caressed Jade's nose, urging Cassandra to rub her neck. After several minutes more, in which Cassandra tried to familiarise herself with the horse, William said, 'Are you ready to mount her?'

Taking a deep, fortifying breath, Cassandra nodded. 'I suppose it's now or never.'

She was dreadfully nervous as William helped her settle into the side saddle. She felt so high up her head spun. The feeling passed after a moment. William let her sit there and get the feel for the horse before leading it out of the yard and down a path to the park. It was frightening at first and Cassandra was terrified she would fall off. Walking along beside her at a slow, measured pace and holding the side of the bridle, William was wonderfully patient, giving her instructions and correcting errors. Gaining confidence all the time, she began to relax and enjoy herself.

William stared up at her profile, tracing with his gaze the soft lines of her face, the brush of lustrous dark lashes, a stray strand of hair that rested against her cheek, her features rosy with the exhilaration of the ride. 'You're doing well. How do you feel?'

'Better than I imagined—although the horse has something to do with that. She knows how to be extra gentle with me and has helped me to build up my confidence.'

'She has a natural gift of patience, I grant you.'

Glancing down into his eyes, Cassandra saw the soft, smiling warmth there and the last of her fear evaporated. 'It is clear you have a way with horses.'

'I enjoy being with them. When I was in the Peninsula a good mount was worth its weight in gold. It could mean the difference between life and death.'

'Speaking of which,' Cassandra said, 'why did you give Mama and Aunt Elizabeth reason to believe we were set upon by a robber yesterday instead of someone who was out to kill you?'

'Because it is my business and also because your family is already overburdened with problems without adding mine to them.'

'Don't you think you should have told them the truth? After all, it was not only your life that was in jeopardy, but mine, too.'

William's head shot up and he looked most contrite. 'And that was my primary concern, you must believe that. The last thing I want is to put your life in danger, which is why I shall be returning to London tomorrow. I suspect the man who has been following me was a hired assassin.'

'Maybe whoever it is who is trying to kill you will give up now.'

William didn't think so. An inbred caution still told him to be wary until he knew for certain who was behind it.

'Perhaps Mr Jardine will come up with something.'

'That is what I'm paying him for.'

'How do you know that whoever is behind it hasn't hired someone else to execute the deed, and that they aren't watching us at this very minute?' Cassandra asked, her gaze travelling over the vast tract of parkland and imagining a murderer behind every tree.

'I doubt it. Don't forget, there was no identification on the man I killed. It will take some time—if ever—for the authorities to find out who he was. But after saying that, I have no doubt that the person who wants me dead will soon hire someone else when he fails to get results.'

Chapter Nine

Coming to some trees on the crest of a hill, they followed a path down a gentle slope to a brook. The sun was hot and only the gentlest of breezes stirred the trees.

'We should rest the horses. It would be a pity to ruin a good mount.' William reached up and lifted her down. Her perfume was reminiscent of a warm summer day, when blossoms surrendered their scent to the air.

'We should?' As soon as her feet touched the ground she moved away from him.

Fastening the reins loosely to a low-lying branch, William leaned against a tree and gazed at her, a half smile curling on his lips. 'I'm trying to be a responsible and considerate riding instructor,' he joked, his eyes twinkling with humour.

'But we've only ridden across the park—at a sedate pace, too, I might add.'

'True. In fact, you're doing so well, tomorrow we'll progress to a trot.'

'Don't you think that's a bit ambitious?'

'You can do it.'

'And you have more confidence in my ability than I have.'

'Tell me, Cassandra,' he said after a moment in which he

studied her thoughtfully, 'why did you want me to go back to London when Lady Monkton invited me to stay?'

The directness of his question brought the heat creeping into her cheeks. 'Was it that obvious?'

'Blatantly.' Shoving himself away from the tree, he sauntered to where she was standing.

He was looking at her with those seductive blue eyes and Cassandra felt all the power and provocation of that gaze. Feeling decidedly uncomfortable, she wished she hadn't got off the horse. 'Will—will you stop looking at me like that?' she said, devoured by his burning gaze. She walked in a circle to avoid him, but he followed like a predator, backing her up against the tree he had just vacated, his smile taunting.

'Why are you trying to avoid me?'

'Because I think you're playing a game with me and I don't like it,' she retorted, feeling her defences begin to crumble and seeking refuge in anger.

'No? Well—if I am playing a game, perhaps you should know that you cannot win, but I can teach you how to play.' His voice was low and seductive, his eyes fastened on her lips.

'Please stop it, William. I don't like playing games.'

'Why—are you afraid you will lose?'

'No, it's just that I want no part of it. You may want me, if that is what you desire, but I will be no more yours than any man's.'

'Don't you like relationships?'

'It's not forming a relationship I am against. It's the consequences.' His lips were only a few inches from her own and it was difficult keeping her eyes off them.

'Consequences? What do you mean?'

'The same consequences that compel me to avoid practised seducers like yourself. I am fairly independent and I prefer it that way.'

'You, my dear Cassandra, are proud and foolish,' he

mocked while his eyes bored into hers. 'I ask myself, can a young lady be tempting and alluring and still be proper?'

'Yes, of course.'

'Then what do you want from life, Cassandra—besides your independence?'

'I want what every woman wants—and that is not to become the victim of a philanderer who thinks he is some grand gift to womankind.'

'Believe what you will, but unfortunately I cannot undo the years I lived before I met you. I cannot understand why you are so against me when your family has been kindness personified.'

'Yes—well done. I must congratulate you for the way you have ingratiated yourself with my family. Why have you made it your business to befriend us? Emma now thinks the sun rises and sets with you, Aunt Elizabeth looks on you as some kind of saviour and is already making the guest list for the wedding—who to include and who to leave off because of past slights. Mama is relieved Emma is to be wed—and—and I am confused.'

'And am I the cause of your confusion?'

'Yes, you are. Why are you doing this? Why should you care about the ruined reputation of a young woman who is nothing to you? You have come home from soldiering to take up your inheritance—a colossal undertaking for any man— someone may still be trying to kill you and yet here you are, playing Cupid. Why? None of it makes sense.'

His expression became serious and his eyes burned into hers. 'Does it not? Very well. I will tell you. It is you I want. You, Cassandra. I have seen laughter in your eyes, though they have been far too serious of late. You are beautiful in a way that makes men's heads turn again once they have noticed you, even though you have built an invisible wall around yourself, which can be removed only for a man you truly love.'

'And do you think you are that man?'

'I do.'

'You are arrogant if you believe that.'

'That, too. There is something more that attracts me to you. Not only do I feel the urge to sweep you into my arms and kiss you senseless, but I'm aware of some hidden, enticing quality that carries an air of mystery about it and I will not rest until I have uncovered it.'

Cassandra made a move to turn away, but William caught her by the shoulders and forced her to face him, pressing her back against the tree. What he saw in her eyes, plus the slight trembling in her slender body, belied her words. Lowering his head, he covered her mouth with his, but he misjudged her. There was a sharp pain as her small teeth clamped down on his lip. He drew back, tasting blood. His eyes narrowed and his lips curved in a slow smile. 'Why, you little vixen. I always knew you had fire in your veins.'

Cassandra glowered at him, feeling her pulses quicken as she watched his tongue slowly lick the small droplet of blood from his moist lip—a provocative gesture by any means, but to her susceptible heart it could bring about her downfall. 'It serves you right. You take too many liberties. You may force me, William Lampard, if that is your desire, but I will be no more yours after than I am now,' she vowed, her voice ice cold. 'I am merely trying to spare you what will be a thoroughly embarrassing and completely futile effort at seduction.'

'It won't be futile.'

'Yes, it will.'

His reply, though spoken in a hushed voice, tore through her with force. 'That wasn't what you said when I kissed you at Carlow Park—twice, as I recall.'

The bold reminder of that time at Carlow Park, when she had willingly let him hold her and kiss her, was more than Cassandra's taut nerves could withstand. 'No matter how you connive and cajole to seduce me, it won't work. I'm immune.'

William retaliated by taking her face between his hands and forcing her head back. He looked down at her with eyes that were hooded with emotion. 'No, you're not. I remember, you see, how you melted in my arms, and I intend to see if I can still make you feel the same.'

Fires ignited inside her at the touch of his hands on her face that flared to a startling intensity. His taunting smile made her realise the folly of baiting him. 'You will be wasting your time,' she snapped, swamped with humiliation at the brutal reminder of how openly besotted with him she had been at Carlow Park, before…

'Shall I show you how thinly guarded your denials are?'

Cassandra tried to push him away, but his arms snaked around her waist and brought her full against his hardened frame. His mouth swooped down on to hers with hardened possessiveness and his fiery kiss warmed her to the core of her being. The contact was like an exquisite explosion some-where deep inside her. It was unlike any other, because under-lying the ruthlessness of it, there was flowing a demanding persuasion, an insistence that she kiss him back—and if she yielded to it there was a promise that the kiss would change and become something else, something different. The sensa-tion of his hardened body pressing against hers was devastat-ing and she was afraid that her will would crumble beneath the onslaught of his fervour.

She tried to turn her face aside in denial, wanting him to stop before she was consumed, before she forgot her vow to stand against him—before she forgot that shameful, humili-ating wager he had made with Sir Charles Grisham. But still she let him kiss her, allowing herself, just this once, the for-bidden, fleeting joy of his mouth and his body close to her—never had she been so conscious of the nearness of another human body. She was held in an unyielding vicelike grip, her soft breasts crushed against his chest. His lips left hers and traced a burning line down her throat, causing her senses to erupt. Temporarily robbed of the anger that had fortified her resistance, her traitorous body relaxed.

'Kiss me, Cassandra,' he breathed, his hand splayed across her lower spine, forcing her closer to him, and she unwittingly moulded her melting body to the hardening contours of his. The heat of his lips touched her own once more, his mouth insisting, stirring, demanding, working their pagan magic on the warm and supple woman in his arms.

Cassandra's mind cried out with agonised yearning and now, unable to withstand William's passionate onslaught, for a slow beat in time she yielded. Beyond her will, her arms snaked up and around his neck, her fingers feeling the thickness of his hair at his nape. With a small, triumphant moan he gathered her more closely into his arms. His lips moved hungrily over hers, relentless in their demand, forcing hers to open beneath his mounting ardour. Feeling her response, he deepened the kiss, devouring her sweetness, drugging her senses, setting her whole being on fire.

Fighting back the wild desire to thrust her down on to the grass and take her there and then, William dragged his lips from hers and drew a long steadying breath. He studied the flushed contours of her face, the thick crescent of her lashes and the fine line of her eyebrows. Her lips were soft and tender from his assault, her eyes warm and glowing with desire. He longed to run a fingertip down the slender column of her throat, and to continue downwards until his hand cupped her breast.

He imagined how it would be to have her in his bed, to take her in his arms and draw her to him and devour her with a passion he had not felt in a long time. What a glory that would be. She would make a magnificent bed partner—he had sensed it the instant her mouth had responded to his. It would happen. He would make it happen if he expired with the effort.

Surfacing slowly from the depths of desire, Cassandra dazedly rested her head back against the tree. She could only stare into William's hypnotic eyes—still dark from the mysterious forces of passion—as if she could not comprehend what had just happened between them. 'You beast,' she whispered. 'How dare you kiss me when you knew I didn't want you to?'

'Come, Cassandra,' he murmured lightly, though he himself was shaken by the moment. 'It was only a kiss—and you have been kissed before.'

'I have—by you, and not like that.'

'But you did enjoy it,' he stated assuredly.

Cassandra was furious with herself for not only responding to it, but also for liking it. The sensation she had felt when he put his arms about her and lowered his mouth to hers rippled through her body along with all the other strange things she had experienced. 'What if someone saw?'

'There isn't another living creature in sight except for the horse—and it's too busy cropping grass to pay any attention to what we might be doing.'

'Is it right what you said—that you intend leaving tomorrow?'

'Yes, that is what I've decided. I shall leave Boulting here for a few days more to ensure his complete recovery.'

Cassandra drew back and stepped towards the edge of the brook, where she paused and looked down into the shimmering water as it hurried on its way. She was confused and humiliated. What had she done? How could she have allowed such a thing to happen? She had let herself be carried away on a wave of passion. After her vow never to fall for his seduction, she had succumbed to the coercive, compelling force of his masculinity, melting her reason with his kiss, playing upon her vulnerable, naïve senses as a musician plucks the strings of a violin. He had made her a willing, ardent accomplice to his lusts, and she despised him for it. To William Lampard she represented nothing more than the object of a wager he was determined to win. Raising her head, she looked at the sky. Somewhere she could hear a lark. A blackbird warbled and insects hummed softly.

She was aware of William standing a short distance behind her, watching her so intently that he might have been trying to commit every detail to memory. She struggled to free herself from her trancelike state induced by the heat of the day and the intoxicating closeness of the irresistible man behind her; though she could not dismiss him from any part of her awareness, she managed an attitude of cool disdain.

The fragrance of her perfume drifted on the air and through William's senses. Seized by a strong yearning to hold her against him once more, he moved closer and slipped an arm about her slender waist, pulling her back against him as he bent his head and murmured close to her ear, 'Cassandra...'

'Don't touch me,' she retorted angrily and jerked herself away as his voice tore holes in the thin façade of her composure. 'I think we should go back.' She turned to face him.

William nodded and smiled, content in his belief that he had measured the weakness of her character in the strength of her passion. 'It's a bit late for that,' he told her softly.

'Don't twist my words, William. I meant back to the house and you know it. But you must accept this is as far as it goes between us. If you ever attempt to kiss me again, I'll kill you. Please don't anticipate events that will never happen. I don't want you now and I never will.'

The smile died from his lips and his eyes narrowed into glittering dark slits. 'Your lips have just told me otherwise and I already have the answers I sought. Don't fight me, Cassandra.'

'I will,' she flared, tossing her head and flashing her eyes in anger when she met his gaze, facing him with all the indignation of one whose innermost secrets have been exposed to the scrutiny of another. She shrank from him when he reached out to touch her, realising with a jolt that in the future she must avoid him at all costs. 'I will fight you with all the strength I possess. Do you hear me?'

He nodded. 'Every word.' Gathering the reins and drawing the horse towards her, he lifted her into the saddle. Placing his hand on the bridle, he looked up into her stony face. 'But one day you will come to me. You will be mine in the end, Cassandra.'

'Never. I want no part of you! Ever!'

He contemplated her for a moment, his face expressionless. 'Very well. It would seem that we must continue this at another time. Now—are you ready?'

She nodded and stared straight ahead as they set off back across the park.

His face turned from Cassandra's gaze, William was deep in thought, his lips were set in a tight line as he led her towards the stables. When he'd retired from the army and returned to civilian life, his future had been all mapped out. Now that future had been shaken to its foundations and a new aspect of life presented itself in the form of Cassandra Greenwood. He could walk away from her and pretend she never existed, but deep down he didn't want to, and nor did he intend to.

For the rest of that day, and the following morning when he appeared at breakfast, he was his usual polite, cheerful self, but both Cassandra and William knew things had changed between them. He was coolly remote towards her. It was as though an invisible wall had sprung up between them, and it had everything to do with her angry rejection of his kiss.

However, accompanied by Emma on a frisky bay mare, who kicked her mount into a gallop from time to time, William took Cassandra into the park as he'd promised and, true to his word, had her trotting back to the stables, praising her on her developing riding skills and saying she had the makings of a fine horsewoman, that she must definitely continue her lessons with Emma now he was no longer available to teach her.

After partaking of a light lunch and bidding Aunt Elizabeth and her mother farewell, he left for London.

True to William's predictions, the announcement in the papers of the betrothal between Sir Edward Lampard and

Miss Emma Greenwood hit society with all the force of a thunderbolt, along with the arrival in London of the Dowager Countess of Carlow, who had taken up residence at the home of her nephew in Grosvenor Square and immediately made her approval of the marriage known. Such an announcement bearing the Dowager Countess of Carlow's seal was not to be ignored by anyone wishing to remain on that lady's very exclusive guest list.

The morning following the announcement in the newspapers found William at Monkton House. Unaware that he would call without warning, Lady Monkton had taken Emma shopping in Bond Street. Having no wish to accompany them, Cassandra had remained behind—although when the butler announced the arrival of Lord Lampard, she wished that she'd gone with them.

When he strolled into the room she rose from the couch. Placing the book she'd been reading on a table next to her, she clasped her hands demurely in front of her. Splendidly garbed in a finely tailored coat of bottle-green, William crossed the room to where she stood. His chiselled features were touched by the warm light of the sun slanting through the windows, and the growing ache in her heart attested to the degree of his handsomeness.

'William—I—we were not expecting you. My aunt and Emma are not at home just now. If it is Aunt Elizabeth you wish to see, perhaps you could call later.'

'I am delighted to find you alone, Cassandra,' he said softly, his eyes plumbing the depths of her beauty. 'What I have to say you can relate to Lady Monkton later. But you may set aside your fear. I will not abuse you. You have my word that for the time we are alone I shall comport myself with dignity and propriety.'

She regarded him with a widely sceptical frown. 'In truth, William, I find that difficult to believe. Your persistence never ceases to amaze me. Please sit down.' As he seated himself in a comfortable wingback chair opposite her, there was no way to protect herself from his relentless regard. 'Are you as outrageous with other women as you are with me?'

His eyes took on a slumbering intensity. 'Only those I have a yearning for—and I have told you I have a yearning for you.'

'There you go again, reminding me of past foolishness.'

He raised a brow. 'Yours or mine?'

'Both. Those embarrassing moments I forgot myself I remember with clarity, and they cannot be called anything but foolish. I told you then I want you to leave me alone.'

For several endless, uneasy moments, he gazed at her with enigmatic blue eyes, an impassive expression on his face. 'And I wonder,' he murmured at length, propping one booted foot across his knee and steepling his fingers in front of him, 'if what your head tells you to do will outlast the testing of the flesh.'

'And there's nothing like a woman's reluctance to surrender her virtue to heighten desire, is that not so, William?' she retorted coldly. Placing her hands on the arms of the chair, Cassandra leaned forward to press her point home. 'And I will not have my virtue rent asunder in a rake's bed.'

'And therein lies the rub.' William laughed softly. 'But be at ease, Cassandra. Your virtue is safe with me. No one could be more concerned about it than I am.'

'Safe!' she derided. 'Forgive me, but I feel I must disagree. Whenever I am with you I feel there is but one thought on your mind.'

'And yours, Cassandra,' he countered bluntly, reminding her of her passionate response to his kisses. 'As for myself, perhaps I have something else in mind.'

Calmly Cassandra met his gaze, the outrageous wager he had made to seduce her before the end of the Season never far from her thoughts. Her own lack of discipline and restraint when he had kissed her angered her, but she wasn't entirely certain whether to blame it on him or herself.

'And I have no wish to hear it. Please tell me why you are here.'

'Now the betrothal has been announced, if Edward can be released from his military duties I think we should begin our assault on the *ton.*'

'Oh, and how do you propose we do that, pray?'

'I think we should start by visiting Almack's Assembly Rooms this coming Wednesday.'

Cassandra's stunned gaze shot to his. 'Almack's?'

He smiled. 'That's right—the temple of the *beau monde.* The most exclusive of London's clubs.'

'But we'll never get past the *grandes dames* of society. They guard the doors like formidable dragons.'

'I agree. The patronesses retain the right to blackball anyone they consider is in any way undesirable without explanation.'

'But won't we find it difficult obtaining vouchers?'

'That is where my grandmother's influence comes in. She is well acquainted with one of the patronesses and will prevail upon their friendship.'

'But what's the point? Almack's is known as the Marriage Mart, where girls are launched upon society by their mothers in the hope of them finding a rich and titled husband. Since the club's main function is to act as a showcase for débutantes, neither Emma nor myself come under that category. Emma will already be betrothed and I have no intention of being.'

'Nobody will know that.'

Cassandra stared at him in stupefaction. She knew what he was asking her to do and she would have none of it. 'Please stop it, William. I have expressed my feelings to you on this particular matter. I am not a débutante and I don't want to be.'

'Not for just one night—to help your sister become an accepted member of the *ton?*' he murmured in coaxing tones.

'At my expense.'

'Is it not what any caring sister would do to save a sibling from a lifetime of ostracism?'

'Do you think I don't know that?' she flared. 'How can I forget the real purpose of what will turn out to be an expensive charade? Ever since Emma eloped I have been aware of nothing else; now you are asking me to support her in her efforts to redeem herself in the *ton*'s eyes so she will no longer be scorned, ridiculed and snubbed—to make my bow, when all the time I want to bow out of polite society for good.'

'I know, and, for what it's worth, I'm sorry. I know how much the institute means to you and when Emma's future is settled you will be able to resume your duties.'

Wary of the machinations of William's mind, Cassandra slanted him a look. Why did she always feel that Emma and Edward played only a small part in his scheming and that he was more concerned with her? 'You are going to an awful lot of trouble—and please don't insult my intelligence by saying it is for Emma. You don't know her, so why should it matter to you what happens to her?'

'Because I want what is best for both Emma and Edward. Edward is important to me. Emma is important to him. Need I say more?'

'I will not be forced into this, William.'

'Not forced, Cassandra,' he hastened to assure her softly. 'Persuaded, perhaps.'

She glowered across at him. His flat conviction that she had no choice except to agree to this was almost more than she could bear. 'If I agree to this ridiculous scheme of yours—which I haven't, I hasten to add—how can you be sure it will work?'

'Oh, ye of little faith,' William said, a wicked, knowing gleam in his eyes. 'It cannot fail.'

Just then Lady Monkton, followed by Emma, bustled in. She was delighted to see William and, after ordering refreshments, lost no time in asking the purpose of his visit. At his suggestion that they attend Almack's she positively beamed, thinking it a splendid idea—Emma was less enthusiastic.

'But my betrothal to Edward has been officially announced. I cannot enter Almack's as a débutante.'

'That's right.' William's eyes settled on Cassandra. 'But your sister can.'

Cassandra's eyes shot to his with a flare of anger and found, as she suspected, the amused and mocking grin challenging her.

Emma's head spun round and she looked at her sister, her eyes shining with happiness and hope. 'Oh, would you, Cassy? Would you really do that for me?'

'You can surely see that this is the perfect solution,' Lady Monkton was quick to remark approvingly. 'Almack's will be the stage for you both to make your marks upon the world. The mystique of the club is based upon snobbery and social cachet and is more important than a presentation at court. To be admitted through the club's exclusive doors will set the seal on Emma's and Edward's betrothal and they will be virtually assured of acceptance at all the *ton*'s functions. You, too, Cassandra. I can't tell you how happy it will make me, how proud— to formally present you to society. It's unfortunate we didn't decide this earlier and had you fitted out with the whole new extensive wardrobe of a lady of quality, which is the custom.'

'But I am not a lady of quality, Aunt Elizabeth, and I maintain that it would be an unnecessary extravagance,' Cassandra retorted testily. 'I have enough day dresses, evening dresses, dresses for routs, balls, assemblies and cloaks and hats and all the necessary accessories to see me through to my dotage.'

'I would still have liked to have you properly fitted out.'

Cassandra looked at the three faces watching her expectantly, realising that it was quite useless voicing her objections. She sat perfectly still, her hands clenched in her lap, glaring at the clever, unscrupulous manipulator across from her. She was being tricked by a master player and there wasn't a thing she could do about it. She was trapped and he knew it.

'Are you familiar with Almack's?' Lady Monkton asked William, unaware of Cassandra's inner turmoil.

'I haven't set foot in the place in over a decade,' he told her, unable to prevent his distaste from showing.

'Why, when it's so popular?'

'Lord knows why it is since there's nothing particularly attractive about it or the entertainment it offers. Almack's is a place of insipid propriety. It may hold the most exclusive parties in London, but they are sedate to the point of boring.'

'Then, since you find it so dull, you needn't attend,' Cassandra suggested coldly, hoping he would do just that. 'Aunt Elizabeth will be more than happy to chaperon Emma and me.'

William looked at her. His smile was infuriating. 'What? And deny me the pleasure of escorting you? I wouldn't hear of it. I insist you give me two dances and you must promise there will be no touting for donations for your precious institute. Afterwards we will finish the evening off at my residence in Grosvenor Square. Grandmother will be entertaining a few friends and we are invited. She is most anxious to meet the young lady who is to wed her grandson.'

When William had departed and Aunt Elizabeth and Emma began excitedly making plans for the forthcoming event, the full realisation of what was expected of her hit Cassandra and it began to appear as if she could hardly avoid it. The thought made her breath catch. It was a realisation that against so much opposition there was nothing she could do. Her mind formed a vision of herself at Almack's as a débutante and she angrily shook her head to make the image depart. Her mind did not extend beyond her immediate escape, but there was none.

Her mother shared her doubts about what she was doing, knowing how her daughter felt about society's mores and how she mocked the ludicrous lengths to which people went in order to do only what propriety would allow. She had no wish, however, for Cassandra to set herself apart from it completely, and realising why her daughter was doing it, she gave Cassandra her blessing.

* * *

After prolonged, painstaking primping and preening in front of the cheval mirror, the preparations were complete. Exquisitely coiffured and gorgeously attired, in a gold-spangled gown of cream satin and lace and clutching her fan in her gloved hands, Cassandra joined a radiant Emma, Edward and Aunt Elizabeth in the carriage that was to take them to Almack's in King Street. Edward had come alone, explaining that William had been unavoidably detained and sent his most abject apologies. He would be along later—probably after ten o'clock—and Cassandra was to be sure to reserve a dance for him. Cassandra was both vexed and disappointed to hear this, but she was determined not to let thoughts of William occupy her evening.

Prepared to make her mark upon a world from which she sought to be excluded, when Cassandra passed through the exclusive, holier-than-holy portals of Almack's Assembly Rooms she felt the trap closing around her. Beneath her calm, controlled exterior she endured a nauseating turmoil of anger.

When they entered the huge ballroom, decorated with gilt columns and enormous mirrors, it was filled with animation, laughter and music, dancers and swirling dresses and sparkling jewels. Suddenly the conversation became muted as every influential head swivelled towards the new arrivals, then escalated to frantic whispers. The city was afire with talk of Emma and Edward's betrothal and Cassandra was aware of the amount of gossip and speculation their appearance at Almack's was causing.

There were so many people it was clear the ball was going to be a crush. Most of the débutantes were making their formal bow to the *ton* that night. Blondes and brunettes waited with heightened colour and eager gazes, while the hunting instincts of their mamas and chaperons for the male species were at fever pitch, which meant they had scented prime prey and were making sure their charges' cards were full, as young swains—attractive, well-favoured and well turned out—lavished attention on them.

Cassandra surveyed the scene with disdain. She sighed. It was going to be a long night.

Having fully expected Cassandra—noted for her sobriquet, the Ice Maiden, and for the fact that she frequently turned down prospective partners—to be escorted to Almack's by the renowned Lord Lampard, the young bucks hung back, expecting the illustrious earl to appear at any moment, but when he failed to do so, within minutes she was creditably besieged and her dance card began filling up.

'Miss Greenwood. I am both delighted and surprised to see you here this evening.'

Cassandra started and took a step back as the indolent figure of Sir Charles Grisham, who had just come out of the card room, bowed before her. 'Why, good evening, Sir Charles.'

He beamed delightedly at her. 'Well, now you are here, if your dance card isn't full, perhaps you would honour me with a dance—or two?' he asked expectantly, a bold gleam in his eyes.

She looked at him—Sir Charles Grisham, the dashing and flamboyant Corinthian, the other half of William's wager. Her interest was pricked. Suddenly the evening might not be such a disaster after all. Perhaps she could have some fun—wield her wiles under Almack's glittering chandeliers. Suddenly a cunning light entered her eyes, and she smiled with deep satisfaction. She would make it doubly difficult for William to succeed in seducing her by feigning an interest in his friend. Anticipation laced with excitement flowed through her, and determination to get her own back and bring the conceited William Lampard down a peg or two drove her.

Perhaps she could make him angry enough—or jealous enough, she hoped—to lose control completely and confront her with what he had done. And when he did, she would coldly tell him that she had known about the wager all along and make him grovel at her feet and beg for her forgiveness—

although a picture of William Lampard grovelling at anyone's feet was a difficult one to conjure up. It would be such a lark. Suddenly she brightened and gave Charles a favourable, dazzling smile.

'Why, Sir Charles, I would be delighted, although you must realise that it's a mistake to show partiality by dancing twice with the same partner.'

'As to that, I really could not care less,' he drawled.

'And I do have my reputation to uphold,' she teased.

His grin was impudent as he subjected her to a long, lingering gaze. 'I would not dream of doing anything to damage that. You will pencil me in?'

'You are a determined man, Sir Charles.'

'And you are lovelier than I remember, Miss Greenwood.'

'Flatterer. In which case I shall reserve two dances for you,' Cassandra heard herself say.

Within half an hour every dance of the night except the one she had reserved for William after ten o'clock had been claimed. The strict rules of the club stated that the doors closed at eleven and after that no one was allowed in. Under the watchful and profoundly proud eye of Aunt Elizabeth, both her charges took to the floor with their respective partners for a lively country dance.

When Cassandra had danced with more gentlemen than she could remember, gentlemen who flattered her outrageously, and she was dancing her second dance with Sir Charles Grisham, William arrived just before eleven o'clock. Unbeknown to him, he was too late to claim his dance with Cassandra—she had given it to someone else. At the sight of him she experienced a rush of feeling, a bittersweet joy in view of what stood between them and her intention to make him realise that there were several rivals for her company.

There was a whispered stir among those standing on the side lines of the crowded ballroom. Almost every eye turned

towards the entrance as the man who had just arrived attracted
their total attention. It was none other than Lord Lampard, the
Earl of Carlow, who had not attended Almack's for many years.

Like every other male present he was attired in formal
black tail coat, white waistcoat and neckcloth and regulation
knee breeches. A tall strong-looking man, his brooding good
looks turned heads wherever he went and caused several
young women to heave a quiet sigh—and tonight was no exception. When his gaze swept the room, acknowledging his
cousin dancing with his radiant betrothed with a slight nod,
before coming to rest on the exquisite creature dancing with
Sir Charles Grisham, they did not have to ask which female
it was that had lured him to the club tonight. Was there any
truth in what was being said about them? Were they really
caught up in a torrid affair? It was clear from the way he was
looking at her that Lord Lampard would not be inclined to ask
anyone else to dance.

Completely impervious to the stir he was creating,
excusing himself to Lady Cowper, just one of Almack's arbi-
trary and despotic patronesses trailing in his wake, William
strolled further into the ballroom. He regretted being unable
to escort Cassandra to the club, but, when he'd received Mr
Jardine's note informing him that he was to call on him at
eight o'clock with interesting news regarding the assassin,
he'd been keen to know what he had found out, so he'd
decided to let Edward do the honour of escorting the ladies.

The effect of seeing Cassandra dancing with Charles surprised him—the sudden tightening of possessiveness, the unexpected tug on his vitals. At the same moment, combining
the perfect amount of boldness and maidenly demureness,
Cassandra raised her eyes to Charles's attractive face and
smiled favourably. It was a small encouragement of sorts, for
William saw Charles's hand tighten about her waist as he
spun her round. He felt a dart of anger course through him.

Had it been any other man she was dancing with he would

not have felt so put out, but, knowing Charles's penchant for a pretty face and how mischievous he could be, and that for some perverse reason of his own he might be tempted to mention their wager, he felt decidedly uneasy. Having completed his business with Mr Jardine, and eager to see Cassandra, he'd hurried to Almack's to be with her, but now, feeling thwarted, his high spirits faded.

Propping his shoulder against a pillar, he continued to watch her in brooding silence. Dazzling and vivacious, she shone out among all the débutantes, and she was smiling into Charles's eyes in a way that made him want to wring her neck. Considering her opinion regarding this kind of event, he'd fully expected to find her looking bored to death, but instead she was enjoying herself in a way that astounded him—a mite too much for his liking.

Cassandra was fully aware of William watching her from the sidelines and with glee she deliberately set out to put his teeth on edge by flirting quite shamelessly with Charles. When the dance ended and Charles escorted her back to Aunt Elizabeth, Cassandra, glancing in William's direction, felt the turbulence of his desire and the violence of his anger reach her with equal intensity.

There was not a man in the room to compare with him. She had not failed to notice the women who glanced his way, their glances lingering an extra fraction of a second. She should be flattered that a man such as he had come to Almack's because of her, but how could she be? Something cold fell in her chest. He wasn't sincere, she knew that, and that hurt.

Pushing himself off the pillar, William approached her. 'I'm glad to see you are enjoying yourself,' he commented with calm emphasis.

A brilliant smile dawned across Cassandra's features as she met his gaze. 'Yes, I'm enjoying myself enormously,' she replied, managing to look extremely innocent, despite the seductive allure of her gown and rosy face. 'It's the most wonderful evening I've had in years. It's a shame you couldn't come earlier. You've missed a splendid evening.'

His eyes narrowed as they looked pointedly into hers. 'It's not over yet. I have a dance to claim from you, don't forget.'

She managed to feign a look of disappointment and mortification. 'Oh, what a pity. I thought you must have forgotten. I did reserve one, but when you failed to arrive I thought you weren't coming so I danced with someone else. Unfortunately, my dance card is full and I'm afraid there's not a thing I can do about it.'

William's face darkened with annoyance, and Cassandra could almost feel his struggle to hold his temper in check, but before he could reply a smiling swain of medium height and pink-faced stepped up to her to claim her hand. With a dazzling smile on her pink lips, she turned her back on William and stepped on to the dance floor without a backward glance, leaving him to exist in a state of seething frustration.

William glared after her. His jealousy and fury mounted as he watched her throw herself into a Scottish reel. He saw how heads turned to look at her—honey-gold hair glowing like the sun, a gown of gold-spangled cream satin and swirling lace. For a moment she caught his angry eyes and smiled, secure in herself, secure in certain victory.

Gritting his teeth, William thought every unpleasant thing about the young man she was with. When the dance ended he advanced towards her, but before he could reach her she had been claimed by another swain.

'You are not gaining headwind tonight, William,' a calm voice said next to him. 'Cupid must have smitten you,' Charles observed, 'if you have to follow Miss Greenwood all the way to Almack's. Wouldn't have thought this would appeal to you.'

William whirled round, but stopped when he saw Charles's slumberous eyes watching him, and the unthinking response that sprang to his lips died. For, he thought angrily, Charles was right. He was bewitched and beguiled by the wench. In short, for the first time in his life his heartfelt emotions were overruling his head, and he didn't suffer the affliction well.

'She's out to collect as many fawning admirers as she can tonight,' Charles went on. 'You appear to have a great deal of competition—and small wonder. Miss Greenwood is quite out of the ordinary. She shines tonight. She is also warm, witty and an exquisite dancer—and she appears to be avoiding you.' Helping himself to a pinch of snuff, he lifted his arrogant brows and turned to William, his look both suspicious and intrigued. 'Why, I can't imagine. Would I be right in thinking you've had a change of heart and would like to seduce the lady after all?'

'Mind your own damned business,' William growled.

Charles smiled lazily, not in the least offended by his friend's offhand remark. 'If I didn't think you were after her, I'd make a play for her myself.'

William slowly turned his head and gave him a bland stare. 'If you value our friendship, Charles, you will forget you made that remark.'

Charles slanted him an amused look. 'You're beginning to sound like a jealous swain, William. Don't tell me your attentions towards Miss Greenwood are honourable. Good Lord, perish the thought. I am trying to imagine what the *ton* will make of it if the renowned Earl of Carlow, libertine *par excellence,* has decided to wed the daughter of a penniless professional.' Adopting a bored expression, he glanced around the room. 'I always find evenings at Almack's unbearably flat— don't know why I bother coming. Perhaps you'd care to join me in the card room.'

'If I'd wanted to play cards, I would have gone to White's,' William ground out ungraciously. He frowned. 'A drink wouldn't go amiss.'

'Forget it. Unless you have a fancy for lemonade and orange water, there's nothing else.'

William gave Cassandra another half an hour of flaunting

herself on the dance floor before he approached Lady Monkton and informed her it was time to leave for Grosvenor Square. He wasn't unpleasant and was amiable to everyone who spoke to him as they were leaving; in fact, Cassandra was put out that he didn't seem to mind that he'd missed dancing with her and that she'd totally ignored him.

Chapter Ten

Light blazed from every window of William's house in Grosvenor Square. In the large, sumptuously furnished white-and-gold salon, tables and chairs and sofas had been placed so that the thirty guests could gather in intimate little groups to chat or play cards. Several gentlemen were in the adjoining billiard room, wreathed in the smoke of their cigars. Into this serene company entered the newcomers. A hush descended as conversation ceased and every eye turned in their direction. When they saw it was the master of the house conversation and cards were resumed.

Lady Monkton paused to acknowledge an acquaintance, leaving William to escort Cassandra and Emma to be presented to the dowager countess, where she was seated at a small table playing bridge. She was a handsome woman with a majestic bearing, an aristocratic nose and imperious expression. Her eyes brightened as she observed her grandsons' approach—William, proud and arrogant, who attacked life with a vigorous purposefulness, and Edward, who was good-natured and easy to get on with. Edward had felt a wrenching sorrow over the demise of his parents, and the dowager had thanked God that he'd had William and his brother Robert to guide him.

'Ah, William, I'm delighted you were able to join our festivities, even if tardily.'

William bent and kissed her proffered cheek. 'I apologise if we've kept you waiting, Grandmother. The ladies were enjoying themselves greatly. It was difficult to drag them away.'

'I'm happy you were successful. I'm eager to meet the two young ladies who have so bedazzled my grandsons.' Completely ignorant of the unease her casual remark stirred in the older of the two young women, or the look of indignation she darted at William, the dowager watched them execute their flawless curtsies.

Taking Emma's hand, Edward proudly drew her forward and introduced her.

The dowager raised her lorgnette to her piercing eyes and inspected her from top to toe. She nodded her approval. 'Yes, you have chosen well, Edward. I must compliment you on your excellent taste.'

'You are very kind,' Emma said, radiant with happiness as she hung on to Edward's arm.

Not to be won over so easily, in response the dowager raised her brows and disdainfully looked at her. 'I have admonished Edward most severely and I will tell you, young woman, what I told him. I do not approve of couples eloping—unpleasantness always ensues. It was badly done by you both and was in danger of creating a scandal of the worst kind. Still, I am glad William decided to handle it. If one cannot stop gossip, it's as well to turn it in another direction—a feasible solution.' She looked at William. 'How did it go at Almack's? Have we pulled it off?'

William nodded. 'Just as I planned it would,' he told her, still seething over the let-down Cassandra had given him earlier and impatient to take her to task over it. 'The betrothed couple were a tremendous success. I have no doubt that tomorrow morning Monkton House will be swamped with invitations for them to attend every social event in London.'

'Splendid.' She looked at the butler who was bearing a tray of goblets. 'Bring in the champagne, Siddons. We will all raise our glasses and drink a toast to the happy couple.' Her gaze shifted to Cassandra. It was slow and pointedly bold as she perused the young woman. She carefully studied the blue-green eyes regarding her from beneath a heavy fringe of dark lashes. 'And you are Cassandra. You are very young,' the dowager countess observed, studying the lovely visage, 'and very lovely.'

Cassandra smiled at the elegantly attired woman while thinking that the Dowager Countess of Carlow was the most intimidating woman she had ever met—and that William was so like her. 'Thank you. It's kind of you to say so.'

The dowager looked at William with an expression of approval and satisfaction. William's reply to her look was merely a sardonic lift to his brows, which caused a *frisson* of alarm to shoot through Cassandra. Since leaving Almack's he was all charm and politeness personified, but she knew that beneath that veneer of calmness he was burningly angry.

'Now circulate. Introduce them to my guests, William,' the dowager ordered, picking up her cards to resume her game of bridge, a sudden humour lighting her eyes as they swept over the collected throng, 'before they expire with curiosity.'

William skilfully guided them from group to group and introduced them. As they mingled, all attention should have been focused on Emma as Edward's betrothed, but Cassandra had the uncomfortable feeling that she was the one under scrutiny and the dowager countess in particular was showing more interest in her than was acceptable to her peace of mind.

When introductions had been duly made the champagne was brought in. There was a bubble of laughter and shouts of congratulations as everyone toasted the betrothed couple, touching glasses so that they made crystal chimes. Cassandra, feeling the need to escape, was leaving the salon for the ladies' retiring room when she came face to face with Lady Lydia Lampard, Mark's wife.

Wearing an expression of civil disdain, Lydia smiled thinly. 'Ah, Miss Greenwood. How nice to see you again. We have met, albeit briefly, at Carlow.'

Cassandra met the appraising stare of the proud and haughty woman. Her eyes were expressionless. It was difficult to know what she was thinking. She was attired in watered grey silk and diamonds sparkled coldly at her throat. They suited her, Cassandra thought—in fact, she could not imagine her wearing any other jewel. Mark Lampard and this woman were well matched—both cold and remote. Cassandra could not imagine her glowing with passion. There was something deadly about her, as there is about a snake.

'Yes, I do remember. I must apologise for rushing off. My sister was unwell and I was most eager to get her back to London.'

'Of course. I do understand. Mark and I are in London for the wedding. We are staying with my sister and her husband in Greenwich. You must be delighted with the way things have turned out.'

'I'm sorry? What can you mean?'

'Only that you must be relieved the situation has turned out so well.'

'If you mean the wedding has been arranged to silence the gossips then, yes, I am. But I am also happy for Emma and Edward since they are clearly so much in love. It is a good match.'

'Yes, of course it is,' Lydia murmured, sounding quietly unconvinced and without enthusiasm. 'Please excuse me. My husband is beckoning.'

Relieved when Lydia moved on, Cassandra made her escape. Spending as much time as was possible in the retiring room, when she did return to the salon, William suddenly appeared in front of her. Seeing his fixed expression, she was filled with unease and foreboding.

'A word, if you please, Cassandra.'

'If you don't mind, William, I would like to return to the others,' she told him coldly.

William clamped his hand on her elbow. 'I insist.'

Cassandra beheld a face of such dark menacing rage that she shuddered. 'Let go of my arm.'

'Shut up,' he hissed, maintaining his hold and propelling her inside a room and closing the door. In the oppressive silence as he walked into the middle of the room, Cassandra took note of the judicious set to his jaw. She realised that beneath his bland exterior he was furious. She waited, enduring the icy blast of his gaze. It dawned on her that he was striving to control his anger and she prayed he would gain it.

'Were you deliberately trying to publicly humiliate me tonight?' he demanded at length. 'Come, Cassandra,' he sneered when she merely stared at him, 'don't tell me you are stuck for words. You seemed to have plenty to say to your doting swains when you flirted and hung on to their every word. You are clearly a woman of many pleasures, and it would seem one of them is to try and humble me—you didn't succeed, by the way. I'm too experienced and too thick skinned to be baited by a mere chit of a girl. Why, if you feel compelled to show me you care nothing for me, for my advances, did you need to prove it in such a petty, small-minded way?'

William's reprimand for her behaviour was deserved, but Cassandra had done it with good reason and was not sorry. 'Don't you dare talk to me about being humbled and humiliated,' she uttered irately, slowly walking towards him. 'You seem to believe this is all about you. What did you expect? It was more than you deserved.'

'Really! I disagree.'

Cassandra's mouth went dry when he moved closer. She stepped back. 'Don't you dare touch me. I hate it when you do. I hate you.'

William's dark brows drew together. Reaching out, he

dragged her into his arms and before she knew what he was about his mouth swooped down on to hers. She struggled and tried to pull away, but his arms tightened about her. His lips were hard, the kiss meant to punish—but it had the opposite effect. When his hand closed over her breast and caressed it, teasing the hardening nipple, tingling, pleasurable flames began shooting through her body.

When he felt her begin to respond, William raised his head and looked down at her upturned face and smiled sardonically. 'Now tell me you hate it when I touch you, and perhaps next time you decide to humiliate and embarrass me in public you will reconsider.'

Drowning in shame at her inability to control her own treacherous body, with flaming cheeks Cassandra twisted free as the bewildered terror that had gripped her when he had forced her inside the room evaporated.

'You? Humiliated? Embarrassed? How dare you say that—you despicable hypocrite,' she fired back and had the satisfaction of seeing shock crack his hard, handsome features. 'From the very beginning you set out to degrade me in the most shameful way of all, and yet you accuse *me* of humiliating *you.* Believe me, William Lampard, what happened to you at Almack's tonight was pretty tame considering what you had intended for me. And how dare *you,* the biggest hellion in London, lecture *me* on how to behave when your own behaviour is anything but honourable. You do not deserve to be called a gentleman.'

William cocked a dubious brow, somewhat amazed by the spirit of the woman. He reached out to draw her to him. Furiously she shrugged him off.

'Keep your hands off me. I haven't finished. I'm not too proud to admit that in the beginning I was foolish enough to fall for your charms. It was quite wonderful, the most wonderful and remarkable thing that had ever happened to me, and now I am so ashamed—it was so trite. You're no doubt accustomed to that sort of feminine reaction wherever you go,' she said scathingly. 'I succumbed just like every other unsuspecting woman you take a fancy to—a foolish inclination on my part not supported by anything other than infatuation and my own imagination, because you felt nothing for me at all. That I knew.'

'How? How did you know?'

His shocked expression and the question told Cassandra her mistake, that she had almost revealed her secret, but she was so angry it no longer mattered.

'Because I heard you. I heard you,' she flared, looking him in the eyes, ashamed of the feelings she carried for him in her heart. 'It was at Carlow Park—the morning after you kissed me. Naïve fool that I was, I was so eager to see you I couldn't wait. You were in the library with Sir Charles Grisham. I paused in the doorway, not wishing to interrupt you. I heard every word you said. Do you recall that conversation, my lord?'

Comprehension and a hint of dismay dawned on William's face. 'I do remember,' he murmured. 'How much did you hear?'

'Enough. Enough to learn of your disgusting wager—that if you failed to seduce me before the end of the Season, Charles Grisham would be richer by a horse. A horse, for heaven's sake! Is that all I am worth?'

'Cassandra, I am grieved that you heard that conversation, and please believe me when I say I regret that wager. I give you my word I never intended to hurt you.'

Her eyes were alive with pain and fury. 'Liar!' she cried contemptuously, her chest heaving. 'Your word? Your word means nothing to me.' She was looking at him as if he was obscene.

White faced with guilt and remorse, William tried to placate her. 'It was a temporary madness. It was cruel and thoughtless and I realise you must be deeply hurt.'

'That's correct,' she flared, her eyes blazing with turbulent animosity, 'and there is no excuse. It was my knowledge of what you were doing that kept me ahead of the game. Lord knows how much of a fool I would have made of myself had

I not found out about that sordid wager. What is true of most scoundrels is doubly so of you. You would have ruined me, defiled me without any regard to my feelings and then cast me off as you would a common trull, you—you loathsome, despicable letch. Although I am hardly surprised. You were merely living up to your name.' She turned from him and walked away, as if she couldn't bear to look at him.

'Cassandra—' William began tautly, but she whirled on her heels like a dervish and stalked back to him, her hips swaying provocatively while her eyes flashed.

'What was I, William?' she scoffed sneeringly, jabbing her finger hard into his chest. 'Was I some tender titbit you decided to play with, a simpleton to fill your needs for a night or two? What amusement you must have had playing your sordid little game with me. And how disappointed you must now be feeling, knowing you have lost your wager.'

Nothing moved in William's face, but his eyes darkened. Quietly he asked, 'Will you listen to what I have to say?'

'No. I am not interested. I will never be able to forgive you. But you listen to me, William Lampard,' she said, her chilled contempt meeting him face to face. 'The harm you have done me will stand between us for ever. From now on you keep your distance. Any future contact between us will be impersonal, brief and in public. The wedding means we cannot avoid coming into contact with each other—at such times we will be polite and cordial as protocol dictates. But that is all. Now, if you don't mind, I will return to the others before I am missed and someone comes looking for me. The last thing I want is to be found alone with you, which would no doubt start another scandal.'

With her head high she marched towards the door. As she reached it she turned and glared back at him. 'I don't like being made sport of, but you obviously enjoy causing discomfort in any manner. Someday I sincerely hope you meet someone who will get the better of you.' Stalking out, she slammed the door behind her, leaving him to bear the oppressive silence alone.

Weighted down with unbearable guilt and hating himself with a virulence that almost choked him, William walked over to the hearth. Propping his foot on the fender and resting his arm on the mantelpiece, he stared down into the flames. So that was what all this had been about. In the space of a fraction of a second everything was made clear, presenting the whole sordid picture in every profane detail. Cassandra's revelation answered so many questions—why she had behaved as she had on leaving Carlow Park, why she had told him she wanted no part of him, ever, when he had kissed her at Netherton Hall, when he knew by her response to his kiss that she was lying.

Dear God, he had hurt her very badly. She hated him, and with good reason. And knowing how deeply he had hurt her, the pain William felt was a thousand times worse than any wound he had ever received. But when she had overheard his conversation with Charles at Carlow Park, she must not have stayed long enough to hear him tell Charles the wager was off—and the mood she was in now, she wouldn't believe him if he told her. He was going to have to figure out a way to redeem himself, but it was not going to be easy.

When Cassandra returned to the salon there was no sign of the bitter altercation that had just taken place on her smiling face. William appeared fifteen minutes later. His eyes swept the room, coming to rest briefly on her before he looked away and disappeared into the billiards room.

Cassandra turned and saw Lydia across the room speaking to Aunt Elizabeth. She was also looking at William and Cassandra noted a cold glitter in her eyes—what secrets did those eyes hold? she wondered. She was looking at William as if she hated him.

For the rest of the evening Cassandra stored up a terrible burden of emotion and not until she was back at Monkton

House and in bed did she allow herself to dwell on her confrontation with William, firmly believing he didn't feel any remorse at all for what he had done to her. As she buried her head in the pillows she succumbed to tears.

Her mind had always shied away from delving too deeply into what her feelings were for William, but now she had to ask herself. She did care for him, there was no use denying it merely to keep the fires of resentment burning. Thinking about the times they had been together, she began with their meeting in Green Park. He could have died that day had she not been passing through at the time.

She could not blot from her mind the exquisite sweetness of the times she had been in his arms, the memory of his kisses, of his whispered words of passion that tormented her every day. No matter how hard she tried to think otherwise, nothing had been the same since she had met him. The pleasure, the intensity she had experienced at Carlow Park before she knew about the wager, still vividly etched and clear, were now too painful to contemplate.

Recalling the day he had searched her out at the institute, how he had patiently listened with superior understanding and compassion when she had spoken about the children, she had thought he cared, but it never existed, only in her imagination. She reminded herself that he was a rake and that righteousness was on her side, and she would insulate herself against heartbreak, but, if so, then why did it hurt so much and why was she crying so desperately?

Suddenly Edward and Emma were the darlings of society, London's most talked-about couple—theirs was a heady triumph. The gossips and society columns were full of the forthcoming wedding, and instead of the cruel, ridiculous tittle-tattle that had followed in the wake of their elopement, they suddenly made a fine couple and were clearly very much in love.

Lady Monkton, used to dealing with the pressures of public

life, immersed herself in the extensive wedding preparations that required the efforts of modistes and an army of servants. Harriet, her duties at the institute taking up more of her time as she struggled to keep it open, was more than happy to let her cousin take over. Emma moved into Monkton House where she found herself skilfully guided by Aunt Elizabeth. Visitors were received at the house in staggering numbers and invitation cards piled up on the hall table thick and fast. She was presented to this and that and readily accepted by everyone she met.

Listening intently to what was being said, Cassandra heard the odd speculation about her family—not much money, father a professional man, mother heavily involved with destitute children—but for the most part the comments were complimentary. Emma had youth, beauty, good connections through Lady Monkton and a certain fashionable notoriety.

As Emma was being carried along on the crest of a gigantic wave, and considering she had done quite enough to help her sister become an accepted and popular member of society, Cassandra purposely kept a low profile and kept herself too busy to think of William. He had given Aunt Elizabeth *carte blanche* with the wedding preparations and they saw nothing of him, and Cassandra hoped fervently that this was how it would remain—but she had never felt so wretchedly unhappy.

If she wasn't at the institute, although she refused to attend the levees and soirées she was invited to, or receive suitors following her début at Almack's, she did accompany Aunt Elizabeth and Emma to the theatre and musical evenings. She also went driving in Hyde Park and along Pall Mall and often rode out with Emma and a groom in attendance, now she had conquered her fear of horses and was more confident in her prowess as a horsewoman.

They strolled in London's flower-filled gardens that were dotted all over the city and open to all for a few pennies, and in particular the splendour of Vauxhall, with its rotunda, its lights and groves and whispering lovers. Then there were the shopping expeditions to Covent Garden, Bond Street, the Strand and St James's, which was a predominantly masculine preserve, with streets packed with bachelor lodgings and expensive shops. Its main street was dominated by gentlemen's clubs, such as White's, Brooks's and Boodle's, all out of bounds to ladies of quality.

Lady Monkton would order the driver to take the open carriage slowly past so the bucks and the beaux—foppish young gentlemen, with exquisite clothes and manners so indolent that they seemed half-asleep—seated in the bow windows could ogle her young charges with their quizzing glasses.

The afternoon was warm, the air sultry as they circled the ring in Hyde Park—a rendezvous for fashion and beauty, the preserve of the upper classes. The cavalcade of handsome equipages and men mounted on splendid high-stepping horses with gleaming flanks moved at a leisurely pace. It was one of the ways to see and be seen, to show off new clothes and meet fellow members of the *ton*.

Cassandra and Emma were seated across from Aunt Elizabeth. When the driver stopped the carriage so Aunt Elizabeth could speak to an acquaintance, Cassandra sighed, quite intoxicated by the sight.

'It's quite a turn out, don't you agree, Emma?' she commented, letting her gaze wander aimlessly over the crowd.

'Yes, quite a turn out.' Emma echoed her words with a full heart, seeing little from beneath her pretty parasol beyond the elegant, glittering throng.

Cassandra let her gaze drift over the languidly moving crowd, past a carriage holding three vivacious young women under the stern eye of a chaperon, past a tall man on horseback—her heart gave a leap and missed a beat. He was engrossed in conversation with another gentleman also on horseback and seemingly taking little notice of what was going on around him. In stricken paralysis she stared at him. Everyone else became faceless and anonymous to her. They fell away like shadows. All she was conscious of was William.

He had appeared too suddenly for her to prepare herself, so the heady surge of pleasure on seeing him following her initial shock was clearly evident on her lovely features. Since that night when she had last seen him almost two weeks ago, she had managed to avoid a confrontation with the only man who posed any threat to her control, and already she could feel it crumbling.

He moved with an easy grace, at one with his mount, cutting a dashing swath through the crowd. Cassandra's heart gave a sickening lurch. She could feel his seductive power reach out across the ring to stir her senses, and now he was looking straight at her.

Sensing her sister's disquiet, Emma turned and looked at her. 'Cassy, are you all right?' she asked with concern.

Dragging air into her constricted lungs, Cassandra averted her eyes. She must not allow Emma to see the devastating effect that infuriating man had on her. 'I am quite all right, Emma. I just wish the carriage would move on.'

Unconvinced, Emma glanced in the direction Cassandra had been looking. Seeing Lord Lampard, she believed she had found the cause of her sister's unease. She looked back at her sister, her eyebrows drawn into a frown. 'Cassy, why are you so determined to avoid Lord Lampard?'

'I'm not,' she replied stiffly. 'It's just that I don't care for his company, that's all.'

'So you still haven't changed your opinion of him.'

'No. He's everything I accused him of being on the night of Aunt Elizabeth's ball—the night before you and Edward eloped. He is still a rake and a blackguard and I want nothing to do with him.'

'Rake he may be, but he is the one Edward and I have to thank for being allowed to wed. It is all his doing and I shall be eternally grateful to him. Edward says that at heart he's as honourable a man as you are likely to find. With the wedding looming, sooner or later you'll have to speak to him.'

'Then let it be later.'

Emma looked sceptical. 'When we were in Surrey you spent a good deal of time together. I thought you were beginning to get on better, that you were beginning to warm to him. Did anything happen between you to change that?'

'No.' Cassandra averted her eyes, glad that Aunt Elizabeth was too engrossed in animated conversation to notice their altercation.

Emma's hand tightened on her arm. 'Cassy,' she whispered, 'what did Lord Lampard do? It is clear to me that something must have happened between the two of you, so you might as well tell me.'

'Nothing happened, Emma.'

'It did,' Emma persisted forcefully. 'It's written all over your face.'

Cassandra's face flamed. 'All right, Emma. If you must know he—he kissed me,' she confessed quietly, wondering what her young sister would say if she were to disclose the full facts of that wretched, humiliating wager.

Emma's eyes widened with amazement. 'Kissed you? Goodness! And didn't you like being kissed by him?'

'No—yes—oh, Emma, I don't know. It's just that I don't want to become involved with him. I can't and I shall do my best to avoid him.'

'Well, you won't be able to for much longer because he's seen us and is riding this way. Who's that with him? He looks slightly familiar, but for the life of me I can't think where I've seen him.'

Cassandra glanced at William's companion. 'That's William's cousin Mark Lampard. You met him briefly as we were leaving Carlow Park and you will have seen him at Grosvenor Square two weeks ago.'

'Oh, yes, now I remember. He's terribly serious and his wife was a mite too superior to be nice. Still, I suppose I'd better try and like her since I'm to be family.'

Astride his restive horse, William and his cousin joined the languid promenade of carriages and eventually stopped beside their carriage. Sunlight glittered on the backs of proud, prancing horses; it touched the leaves and lighted on Cassandra's bewitching face. The sight of her after almost two weeks of not seeing her had a devastating effect on William. Never had she looked so radiantly lovely or serene. The truth was that neither time nor distance had blunted the feelings he had for her.

Bitter regret twisted his heart. No matter where he was or what he did, thoughts of her consumed him. Looking into her eyes, he felt as if he were being tortured. His muscles tightened and his whole body ached for her, but it was a hurt he didn't want to be spared.

If William was surprised to see Cassandra in the park, beyond a slight lift to his eyebrows, he made no show of it. She had dressed with special care, deliberating on what gown to wear, as though she was aware that she must look her best. She had chosen a deep pink. Afterwards she had her doubts about the colour, but she had been wrong, for it seemed to reflect in her face, giving it a flush that was extremely flattering. Beneath her small matching hat, her honey-gold hair had been arranged in bright glossy curls. Whatever he had to say, she resolved to appear and speak calmly.

His eyes were cool and expressionless. 'Cassandra. You are well, I hope?'

'Perfectly, thank you,' she replied, her voice toneless, recollections of the last time they had met uppermost in her thoughts. There was a strange silence while she searched her mind for something to add, but he had turned away and entered into conversation with Aunt Elizabeth.

Her acquaintance having moved on, Lady Monkton

focused all her attention on Lord Lampard. 'This is a pleasant surprise, Lord Lampard.'

'You remember my cousin, Baron Mark Lampard. As you know, he's in town with his wife for the wedding.'

'I am delighted to meet you again,' Lady Monkton said pleasantly.

Mark inclined his head. 'Likewise, Lady Monkton. I trust the wedding arrangements are going to plan?'

'They are indeed. We're all impatient for the happy day. Of course you have met my nieces—Cassandra, and Emma, the bride-to-be?'

Mark's cold, humourless eyes skimmed over Cassandra before settling on Emma. 'I have had that pleasure.'

'And how is your grandmother?' Lady Monkton enquired politely.

'She is well, thank you,' William replied. 'You must call on her to discuss wedding plans. She would like that—all of you,' he said, his eyes on Cassandra.

'We would be delighted.'

While William conversed with Aunt Elizabeth, Cassandra studied this strikingly handsome man surreptitiously. People passing by looked openly at him, but he seemed oblivious to them. His long muscular frame was well turned out in a midnight-blue jacket, the colour's starkness being broken only by a waistcoat in light grey satin and a crisp white neckcloth.

It was like coming face to face with a stranger. It unnerved her when those penetrating eyes locked on her and with threatening boldness slowly raked her as if he were stripping her bare. She had forgotten how brilliant they were. It was all she could do to face the unspoken challenge and not flee from the carriage.

While Lady Monkton and Emma continued to banter with Mark, William rode his horse to her side of the carriage. His gaze rested warmly on her face.

'I don't believe I apologised for not escorting you to Almack's, Cassandra.'

'I don't recall whether you did or not,' Cassandra replied coldly, avoiding his gaze. 'Whatever the reason was that delayed you, it must have been of far more interest and importance than escorting some silly débutantes to a ball.'

'It wasn't, but it was important.'

'It has nothing to do with me,' she bit back. 'Go away. I don't want to talk to you.'

'Stop it, Cassandra,' he rebuked in a low voice. 'I want to talk to you without your eyes hurling daggers at me. I desire a few moments of your time, if you can spare them. Kindly have the courtesy to listen to what I have to say. What kept me that night has everything to do with you since apart from myself you are the only one who knows about the attempts on my life.'

Cassandra's eyes flew to his. Deeply anxious for his safety despite everything, her interest was roused and her animosity for the moment forgotten. 'Has anything happened—have they tried again?'

Both happy and touched to see concern for him in her eyes, William's mouth curved in that sensuous smile of his. 'Soothe your fears, my love,' he murmured, 'not since the day I shot that blackguard on the road to Guildford. Mr Jardine, the private investigator I've hired, sent a note wanting to see me urgently that evening. You will understand why I had to speak to him. You may be interested to learn that the man I shot was called Daniel Sharp.'

'How does he know this?'

'The authorities in Guildford found his horse not far from his body. His name was on some correspondence in his saddlebags. Unfortunately, apart from his name we have nothing else to go on, but it's a start.'

'And the name means nothing to you?'

He shook his head. 'Not a thing.'

'Then Mr Jardine is going to have his work cut out.' Aching to tell him to take care—not to ride out alone and to look behind him at all times—at that same moment Emma turned to speak to her, so all she could manage to say was, 'Thank you for telling me.'

Returning to her home in Kensington later that day intending to visit the institute, she was happy to find her mother, who had just returned, waiting to disclose some uplifting news. Harriet told her that there was fresh hope for the institute and it would not have to close after all. Doctor Brookes had called at the institute to tell her that he had had a meeting with a lawyer who was representing a benefactor who wished to remain anonymous for the time being. Apparently he was so impressed by their work at the institute that he had made a considerable donation and would continue to do so on a six-monthly basis. Indeed, it was so generous that they might even be able to look for larger premises and possibly consider opening an orphanage.

Cassandra was overwhelmed with relief. It was like having a huge burden lifted from her shoulders. She was also relieved and happy to see her mother smile again and fresh animation light her eyes—although she thought this had as much to do with her meeting with Dr Brookes as the mysterious benefactor's generous donation. Still, with such a big sponsor, hopefully it would inspire others to donate. Not until she was in the carriage heading for the institute did she begin to wonder as to the identity of the benefactor. He seemed too good to be true—or was he?

He! Suddenly she sat bolt upright. In the space of two seconds blinding realisation dawned. There was only one *he* she could think of who would do something like this. Were there no lengths that man would go to to get her into his bed? Cold fury engulfed her. Of all the treacherous, underhanded tricks... Horrifying clarity had her ordering Clem to change direction and head for Grosvenor Square instead.

She was admitted to the house and told by Siddons—who, recalling another time when this same young lady had stormed into the house without a by your leave, eyed her with wary suspicion—to wait in the salon and he would inform Lord Lampard that she was here. As soon as William saw her pacing irately to and fro, her face like black thunder, he had the distinct impression that he had somehow stirred a volcano.

The sound of the double doors closing brought Cassandra immediately whirling round and she faced him with eyes blazing.

'Cassandra! I am surprised,' he said, coming further into the room with a graceful, half-animal saunter. 'To what do I owe the pleasure of your visit?'

Slowly she moved towards him, planting her small feet firmly in front of him. She faced him squarely, her elbows akimbo. 'This isn't a social call. Far from it. Didn't you hear anything I said to you two weeks ago? Are you deaf as well as stupid? What kind of man are you? What kind of man is it who will go to such lengths as to secure a children's institute in the belief it will lure one of its trustees into his bed?'

If he was surprised that she had found out about his donation, he gave no hint of it. Perching his hip on the edge of the table behind him, crossing his arms over his chest, he studied her impassively. 'I had an idea you would soon work out the identity of the anonymous benefactor.'

'In no time at all. So you don't deny it is you?'

He shrugged, immune to the wrathful expression on her lovely face. 'Since you ask me so pointedly, no, I do not deny it. Come, Cassandra, there's no need to take umbrage. I thought you'd be pleased. You cannot deny I have been helpful.'

'Because you had an ulterior motive—namely seducing me.'

'You make it sound sordid,' William said with an infuriating calm.

'That's because it is. In all the time I have known you, you have not been honest with me. You have used your mercenary qualities to manoeuvre me into your bed. I will not be your plaything. Thank God I found out in time.'

William smiled in the face of her fury, knowing he trod the trembling ground with a fool's boldness. 'I'm trying to reform.'

How she yearned to wipe that look from his face. 'An impossibility for you.' The rising fire of the volcano showed in her eyes. 'I care nothing for good deeds.' He did not seem surprised or offended. Undaunted, he lifted his brows quizzically, a twist of humour about his beautifully moulded lips.

'I recall you telling me not so long ago that your dream was to open an orphanage. You've got your wish, Cassandra, so stop glaring at me. Are you too proud and stubborn to accept my gesture? I thought there was more at stake than pride and money.'

'You're right,' she snapped. 'The children.'

'Would you like me to withdraw my offer? Is that what you want?'

He was looking at her with the patience of a teacher discussing an illogical subject with a troublesome pupil. His calm made her want to kick his shin. 'Damn you, William Lampard. It's not up to me and you know it. Mama and Dr Brookes hold the purse strings and they're absolutely elated about what you're doing. Besides, how can I deny the children? But I don't like it. I don't like the way you've gone about ingratiating yourself with my family.'

William gazed at the tempestuous beauty standing merely a foot away, her eyes flashing angry sparks, her breasts rising and falling with suppressed fury beneath the grey dress she always wore for her work at the institute, and he felt a tremendous admiration for her honesty and courage in this stand she was taking because she believed he had wronged her. However, he hadn't expected her to react quite so violently to his donation to the institute, or his promise for its future.

Calmly he said, 'I thought you'd be pleased.'

'Pleased? You unspeakable cad,' she flung back. 'I'm pleased the children won't be deprived—of course I am, but I wish the money had come from another source. I find the idea of being indebted to you distinctly distasteful.'

He cocked a sleek black eyebrow. 'Beggars can't be choosers.'

'You're right, they can't.'

'Why does the idea of me funding the institute bring you such anger?'

'Because I know the reason why you're doing it. And don't insult my intelligence by telling me it's for the children, because I will not believe you.'

William studied her angry, rebellious face impassively for a long, silent moment. 'I'm very sorry to hear that,' he said softly, 'because it is true. It's time I did something worthwhile and it is a worthy cause. Besides, I have plenty of money. I can afford it.'

'And what is the price to me? Say what you like, but I know you never do anything without a motive. How long will it be before you demand some form of payment?'

'Damn it, Cassandra,' he cried, unable to repress his annoyance over her argumentative attitude. 'I don't want you to feel obligated to me.'

'I don't. I don't owe you anything and I will take nothing from you.'

Shoving a heavy lock of hair back from his forehead, William sighed heavily. 'You are a stubborn woman, Cassandra Greenwood.'

'You have no idea how stubborn I can be. So far you have only scratched the surface.'

'Are you always so unreasonable?'

'Ha! Because I won't be coerced and cajoled to bed down with you? You are the one who is being unreasonable.'

'That isn't what I want.'

'No? Then the wager was pointless.'

'Then marry me.'

For a moment Cassandra was stunned by his suggestion. She stared at him in astonishment. He was watching her reaction to his offer from beneath lowered lids. 'Marry you? Never.'

He sighed as if forlorn. 'Alas. I am to be tortured more, then. Have you any idea how the merest sight of you is enough to bring me pain?'

His voice had become low and soft in her ears, and Cassandra had to delve deeply into her reserve of will to dispel the slow numbing of her senses. 'What's this? Are you still lamenting the loss of your wager, my lord ? Have you and Sir Charles raised the stakes since we last spoke? Careful, William,' she mocked scathingly, 'he might want another of your horses. At this rate, his stables will be full to bursting with mounts from Carlow Park.'

'But I want to marry you.'

He had to be jesting. He must be—she simply dare not think that he might not be lest it destroy her control. 'I don't want to marry you,' she seethed.

'Does the idea of being a countess not appeal to you?'

Cassandra lifted her chin in scornful resentment. 'I wouldn't marry you if you were offering me the position of Queen of England. Now, no more. Let this business with the institute be enough.' She turned and stalked towards the door.

William's brows drew together. As she had turned from him he had been struck by an astonishing realisation—for despite her magnificent show of spirit and courage, Cassandra was apparently on the brink of tears. 'There—is just one more thing'

She paused. Something in his tone sent a warning shooting along her nerves. Turning, she looked at him warily, waiting for him to speak.

'I've spent some time at Westminster—in the House, recently. You will be relieved to learn that I've succeeded in obtaining some Government funding for your project.'

For the first time since entering the house, Cassandra was rendered speechless. All she could do was stare at him.

'And one more thing,' he said softly. Standing straight, his broad shoulders squared, his jaw set with implacable determination, he emanated the restrained power and unyielding authority Cassandra had always sensed and resented. 'Everything I've done I've done for you. I will stop at nothing to win you. Believe that.'

Unable to find words to answer, drop by precious drop Cassandra felt her confidence drain away. In a blinding streak of suffocating humiliation, she asked herself how she could ever have deluded herself into believing that she could sway him from his purpose. Almost choking on the lump of emotion that had risen in her throat, she went out.

Cassandra leaned her head back and closed her eyes as the carriage bore her away from Grosvenor Square back to Kensington. Feeling much abused and angered, she had decided not to go to the institute after all—she had no heart for it. It was impossible to shut out thoughts of William—when she closed her eyes, the image of his handsome face and blue smiling eyes mocked, challenged and consumed her. Bitter bile rose up in her throat as her thoughts marched in a circle of misery and anger. She would never forgive either William or Charles Grisham that wager, but what could she do? And so she was forced to bear her hurt and shame alone, with no way of avenging herself on either of them. But it was done with and her honour still remained intact.

But she was not content. As much as she forced all her determination to put William from her mind, it had an empty ring. The weakness of it echoed through her brain and the heady memory of his kisses became all the more intoxicating and seemed to ferment in her woman's body.

Over the days that followed, never in her life had Cassandra been so miserable or confused. She could think only of William. It was becoming an obsession. She had never known what obsession was except for the dictionary definition, which could not begin to describe how she felt for him. She hadn't known what it was to think of two things at the same time: to read a book and, while comprehending what was written, to see a darkly handsome face and two flashing blue eyes; to be in a room full of chattering people and at the same time distinctly hear another one. If this was obsession, then it was a miserable condition from which she could see no relief.

Chapter Eleven

The Season was at an end and almost everyone would be leaving town for their country estates. When the day of the wedding finally dawned after weeks of frenetic preparations, a radiant Emma, beneath an enveloping cloud of lace, walked down the aisle to stand beside her beloved Edward to recite their vows. She was accompanied by her bridal attendants with Cassandra as Matron of Honour.

Before going into church, as Cassandra had fussed and straightened her train, Emma whispered, 'You'll be next, Cassy. I just know you will.'

Cassandra had looked at her and smiled wryly, doubtful of that. The only man who continued to occupy her thoughts every waking moment, she had not seen since she had walked out of his house in angry confusion two weeks ago.

And then there he was, standing beside Edward in the church, his head rising above most of the guests assembled, his hands clasped behind his back, his legs a little apart. Her heart gave a joyful leap. His clean-cut profile faced the altar, his powerful shoulders moulded by his dark blue coat. To her at that moment he was pure perfection. Sensing her eyes on him, he turned his head and met her gaze, his deep-set eyes unnervingly intent.

All through the ceremony, Cassandra was conscious of

those eyes on her neck and shoulders and then her face when she turned. She found herself avoiding them because, for all her courage, she found it hard to meet them because of what was in her heart.

The ceremony over, it was a proud moment for Harriet and Elizabeth, dabbing away their tears, as the newly wedded pair walked down the aisle, past the crowded pews and out of the church. The mass of guests in a sea of silks and lace flowed together and, pushing and shoving, twittering and laughing, followed in their wake.

Cassandra's mind was in a strange, feverish state, raging impatiently against all these people who were separating her from William. He had vanished amid the swell and, despite all her efforts, she did not catch a glimpse of him until later at the wedding banquet at Monkton House.

It was a sumptuous feast. William fulfilled his role as best man with his usual careless elegance, engaging in brilliant conversation and seeming to welcome the attentions of the women who fawned and flirted shamelessly with him, much to Cassandra's indignation and dismay as she observed it all from a distance.

Gradually her patience began to fray. Not once did he approach her. It was as if she didn't exist for him. Perhaps now that he had lost the wager, she no longer interested him and the pursuit would be off. Stiffened by pride, she succeeded in being her most dazzling, vivacious self and managed with a painful effort to dominate her disappointment and accept the slap that fate had dealt her.

Their last meeting uppermost in William's mind, until he could speak privately to Cassandra—who seemed either afraid or unwilling to meet his gaze, without being surrounded by strangers—his decision to avoid her became harder to adhere to as the evening drifted on. In her pink satin gown and pink and white roses to match the bride's bouquet twined in her hair, never had she looked more lovely.

After what seemed like an eternity the guests at last rose from the banqueting tables and adjourned to the ballroom, where Edward led his bride of a few hours into the centre of the floor. Others began dancing and Cassandra drifted into the arms of first one partner, then another.

It was while she was taking refreshment in a break from dancing that she sensed William's presence behind her. She even recognised the spicy tang of his cologne. Her throat went dry and a nervous quaking jarred through her as she waited for him to speak to her.

'Dance with me, Cassandra.'

She spun round. He was watching her, white teeth showing in a lazy smile. 'I don't think that would be wise.'

'Nothing you and I have ever done has been wise. Come, all my duty dances are over except one.'

'And that is?'

'To dance with the Matron of Honour—it is the custom at weddings for the best man to dance with the Matron of Honour. Do you intend to refuse me?' he challenged her stunned appraisal. 'Have we been apart so long you do not recognise me, perhaps?'

Cassandra's pride demanded that she show him contempt, but her heart said otherwise.

'I may not be the most popular of your suitors, but I am the most determined, so do not even think of refusing. Come, Cassandra, we've teetered on the edge of scandal once, don't give them more grist to grind by walking away from me. Everyone is watching us.'

Taking her hand, he drew her on to the dance floor and into his embrace. It was a waltz, a swirling, exciting dance that brought couples into close contact as no other—a dance considered to be fast and daring and banned at Almack's. He swung her into rhythm with a sureness of step and she followed with a natural grace.

'I meant what I said, Cassandra.'

'Remind me. I have forgotten.'

'I will not accept your refusal to marry me.'

Leaning back in his arms the better to see his face, she looked at him as if he'd taken leave of his senses. 'Are you telling me you actually meant it, William?'

'I never say anything I don't mean. At some point very soon I will have persuaded you to overlook that damned wager and marry me in spite of it.' The heat of his stare lent the weight of truth to his words. 'My grandmother liked you, by the way. She approves of the match.'

'What?' she gasped. 'Do you mean to tell me that you've discussed me with your grandmother?'

'Of course.'

Cassandra's eyes narrowed in a glare. 'So that's why she directed so much attention to me when we met. How impossibly conceited you are, William Lampard. When I think of what you are guilty of where I am concerned, how can you expect me to marry you? Why, you don't even sound sincere.'

'You are refusing me?' he asked, pretending to sound mortified.

'It's no more than you deserve. Why do you constantly refuse to hear what I say?'

'Because I cannot get you out of my thoughts.' His voice became soft and serious. 'I think of the times we have talked. I remember what it felt like when I held you, how soft your skin and how warm and willing your lips. I remember how you looked that day by the lake with the sun shining on your face. I remember everything, and were we alone I would swiftly prove the ardour you have stirred.'

'William, please stop it.' Blushing under his intimate, predatory gaze, she noticed the increasing interest of the gazes being directed at them. 'People are looking at us.'

'Let them look,' he murmured, his eyes shining softly, hungrily as he gazed down into hers.

'At least try to behave yourself.'

'I am a man and you are a very beautiful and desirable woman. How else should I behave?'

'Like a gentleman would be a start.'

'Ah, Cassandra, my love. Am I really to believe that you care nothing for me at all? How can I believe you when I know you took pleasure in my kisses—and I can pleasure you again. Do not deny yourself, Cassandra.'

His gaze was now direct, challenging, almost insulting, raking her face upturned to his. The bold stare touched a quickness in Cassandra that made her feel as if she were on fire. He was close, much too close, and she was embarrassingly conscious of his hand resting on the small of her back. 'Be quiet, William. Have you no sense of honour?'

His lips twisted in a smile. 'Where you are concerned? At this moment I feel quite dishonourable. Come, Cassandra,' he said, swinging her in a dizzying whirl, 'you want me as much as I want you. Admit it.'

She did want him. She wanted him more than she had ever wanted anything in her life. But she would not admit it. 'It is cruel of you to say such things to me when I cannot retaliate. This is Emma's wedding and I will not spoil it by causing a scene and leave you standing on the dance floor. I will not embarrass you.'

The dance over, he returned her to her place beside Lady Monkton. Defying the stares, he bent and whispered in her ear, 'You cannot have forgotten what it felt like to be in my arms— if you have forgotten, I will remind you, I promise you.'

Some of the guests watched him walk away. A few heads turned to follow him, either because he was an impressive man, or because people were aware that something interesting or maybe scandalous had been going on between these two.

The sun was going down on Monkton House when Cassandra went in search of her mama, realising she hadn't seen her for most of the afternoon. Looking out of the French windows, she saw her on Dr Brookes's arm, strolling on the terrace. Her head was tilted to one side and she was looking up at him with her mouth slightly parted and a look on her face that Cassandra did not know. Why, it was the look of a coquette. Dr Brookes bent his head to her and she laughed at something he said. Cassandra thought what a handsome couple they made, and with a smile she turned away.

The day after the wedding, accompanied by a groom, Cassandra was riding in the park when she saw Sir Charles Grisham galloping across the turf astride a rather splendid dark brown stallion. Impressed more by the horse than by its rider, she reined in her horse and watched him. On seeing her, Charles pulled on the reins and slowed the stallion to a walk, eyeing her with lazy interest.

As he approached, Cassandra quickly weighed the relative merits of letting him know that she knew all about the wager he had made with William. Recalling the humiliation she had suffered since that awful day when she had overheard the two of them at Carlow Park, she decided to be daring rather than cowardly.

Coming to a halt directly in front of her, Sir Charles lifted his arrogant brows and drawled, 'Miss Greenwood! What a pleasant surprise. You have no idea of the effect that simply being near you can have on my poor heart.'

Her smile was cool. 'And I think you must be taking too much sugar in your tea, Sir Charles.'

'Since our last meeting at Almack's I've long been desiring to see you again—but you rejected all my cards asking if I could call on you.'

'As I did all the others. I've decided I don't like being a débutante.'

'Well, I am most put out about it—stricken to the quick, in fact.'

'You'll get over it. I have decided that society is not to my liking.' She regarded him with a bland expression. 'It's a fine horse you're riding. Is it a recent acquisition?'

'Not quite,' he replied, clearly proud of his mount as he patted its glossy neck. 'As a matter of fact, he's been in my possession for several weeks. His name's Monarch—out of the stables at Carlow Park—fastest devil I've ever owned.'

Cassandra's eyes widened in mock-surprise. 'Really! How very interesting.'

His look was sharp and guarded. 'Why so?'

'You will be pleased to know that you will acquire another mount from Lord Lampard's stables shortly.'

He frowned. Clearly he had no idea what she was talking about. 'I'm sorry? This is news to me.'

Cassandra lifted her brows and her smile widened. 'I don't see why it should be if it isn't to me. Lord Lampard has lost the wager, Sir Charles—surely it cannot have slipped your mind.' Her eyes were dancing with laughter as she watched his shock register.

'Well, I'll be damned!' he gasped.

Immediately Cassandra's humour left her. 'And so you should be,' she remarked with no sympathy, 'for trying to make me an object of ridicule.'

'How did you find out about it?'

'I overheard the conversation you had with Lord Lampard when you visited Carlow Park.'

'You were there? You heard?'

She nodded. 'Every damning word.'

Charles cocked a brow imperturbably. 'Not quite all. If you had, you would have heard William renege on the wager—no stomach for it, apparently.'

Cassandra stared at him, a feeling of unease beginning to creep over her. 'What are you saying?'

'He folded, told me he had developed a deep regard for you and he would not dishonour you. But, true to his word, he honoured the wager that same day—Monarch here is proof of that.'

The blood drained out of Cassandra's face and she almost stopped breathing when the implication of what he'd told her rammed home. 'I see,' she said tightly. 'In that case allow me to offer you my belated congratulations. Please excuse me.' Pressing her lips together, she jerked the reins and turned the horse around.

'Miss Greenwood.'

She turned back.

'For what it's worth, I do apologise for the wager.'

'So you should. I do not like being made sport of. Find someone else to play your childish games with next time.'

Her mind was in turmoil as she rode back to Monkton House. What had she done? She felt as if she had lost something very precious, that she had thrown it away, considering it to be useless, and her heart was breaking with the loss of it. But how was she to have known? How could she possibly have known that William had reneged on the wager because he had no wish to dishonour her?

Why hadn't he said anything? Now she saw the truth of it, unobstructed by impractical notions as to his disreputable character or her high belief in human nature. He had been there in the background, understanding her and her desperation to keep the institute from going under, ready to help. He had been there to offer Archie a place in his stables, reading her anxiety and impatience in her eyes when Emma and Edward had eloped and agreeing to let her accompany him to Scotland. He had shown concern for Emma in her illness, been generous when he had put his house at their disposal, had made everything right when the scandal of the elopement had burst on to the social scene, and now this latest—his offer to become a beneficiary in the institute while quietly petitioning Parliament and being granted Government funding.

No man did that for a woman without caring for her. He'd cared for her all along and she hadn't seen it and had been so dreadful to him. Once she thought she had hated him for causes she had thought were justified, but the sting had been taken out of her anger by small degrees and now she regarded him with new respect. The stabilising force of anger had gone, leaving her prey to the softer emotions. Recalling their kiss at Netherton Hall and her angry words afterwards, she realised how much she must have hurt him and he'd been too proud to show it.

Riding a little ahead of the groom, other people on horseback and those strolling through the park gave friendly greetings and she smiled, but did not see them. For when she thought of William, with his handsome face, a trembling came over her and she knew that she loved him. She accepted the truth of it as she would a precious gift, without wonder, without awe, because that was the way of it. She loved everything about him—his smile, his strength, his passion—and she knew he would never let her down.

She didn't know how long she had loved him, but it was true, and if it hadn't been for that wretched wager she'd have realised it long before now. What a complete and utter fool she had been, and how could she go about making amends?

Siddons showed Cassandra into the salon where she was surprised to be greeted by Mark and Lydia. They were seated in plush chairs opposite each other and Lydia was pouring tea on a small table between them.

'I'm sorry,' Cassandra said, feeling a sudden awkwardness. 'I have no wish to disturb you. I hoped William would be at home.'

'I'm afraid you've just missed him,' Mark informed her, standing up and offering her a seat. 'Would you care for some tea?'

Cassandra perched on the edge of a chair, but declined the tea.

'William's accompanying Grandmother back to Carlow,' Mark went on, 'said she'd had enough of the city and wanted to leave early.'

'Oh, I see,' Cassandra replied, careful not to let her disappointment show. 'Will—will he be returning to London?'

'I don't believe so. What with the wedding and everything, matters awaiting his attention at Carlow Park are piling up. Lydia and I stayed here last night, rather than travel all the way to Greenwich. We are to leave for Carlow later, but first we have to go to Greenwich to say farewell to Lydia's sister.' Mark stood up. 'Excuse me a moment. There is a minor matter I wish to discuss with Siddons before we leave.'

'Miss Greenwood,' Lydia remarked when her husband had closed the door. 'I am all amazement. Your visit is most unusual. Is it a habit of yours to call on gentlemen at their homes unchaperoned?'

Cassandra stiffened at the unexpected and unprovoked attack. The tone, lightly contemptuous and at the same time more than a little suspicious, made her hackles rise. A spark of anger momentarily diverted her thoughts from William. She smiled, and in a voice no less disdainful said, 'I do all sorts of things young ladies shouldn't.'

The beautiful brows rose slightly. 'And does your unladylike behaviour not concern Lady Monkton?'

'If anyone should feel any concern for what I do, it is my mother, and she, like me, is open minded about these things.'

'How very odd,' Lydia remarked, reaching for her tea. 'Forgive me, Miss Greenwood, but there is one thing I don't understand. You seem to have developed a peculiar relationship with William. Why, it is almost as if the two of you are…' she gave a low, humourless laugh '…lovers—and there is a rumour that the two of you have been—close—for some time. Can you say there is no foundation in the rumour?'

Cassandra's brows lifted in surprise at her malicious impertinence. 'Whatever the truth of it, I do not choose to answer. That is my business.'

'Of course, but since your sister has succeeded in making a prestigious marriage, in the wake of it perhaps you have aspirations of a similar kind. Are you hoping William will offer for you?'

Cassandra's cheeks burned. How dare she? What she was saying was that Emma was some upstart with pretensions above her station, who had wormed her way into Edward's affections. Her rudeness was not to be endured.

'If William asks me, I shall most certainly accept him if that is what I want. Perhaps you think a connection with me will disgrace him.' There was a flash of something indefinable in Lydia's eyes. For a moment Cassandra couldn't think what it meant and then she recognised it. It was the assessment of one woman for another—from the one who had lost to the one who might triumph.

'I am not ignorant of your condition, and that your connections come through Lady Monkton. Your mother must be feeling extremely relieved this morning to have one of her daughters in a very satisfactory marriage—advantageous for your family, I would think. And consider this. If the scandal of the elopement hadn't come out and William hadn't foolishly intervened, there would have been no wedding.'

Cassandra stared at her as the realisation dawned that this woman might have been responsible for spreading the scandal and causing Emma and her mama such distress. What she felt was beyond expression. Her face became pale with anger.

'Is it possible that you had something to do with that? Were you the one who gossiped and spread the scandal in the hope that my sister and my family would be so shamed that they would be forced to retreat into obscurity?'

Unmoved by any feeling of remorse, Lydia's smile was thin, her eyes hard and brittle. 'One thing you should know about me is that I never gossip. There is always a motive behind what I do. The Lampards are an old and distinguished family—as is my own. To form such a close attachment to a family whose connections and conditions in life are so inferior is not acceptable. Water and oil don't mix, Miss Greenwood, and never will.'

At that moment Mark entered the room, putting an end to their heated discourse, but on observing Cassandra's tense countenance he asked if everything was all right. Forcing a smile to her lips, she told him that she and Lady Lampard had engaged in the most interesting conversation—to reveal the substance of their conversation would only cause unnecessary unpleasantness.

Mark sat down and half-smiled at Cassandra. 'Miss Greenwood, I would like to apologise if anything I said concerning your sister when we met at Carlow Park upset you. Believe me, it was not my intention. I am fond of Edward and that particular escapade made me very angry indeed. However, I realise that in relieving my own feelings I may have wounded yours.'

'I understand. I was angry and upset myself at the time,' Cassandra confessed, thinking that she might have misjudged William's grave cousin and that underneath his seriousness he was really quite agreeable. Perhaps he did not believe in showing emotion, or maybe it was not in him at all. 'My sister can be unpredictable and rather trying at times. Do—you have any siblings?' she asked Lydia pointedly, refusing to appear in any way submissive to this arrogant, dreadful woman.

Lydia stirred her tea and stared into the cup. 'Two, one younger sister and a half-brother, Daniel. We—see each other rarely.'

Cassandra stayed a little while longer, making awkward, polite conversation before making her escape. Still incensed by the conversation she had had with Lydia, it was with a distinct feeling of unease that she recalled the look she had seen on Lydia's face when she had watched William on the night of Almack's—as if she hated him.

She also recalled the conversation she had had with William when they had been travelling to Netherton Hall and she had cautiously asked him if it might be possible that Mark, with much to gain from William's death, could be behind the attempt on his life. William had refused to consider it and now she had spoken to Mark she thought that maybe he was right.

But what of Lydia? And was it a coincidence that her half-brother was called Daniel?

How well did William know the woman who was to have married his brother? Had it been a love match or was she ambitious? How much had Lydia aspired to be Countess of Carlow? When Robert had died she had married Mark. Had she thought William might be killed in the Peninsula, which would have enabled her to realise her desire to be Countess of Carlow?

Cassandra shook her head. Now she was being foolish by letting her mind run along these lines. It was silly and far-fetched to be thinking like this and she must stop it. What an absurd, overactive imagination she had.

But it was too late. The seed had been planted, took root and began to grow, and by the time she reached Monkton House it was a full-grown tree.

Finding her aunt in her sitting room dealing with her correspondence at her writing table, after they had talked and enthused about the wedding and wondered how the newly-weds were settling into their new home, Cassandra casually asked her what she knew about Lydia Lampard.

'As a matter of fact, very little. Her family were gentry and resided in Kent. I know she was to have married William's brother, but when he died in that dreadful riding accident she married Mark instead.'

'Did you ever meet her parents?'

'Yes, several times, though we were never friends. Her mother married twice. I believe her first husband was a soldier—killed in some battle or other abroad.'

Cassandra braced herself. 'Can you remember his name?'

Elizabeth frowned thoughtfully as she forced her mind back over the years. 'Why—now, let me think—although why you should want to know I really don't know.'

Cassandra shrugged. 'No reason really. I'm just curious, that's all. Can you remember, Aunt Elizabeth?' she pressed.

'George, his name was. Yes—that's it, George.'

'George what?'

'Sharp. There, I do remember. He was from Blackheath— and a bit of a blackguard, if my memory serves me right. There was a child—but don't ask me what he was called, because that I don't know.'

Cassandra couldn't believe what her aunt had innocently disclosed. Daniel Sharp was Lydia's half-brother and he had tried to kill William. If Lydia had knowledge of this, then she had to be in on it, too. And, if so, William was still in danger. It was imperative that he knew what she had uncovered.

The following morning, she had a long talk with her mother, in which she gave her a full account of the attempts on William's life and that she, Cassandra, had discovered who was behind it and must now go to Carlow Park to tell him immediately. When her mother had recovered from the shock of it and considered the importance of it, she reluctantly gave her permission for her to go.

'There is something I have to tell you before I leave, Mama,' Cassandra said, clearing her throat, 'something you should know.' Her eyes met her mother's, which were suddenly sharp with questioning regard. Cassandra quailed inside. What would she say? 'Mama—I—I'm going to marry Lord Lampard.'

Harriet's face was incredulous as she stared at her daughter. 'You? You and Lord Lampard?' she exclaimed quietly.

Cassandra nodded. 'I am in love with him—and I—I believe he is in love with me. He—has asked me to be his wife.'

'I see. And what was your answer?'

'I haven't given him one—but I will.'

'Well, what can I say? I knew there was a certain…attraction between the two of you—I'm not blind—and that he seemed to have made quite an impression on you—'

'He is an impressive person, Mama.'

'Yes, so it would seem, but I had no idea it had gone as far as this. Of course he will have to speak to me. But do you know the full import of what you will be taking on? Oh, I am grateful for all he has done for Emma, of course I am, but—I must voice my concern. I know that he's attractive and that he has a way with women—that he is regarded as a—well—you know.'

'A rake, Mama,' Cassandra said, voicing the word that was so difficult for her mother to say.

'Yes. I must say that he has impressed me and I do like him, but his attitude to women is reputed to be quite light-hearted. How can you know he is serious?'

Cassandra smiled. 'Mama, you worry unnecessarily. Truly.'

'It's a mother's right to worry about her daughter. I want you to be as happy and content as Emma. I don't want him to break your heart.'

'He won't, Mama. I know he won't. I do truly love him and would like your blessing.'

Harriet's eyes filled with tears and she hugged Cassandra tightly. 'You have it, Cassandra. Of course you do.' She stood back and looked at her, composed and in control of herself once more. 'Now, you said there have been several attempts on Lord Lampard's life. Are you in any danger?'

'No, Mama, but William will be if I don't warn him.'

Half an hour later Cassandra left with Clem for Hertfordshire.

Two hours into her journey, she tried imagining her meeting with William. Because of her harsh words to him in the past, would he welcome her warmly, or would he be angry and send her back to London? It was a relief when they reached Carlow

Park and the coach pulled to a stop. Climbing down, Clem lowered the steps for her to alight.

Pearson, the butler, recognised her immediately.

'I wish to see Lord Lampard,' Cassandra pronounced when she'd entered the house. 'Unfortunately he is not expecting me. Is he at home?'

'I'm sorry, Miss Greenwood. Lord Lampard is away on estate business, but he is due back shortly. Perhaps you would care for refreshments while you wait.'

'That would be most welcome. Thank you—and would you see that Clem and the horses are taken care of?'

When William failed to return, remembering how lovely the gardens were at Carlow Park, Cassandra left the house to stroll along the paths. It was a lovely day, the air sultry and pleasantly warm, with insects flitting from one flowering bloom to another. The lake beckoned to her in the distance. Deciding to extend her walk, she looked up at the sky where thunderclouds were gathering. They were hours away, she thought.

It was when she reached the lake and had walked some considerable distance along its banks that she paused. There was a sudden stillness in the air. How quiet it was—the quiet before the storm. She had miscalculated. The sky had gone grey and roiling clouds had come from nowhere. A furious wind rose suddenly and whipped up the surface of the lake. Leaves and branches were lashed dangerously about. A chill swept through the air.

She looked up at the frenzied sky just as a bolt of lightning seared the sky, shattering the grey with a silver blue. Hurriedly she began retracing her steps. Heavy raindrops began to pelt her. Battered by the wind, she was soon soaked through. Disturbed by the elements and thinking it was a long way to the house, frantically she sought the shelter of a giant elm, cursing her stupidity for having walked so far.

* * *

William was incredulous and pleasantly surprised when he arrived back at the house and Pearson told him Miss Greenwood was waiting to see him. His pleasure soon turned to frustration when he found the drawing room empty. The glass doors to the terrace were open; surmising she had gone outside, he went to look. The storm chose that moment to break and a clap of thunder shook the earth. Unable to locate her, he scowled as he retreated to the house to avoid a soaking.

Damn! The little fool. His eyes were drawn in the direction of the lake, obliterated now by the rain. Some instinct told him that was where she would be. If so, she would have to find shelter. Anxious for her safety, he hurried to his room. After several minutes he returned, dressed in an oilskin cloak. Rushing out, his long strides carried him quickly through the gardens and down to the lake.

He shouted her name, his words torn asunder by the wind. Lightning flashed repeatedly, followed by rumbling cracks of thunder. And then he saw her, huddled against a tree. She saw him running towards her and seemed glad that he had come.

Taking her hand, he shouted, 'Come with me. We've got to get out of this.'

Another bolt of lightning sizzled and crackled across the sky, followed by thunder. It was as if the very earth was being riven apart. They had no protection from the rain as a heavier torrent of water was unleashed on them, assaulting them from every angle, wetting Cassandra's garments until they became dead weights and hindered her movements. Her skirt caught on something; she turned to look. William tugged at it and ripped it. Then the vague shape of a low structure appeared in the shrubbery. Cassandra recognised it as the little summerhouse. Why hadn't she thought of that?

William shoved open the door and thrust Cassandra into the dim interior. The space was small with doors on three sides that could be opened to the weather. Her irresponsible act had put him into a fit of temper. 'You little fool,' he berated angrily. 'You must be mad to venture so far from the house when a storm was threatening—and to shelter under a tree. That's the most dangerous place, don't you know that? What were you trying to do? And look at you. You look like a drowned rabbit.'

Her chin trembling with cold, Cassandra was looking at him in abject misery. 'Y-you don't l-look any b-better yourself,' she bit back indignantly. His anger and her wretched state brought tears to her eyes, which spilled down her cheeks.

When he saw her tears, William's anger immediately evaporated and he murmured gently, 'What's this—tears? Dost the Ice Maiden melt?'

Cassandra stared at him. 'I-is that h-how I appear to you—a-as some hard, c-cold-hearted woman? Is that how you th-think of me? I-it may surprise you to know that I have feelings j-just like any other.'

'I know you do,' he said softly.

She was a sorry sight, soaked to the skin and her hair plastered over her face. Her lemon dress was stuck to her body, moulding to every curve and hollow—the round fullness of her breasts, her tiny waist—and clinging to her long legs. William's gaze went to her mouth, watching as rivulets of water ran down her face and over her parted lips.

Lust hit him with such unexpected force that for a moment he couldn't move. Somehow he managed to say, 'You are cold. Let me warm you. Here.' Removing his cloak, he wrapped it round her. 'We'll be safe enough here until the storm has passed.' Sensing her shaking limbs were about to give way beneath her, he pulled her down on to a wooden bench. Enfolding her quaking form, he drew her against his chest, surprised when she neither resisted nor objected. 'If I thought the storm was going to last, I would light a fire and my pleasure would be to remove your clothes.'

She tilted her head to look up at him. 'Why?'

His eyes gleamed into hers. 'To dry them. What else?'

With the torrential rain drumming on the roof and flailing the earth, Cassandra sighed and nestled against him. The heat of his body was making her warm, so very warm, and she had no intention of escaping the wonderful sensations he was evoking in her. 'What else indeed,' she murmured, wanting this, wanting him—how very empty everything was otherwise.

'Tell me why you are here, Cassandra—what it is you want.'

'The same thing you do.' Lifting her head, she studied him in the dim light. She wanted to feel the broad expanse of his chest pressed to hers, to kiss again those beautifully moulded lips that she knew were the most wonderful lips in the world.

'I have been telling you for long enough that I want you. Do not torture me any more.'

She looked into his eyes and he held her gaze in a wilful, hungry vice of blue. 'I am at your mercy,' she whispered, conscious of a fine trembling throughout her body that had nothing to do with the cold. Raising her arm, she slipped her hand around his nape. Tangling her fingers in his wet hair, she drew his head down to hers.

Deprived of her for so long, the days of loneliness had left William hungry for her. With desire beating fiercely in his veins, he clasped her to him, his arms strong and protective. Smoothing her hair from her face, he placed his mouth on her lips. They were sweet and moist and parted beneath his own. Sliding his tongue between them, his arms tightening possessively around her, he groaned and his long-starved passions flared. Their bodies bent in the ardour of their embrace. The kiss was fierce and stirring, devouring and all consuming. Their mouths slanted across each other with hungry impatience.

One hand caressed her, arousing her, stroking and cupping her breasts, until a warm tide of excitement flooded Cassandra's whole being. Dragging his lips from hers, William trailed kisses along her jaw and down her neck, feeling his wits slipping away bit by bit. He had to stop before all sanity left him. She was naïve, innocent and inexperienced with what it all meant, but he did know and he had to call a halt before he acted on it. It took an extreme exercise of will for him to stop kissing her.

With an audible sigh Cassandra looked at him, her eyes languid beneath lowered lids. 'What is it? Is something wrong?'

'We must stop,' he replied huskily, 'otherwise you are in danger of being seduced by a scoundrel, which is what you have been striving to avoid for weeks.'

'I no longer wish to avoid it. I've decided that I want to be seduced by a scoundrel,' she whispered, placing a featherlight kiss at the side of his mouth that set his pulses racing, 'so do not deny me. Please don't stop now.'

'Not here, Cassandra. This is not the place.'

'You're wrong. This is the very place.'

William's caution was ripped away. His eyes held hers for one long, compelling look, holding all his frustrated longings, his unfulfilled desires, everything that was between them. 'Shameless little fool!' he murmured, wanting nothing more than to drag her down on to the dusty floor and make love to her. It was all he could do to control the urges that swamped him. His mouth swooped down to hers once more as if he could not get enough of their dewy sweetness, parting her lips so their breaths merged and became one.

Lost in that wild and beautiful madness Cassandra undid the buttons of his shirt and slipped her hands underneath, touching the hard muscular chest. Sensing his need and responding to an inner heat, with all the repressions and restraints she had imposed on herself ever since she had known about the wager having disappeared, Cassandra tore her lips from his.

Dragging the cloak from round her shoulders, she spread it on the floor. Kneeling on it, seeing how his hair shone with a soft sheen of dark satin in the dim light, she took his hand and pulled him down beside her, and suddenly they were lying side by side and she felt the hard, manly boldness of him. Their bodies met, feverishly intertwining at last. Clothes were unfastened to accommodate questing hands, and teasing kisses placed on bare flesh. Looking into his eyes, Cassandra saw they were not smiling now—they were intense to such a degree that she experienced a moment of panic, but it was soon gone.

William thought of stripping her bare, but decided against it, for even though his mind reeled and his senses were drugged with the soft scent of her and the feel of her shapely form, he was aware of the discomfort she would feel when she had to put the wet clothes back on. He kissed her throat while his hands tugged at the fabric of her bodice, pulling it until her breasts were exposed. His lips trailed down and kissed their full, soft roundness and the cleft between.

Losing her touch of reality, Cassandra closed her eyes, soft and pliable as he stroked and caressed, feeling her nipples begin to throb and rise up proudly against his mouth. Shifting his position, he lifted her skirts and peeled her stockings down, her legs pale and lustrous, his hand moving up her calf, palms and fingers warm, encircling her knee, then spreading and caressing her aching thighs. A warmth spread in her blood, in her bones, a delectable torture that grew and grew and would soon drown her in a flood of pleasure. With the light slanting on them through the windows, uttering a slight moan of surrender, Cassandra willingly yielded to his need, pressing closer against him, meeting his passion with her own, encouraging him, wrapping her arms tightly around his shoulders as he bathed her senses in extravagant pleasure.

His weight pinioning her, Cassandra clung to him as ivy might cling to a tree, the length of her body pressed against his, which was supple, hard and masculine. Her world careened crazily beneath the savage urgency of his need, and she was swept along on a violent storm of passion. While the storm continued to rage outside, their coming together was wonderful and right, and astonishing that it should be instantly so.

As they moved together to the music of love, tasting the

full joy of their mutual union and surrendering to pure sensation, straining to come closer still, each fulfilling the other in a most sublime act of love, the pleasure became unbearable. Cassandra was lost and went soaring into oblivion until she felt bliss; an ecstasy burst upon them, fusing them together into one being until what they shared drove them on to a shattering climax.

Chapter Twelve

Clasped tightly to him as if he would never let her go, Cassandra felt the thunderous beating of his heart against her naked breasts and heard his ragged breathing in her ear. Tucked securely in the curve of her lover's body, sated and spent, Cassandra slowly began to surface from the splendour of his lovemaking. Raising her head, she gazed at his face, unconscious of the vision she presented with her hair tumbling about her shoulders in loose array. Thinking how unbearably handsome he was, she caressed his lips lightly with her own before letting her head fall back, closing her eyes and letting joy and relief wash over her.

'What are you thinking?' William murmured with a tender smile at her upturned face.

An answering smile touched her lips as he splayed his fingers across her cheek. 'That I've dreamed of this moment.'

Cassandra stared up at him; her magnificent eyes, which had taken on a smoky hue, searched deeply into his, amazement etched on her lovely features, soft now with their loving. Drawing away from her on to his side, resting his head on his hand, he gazed down at her. She lay beside him like an innocent golden goddess. Her passion amazed him. The firm voluptuous body that had lain beneath his had been yielding and welcoming as she gave all her desire, passion and love.

His eyes held hers softly. 'Ravaged and ruined, now you will have to marry me,' he whispered.

Her smile was sublime. Suddenly she felt feminine and absurdly happy. 'I fear you are right. You have taken advantage of me and now I am completely and utterly ruined.'

His lips caressed hers tenderly. 'Are you not regretful, my love—full of guilt?'

Cassandra shook her head, and it was no lie. 'I knew what I was doing and I feel no guilt. All I feel is a sense of rightness in being in your arms. I am content. In fact, I feel quite wonderful. How strange and delightful that making love can make a woman feel that way. What an extraordinary thing.' She looked up at him, a gentle flush spreading over her cheeks. 'Did you feel like that, too?'

'I did,' he murmured, brushing a kiss on her forehead.

'Then how soon before we can repeat it?'

He chuckled low in his throat and smoothed some tendrils of hair from her cheek. 'You are without doubt the most shameless and impulsive creature, but the next time I make love to you will be in bed without the restriction of clothes.' He sighed deeply, his expression suddenly serious. 'You do not know how hard you make it for me to resist you.'

A rosy blush stained her smooth cheeks. 'You do not have to resist me any longer, William.'

'I must—for now, but you cannot guess the depth of torment you have put me through of late, for beneath your taunts I have burned with a consuming desire to possess you. I have never worked so hard to win a woman as I have you. Ever since we met I have sought to gain favour in your eyes.'

'And now you have succeeded admirably, my lord.'

His eyes held hers in an enquiring glance. 'I have, but I am confused by your change of heart, my love. Perhaps you should explain what has brought it about.'

'I thought it was time for me to start being honest with myself about what I feel I want, and I decided that, in spite of everything, I want you, William. I want to be with you always.'

William felt humbled and blessed by her unselfish ardour and his lips curved in a smile. He drew his fingers over the slender column of her neck, a tousled mass of honey-gold curls nestling to one side of her head. 'You really are the most unprincipled young woman, Cassandra Greenwood. You never cease to amaze me. You are also lovely, a temptress, not fully awakened to your powers as yet. Of all the women I have known, none has possessed the fire of spirit, of heart and mind as you.'

'Tell me about the wager you made with Sir Charles, William.'

'Ah—that.'

'Yes, that. I need to know the truth of it.'

'The truth of it may surprise you. I told you I agreed to it in a moment of madness. Within an hour of agreeing to it I decided to renege on it. When Charles came to see me at Carlow Park I told him my decision—and had you eavesdropped a while longer, you would have heard.'

'I know.'

'You do?'

She nodded. 'Charles told me.'

'He did? When?'

'Yesterday, when we met in the park whilst out riding. Why didn't you tell me?'

'Because you were so furious with me I felt my protestations of innocence would fall on deaf ears. I was biding my time until your temper cooled. Is it for this reason that you have come to Carlow Park?'

Cassandra sat up and began adjusting her clothes. 'One of them. There is something else. Yesterday when Charles had told me the truth about the wager, I went to your house to see you. I saw Mark and Lydia instead.' Having fastened her bodice, she looked at William directly. 'William, Lydia is the most dreadful woman I have ever met. And—and you cannot know that she has—had, a half-brother called Daniel Sharp.'

William's jaw hardened. 'As a matter of fact I do, and I cannot believe that the woman who was to have married my brother has been calmly planning my murder. Mr Jardine, who has been staying at the inn in Carlow while he made his enquiries, told me earlier today. Like you, he suspected the person who would benefit most from my death might be behind it. When he delved into Lydia's background it didn't take long to discover that Daniel Sharp was her half-brother.'

'Have you been to see her?'

He shook his head. 'In truth, I wasn't looking forward to facing Mark. I am still convinced he knows nothing about his wife's scheming. How did you find out?'

'She told me she had a half-brother called Daniel. It was Aunt Elizabeth who told me her mother's first husband was called Sharp. She also told me she was responsible for leaking the story about the elopement. Did you know?'

'No, but deep down I always suspected it. Her sister is one of the most notorious gossips of the *ton*. If just a whiff of something scandalous reaches her ears, it's out in the blink of an eye and well embroidered on the way.' Getting up, William took Cassandra's hand and pulled her to her feet. 'Listen, the rain has stopped. We'd best get back before Pearson sends a search party out for us.'

'You're right. At this moment I can think of nothing but the luxury of soaking in a hot tub.'

His eyes raked her bedraggled form from head to toe. 'You look adorable.'

Opening the door, they stepped out into a dripping wet and steamy world, only to find a pistol pointing at them.

'Lydia!' Cassandra gasped, and for a moment the pistol swung in her direction.

'Yes—Lydia. What have we here?' she jeeringly questioned, arrogant in her demeanour, confident with a gun in her hand. 'A love nest, no less. How very sweet.'

William stiffened beside Cassandra, and with a glance she saw the muscles in his cheek had tensed with fury. He stood his ground, his tall frame rigid with anger, cursing the fact that he wasn't carrying a pistol. Cassandra's eyes were wide with horror, and her mind raged on in fear.

'After so many attempts on my life have failed, Lydia, it appears you've decided to finish me off yourself.' Each word had a bite, and William's eyes were deadly. 'Who'd have thought it of my cousin's wife?'

Her smile was icy. 'You never did know me very well, did you, William? You didn't know I had a half-brother.'

'I do now,' he replied in a voice of tightly controlled fury.

'You should. You killed him.'

'He was trying to kill me at the time. The two of you were in this together.'

Lydia raised her head aloofly. 'I do not deny it. We devised the plot together to get rid of you. I should have been Countess of Carlow had Robert not died in that wretched accident. I knew, married to Mark, I still could be if you died in the Peninsula. But you didn't die. You came back to cheat me out of all this.'

'And you have been brooding and seething all this time, and the longer your resentment went on, the more bitter and dangerous you became. You're mad.'

A smile playing about her lips, Lydia advanced on William. 'That's right, I am mad,' she hissed, 'and I have no conscience for what I am about to do. When your bodies are found, no one will have any reason to suspect me.'

Instinctively William's arm curved protectively round Cassandra's waist. 'You intend to kill us both?'

'Why not? It would be suicidal to let her go. She knows too much.'

William was about to tell her that Jardine knew of the relationship between her and Daniel, but too late. The pistol was cocked and raised. With a burst of flame and sound it fired.

'No…' Without thinking, Cassandra flung herself in front of William, pushing him back. Her body jerked as the shot entered her and the impact flung her against the door of the summerhouse, where she crumpled in a heap on the ground.

William fell to his knees beside her, looking at her tranquil face. His world turned to ashes.

As she reloaded the gun, Lydia was distracted when two men suddenly appeared out of the undergrowth. Searching for William and Cassandra, the sound of the shot had drawn Clem and Mr Jardine to the summerhouse. Their expressions were frozen with horror as they looked at Cassandra's inert form and William bending over her.

'Lydia, give me the pistol,' a quiet voice said from behind her.

She whipped round. 'You!' she cried, glaring at Mark. 'Do you have to follow me everywhere I go like a lap dog?'

'When you failed to come back from your ride and the storm broke, I came looking for you. I heard the shot.' Not wishing to provoke her into firing the pistol a second time, he spoke calmly, holding out his hand. 'Give me the pistol, Lydia.'

'Go to hell.'

When she turned and it looked as if she was about to fire at William, Mark grabbed at her hand, trying to wrest the pistol away from her. The weapon arched towards him and he leaped aside. There was a frenzied struggle between the two, who seemed to be locked in some devilish embrace. Hampered by her sodden cloak, Lydia struggled as best she could. Suddenly there was a shot and a cry. Mark staggered back. Lydia, a look of surprise on her face, clawed at her chest where the shot had penetrated. She writhed and then collapsed to the floor. No further sound came from her.

Mark looked down at Lydia in dazed stupefaction, unable to believe what had happened and that his wife was dead.

Raising his head, he stared across at his cousin. 'William—what can I say? I'm sorry. I knew nothing about any of this.'

Mr Jardine put his hand on his back. 'It's not your fault. How did she find out about her brother—that he was dead?'

'A constable came to the house earlier. I confess I was troubled by her reaction to the news. Anyone else would have been grief stricken, but Lydia was furious and immediately left the house.' He went to his cousin. William's face was stricken. Kneeling beside him, he asked, 'How is she?'

'Her pulse is weak.' The blood seeping through her dress from the wound in her right shoulder struck terror in his heart. Her head had fallen back and her eyes were closed. Her face held a deathly pallor. 'Dear merciful God,' he prayed with quiet desperation, having seen countless men die of such wounds in battle, 'don't let it be fatal. Please God.'

'We'll get her to the house.'

William gathered her into his arms and lifted her. He looked at Clem. 'Get Dr Tomlinson, Clem, and for God's sake tell him to hurry.'

The doctor came immediately and worked for two hours to try to save Cassandra. He removed the shot successfully. Fortunately it had missed her heart and lung, but she had lost so much blood it would be a miracle if she recovered.

Clem was dispatched to London to fetch Cassandra's mother, who came with Lady Monkton and a weeping Emma, who was comforted by her husband.

William listened to Dr Tomlinson's prognosis with a feeling of impotent rage—the reason being the doctor's failure to give him hope and his own inability to save Cassandra himself.

Going to sit beside her bed, he refused to move. He sat there, holding her lifeless hand and looking down into her beloved face. She was so beautiful it tore at his heart.

'Dear God, Cassandra,' he found himself saying, driven by anger, desperation and a deep and abiding love, 'don't you dare leave me now we have found each other. If you die, I swear I will follow you and give you no peace. Is that what you want, my love?'

The voice penetrated the void in which Cassandra drifted. She liked being in this nothingness where she was cocooned in darkness, where she was so comfortable and warm and she had no worries, no pain…

'Oh, no, Cassandra,' William said fiercely. 'I will not let you go away. You belong to me. I need you. I cannot live without you. I love you. We belong together. Remember our loving—how exquisite it was? It can be so again.'

The voice was loud in her head. It went on and on without ceasing. It gave her no peace. Why didn't he go away and leave her alone? Didn't he know that she liked it here? She didn't want to leave. There was a sigh.

'What about the children? What will you do about them, Cassandra? They need you, you know that. How can you leave them?'

No, her mind cried.

'Yes,' the voice insisted. 'You cannot desert them now. The children, Cassandra. The orphanage you so desire is yours—or perhaps it wasn't that important to you in the end?'

The voice cruelly mocked. Suddenly the void broke and the darkness became light. Her eyes flickered open to see the source of that voice.

A pair of bright blue eyes looked down at her.

'Hello, sweetheart.'

Cassandra opened her eyes. For a moment she couldn't think where she was. She tried to raise herself and a pain shot through her shoulder. She couldn't think what had happened to her. The walls of the room seemed to close in on her. Her head was spinning. Closing her eyes, she tried to remember what had happened to her, and then it all came flooding back and a terrible feeling of foreboding came to her.

'William!' She uttered his name with a cry of utter despair. She had been shot. Lydia had shot her and she was going to shoot William. She began to whimper. Suddenly someone was bending over her. A gentle hand was placed on her forehead. It was Mama.

'Hush, my dear. Don't fret so.' Her voice was soft and soothing. 'You have been ill.'

'William is dead, Mama. Lydia shot him. I know it.'

'No—no, he's here,' Harriet was quick to reassure her daughter. 'He's been here all along and refused to leave you.'

'H-how long?'

'Three days. You were wounded.'

'I remember…Lydia…'

'You lost a lot of blood, Cassandra, and there was a fever. But you are going to be all right. You'll get better now. But we've all been so worried about you.'

'William?'

And then he was there, his anxiety for her etched deeply into his handsome face. With a quiet smile, her mama left the room as he sat beside her. Taking her hand, he raised it to his lips. The memory of the forceful, often mocking, voice came back to her and she smiled.

'You talked to me,' she murmured, her voice husky.

'All the time, my love.'

'I thought it was a dream.'

'It was no dream, Cassandra.'

'Lydia? What happened?'

His face hardened. 'Lydia is dead. It happened when Mark tried taking the gun from her. But it's over and it's going to be a cloud on our perfect horizon for months ahead, but we won't let it spoil what we have.'

Cassandra drew a deep breath and nodded. 'And Mark?'

'He knew nothing about what she was doing.'

'He must be distraught.'

'He's upset, naturally, but he's also angry that his own

wife could have stooped to murder. They never got on, apparently, and she gave him nothing but trouble. Mark realises she only married him because she saw him as a means of realising her ambition to become Countess of Carlow—which she could only achieve with my demise. But we will speak of this later—when you are more yourself.'

'I am beginning to feel more alive by the minute.'

'Do you remember in your dream that I told you that I love you? Remember that?'

She smiled softly, half-teasing. 'No, so you had better tell me again.'

Threading his fingers through her hair, William framed her face between his hands and gazed at her. 'I love you, Cassandra Greenwood. When you lay injured at my feet and I thought you might die, I wanted to die with you. I love you more than life.'

'How can you love me, when I have beset you at every turn?' Her tone was wondrous, her heart soaring with happiness.

'If I could boast to know the wisdom of love, I would be a rich man. But love you I do.'

'And I love you, William. I have loved you for so long. I wanted to tell you, but so much stood between us and I was so busy waging war on you.'

'So you were my sweet, wonderful, aggressive witch. But no longer, my love.'

His eyes grew languid, sending her senses reeling, and there was a soft union of lips as their mouths clung with a leisurely sweetness that held still every moment in time.

Releasing her lips, he gazed down at her. 'I do believe the fever's gone. Your kiss speaks more of passion than of pain.' His eyes darkened and his expression became serious. 'Marry me, Cassandra.'

'Are you quite certain you want me for your wife?'

'Who else could I ask to be my wife but the one who inspires me with feelings that I have never felt before? For good or ill, Cassandra, we two are bound together,' he said with rough sincerity that sent her heart soaring.

The vision of a future stretching endlessly ahead of them was as golden and fertile as Carlow Court itself. Waves of tremendous happiness spread over her as she prepared to pledge her heart and soul to her handsome lover. 'I will marry you, William. I will be proud to marry you.'

Before the end of summer Cassandra and William were married with none of the pomp of Emma and Edward's wedding. With family and carefully selected close friends, theirs was a quiet affair, the ceremony taking place in the family chapel at Carlow Court. And what rejoicing there was.

Cassandra was happy. There was magic in that wedding, with her mama looking on with dreams in her eyes—dreams of the new orphanage—a splendid old house that was being converted to accommodate fifty children—and dreams of her own future with Dr Brookes, who had proposed marriage. This came as no surprise to Cassandra. They were so obviously drawn to each other and were well suited, since they were widow and widower.

When Cassandra walked slowly down the aisle with her hand resting on the arm of Dr Brookes, in the candle-lit chapel, all the radiance in the world was shining from her eyes, which were drawn irresistibly to the man who was waiting for her. He was overwhelming in stature, his dark hair smoothly brushed and gleaming, his midnight-blue coat, dove-grey trousers hugging his long legs, matching silk waistcoat and crisp white cravat simple but impeccably cut.

Unable to contain his desire to look upon Cassandra's gracious form, William turned. The vision of loveliness he beheld, her face as serene as the Madonna's as she carried a bouquet of fragrant white lilies, snatched his breath away. As he viewed her advance, he was convinced she was the most beautiful of women. She looked, in her bridal finery, as if she were moulded of light, ethereal and magnificent in her grace.

An awesome pride and wonder almost sent him to his knees. Unbound, vibrant tresses of honey-gold hair fell in a shimmering cascade halfway down her back, and in her wedding gown of ivory silk and lace, the long tight sleeves forming a point over the backs of her hands, he thought she had never looked so exquisite.

Something like terror moved through his heart. Dear Lord, he prayed, make me cherish and protect her all the days of my life, and give her the joy and happiness she deserves. Stepping out, he waited for her in watchful silence.

Cassandra's eyes clung to his, unable to believe that when she left the church she would belong to this handsome, sophisticated, virile man, who was looking at her adoringly, the passion in his eyes compelling and tender. She felt perfectly calm, her mind wiped clean of everything but this, the most important moment of her life. There was a faint smile on William's firm lips, and her heart warmed as if it felt his touch.

When Cassandra reached him he took her hand, his long fingers closing firmly over hers. She responded to his smile, and in that moment of complete accord, her marriage to William seemed right. Together, side by side, they faced the priest to speak their marriage vows.

Emma and Edward exchanged glances as though there was some delightful conspiracy between them—perhaps memories of their own wedding. When William put the ring on Cassandra's finger and they vowed to cherish each other until death do us part, Aunt Elizabeth wept a little—from pure happiness, she assured everyone. And for her mama, happier than Cassandra had ever seen her before, it was her dearest dream come true to see both her daughters so well married.

There was a wedding reception for the guests, when they were congratulated and their future happiness toasted with the finest champagne, and in due course they were alone. It was a day to treasure and remember for ever.

Deprived of loving for so long, the weeks of preparation

for the wedding had implanted them with a desperate need. Cassandra fell into her husband's arms with utter abandonment. He clasped her to him, their bodies bending in the ardour of their embrace. They kissed deeply, pausing only long enough to cast off clothes and fall into the snug softness of their bed. Their coming together was a feverish intertwining at last. The night was long—they loved and slept and loved again until their bodies were sated and content.

In the pale light of dawn, Cassandra glanced at her husband's dark profile and felt the wonderful hardness of his body pressing closely against her own. Turning on to her stomach, she covered his muscled torso with soft, teasing kisses until he opened his eyes and looked down at her shining head. He smiled that crooked, wicked smile that always made her heart flip over.

'What's this, my love? Are you still not satisfied?' He tipped her chin up so that she could gaze into his eyes. 'Have I told you that you are wonderful?'

Her eyes lit with laughter. 'I'm glad my qualities are apparent.' She sighed, resting her cheek on his hair-dusted chest. 'I couldn't sleep. I can't stop thinking of everything that's happened. You have given me everything, William—I never believed I could be so happy. But—there is something we must discuss.'

'What? Now?' he murmured, feeling his ardour stir once more.

'Why not? We're both awake.'

'Very well, Cassandra—what is it that is so important it takes precedence over my making love to you?'

'The orphanage.'

'Ah!'

'The children have become an important part of my life, you know that. When it opens, Mama will oversee the administration, of course, but you won't stop me continuing to do what I can, will you?'

'Would it matter if I did?'

'Of course it would. I want you to agree and approve of everything I do. It's important to me.'

'How could I object? With my money pouring into the venture—and others before too long, I hope—I'm as committed as you are. I know it's the most important thing in the world to you.'

Cassandra didn't reply immediately. Tilting her head, she looked at him for a long moment, caught up by emotions she could not conceal. 'You're wrong about that, William. The orphanage isn't the most important thing in the world to me.'

'Then what is?'

She snuggled against him. 'Do I really have to show you?'

He smiled. Her voice was persuasive and ever so seductive. 'It might be rather interesting,' he said, covering her mouth with his own.

Here is a sneak preview of
A STONE CREEK CHRISTMAS,
the latest in Linda Lael Miller's acclaimed
McKETTRICK *series.*

A lonely horse brought vet Olivia O'Ballivan to Tanner
Quinn's farm, but it's the rancher's love that might cause
her to stay.

A STONE CREEK CHRISTMAS
Available December 2008
from Silhouette Special Edition

Tanner heard the rig roll in around sunset. Smiling, he wandered to the window. Watched as Olivia O'Ballivan climbed out of her Suburban, flung one defiant glance toward the house and started for the barn, the golden retriever trotting along behind her.

Taking his coat and hat down from the peg next to the back door, he put them on and went outside. He was used to being alone, even liked it, but keeping company with Doc O'Ballivan, bristly though she sometimes was, would provide a welcome diversion.

He gave her time to reach the horse Butterpie's stall, then walked into the barn.

The golden retriever came to greet him, all wagging tail and melting brown eyes, and he bent to stroke her soft, sturdy back. "Hey, there, dog," he said.

Sure enough, Olivia was in the stall, brushing Butterpie down and talking to her in a soft, soothing voice that touched something private inside Tanner and made him want to turn on one heel and beat it back to the house.

He'd be damned if he'd do it, though.

This was *his* ranch, *his* barn. Well-intentioned as she was, *Olivia* was the trespasser here, not him.

"She's still very upset," Olivia told him, without turning to look at him or slowing down with the brush.

Shiloh, always an easy horse to get along with, stood contentedly in his own stall, munching away on the feed Tanner had given him earlier. Butterpie, he noted, hadn't touched her supper as far as he could tell.

"Do you know anything at all about horses, Mr. Quinn?" Olivia asked.

He leaned against the stall door, the way he had the day before, and grinned. He'd practically been raised on horseback; he and Tessa had grown up on their grandmother's farm in the Texas hill country, after their folks divorced and went their separate ways, both of them too busy to bother with a couple of kids. "A few things," he said. "And I mean to call you Olivia, so you might as well return the favor and address me by my first name."

He watched as she took that in, dealt with it, decided on an approach. He'd have to wait and see what that turned out to be, but he didn't mind. It was a pleasure just watching Olivia O'Ballivan grooming a horse.

"All right, *Tanner*," she said. "This barn is a disgrace. When are you going to have the roof fixed? If it snows again, the hay will get wet and probably mold…"

He chuckled, shifted a little. He'd have a crew out there the following Monday morning to replace the roof and shore up the walls—he'd made the arrangements over a week before—but he felt no particular compunction to explain that. He was enjoying her ire too much; it made her color rise and her hair fly when she turned her head, and the faster breathing made her perfect breasts go up and down in an enticing rhythm. "What makes you so sure I'm a greenhorn?" he asked mildly, still leaning on the gate.

At last she looked straight at him, but she didn't move from

Butterpie's side. "Your hat, your boots—that fancy red truck you drive. I'll bet it's customized."

Tanner grinned. Adjusted his hat. "Are you telling me real cowboys don't drive red trucks?"

"There are lots of trucks around here," she said. "Some of them are red, and some of them are new. And *all* of them are splattered with mud or manure or both."

"Maybe I ought to put in a car wash, then," he teased. "Sounds like there's a market for one. Might be a good investment."

She softened, though not significantly, and spared him a cautious half smile, full of questions she probably wouldn't ask. "There's a good car wash in Indian Rock," she informed him. "People go there. It's only forty miles."

"Oh," he said with just a hint of mockery. "*Only* forty miles. Well, then. Guess I'd better dirty up my truck if I want to be taken seriously in these here parts. Scuff up my boots a bit, too, and maybe stomp on my hat a couple of times."

Her cheeks went a fetching shade of pink. "You are twisting what I said," she told him, brushing Butterpie again, her touch gentle but sure. "I meant…"

Tanner envied that little horse. Wished he had a furry hide, so he'd need brushing, too.

"You *meant* that I'm not a real cowboy," he said. "And you could be right. I've spent a lot of time on construction sites over the last few years, or in meetings where a hat and boots wouldn't be appropriate. Instead of digging out my old gear, once I decided to take this job, I just bought new."

"I bet you don't even *have* any old gear," she challenged, but she was smiling, albeit cautiously, as though she might withdraw into a disapproving frown at any second.

He took off his hat, extended it to her. "Here," he teased. "Rub that around in the muck until it suits you."

She laughed, and the sound—well, it caused a powerful and wholly unexpected shift inside him. Scared the hell out of him and, paradoxically, made him yearn to hear it again.

* * * * *

*Discover how this rugged rancher's wanderlust is tamed
in time for a merry Christmas, in
A STONE CREEK CHRISTMAS.
In stores December 2008.*

HARLEQUIN®
INTRIGUE®

BREATHTAKING ROMANTIC SUSPENSE

Shared dangers and passions lead to electrifying romance and heart-stopping suspense!

Every month, you'll meet six new heroes who are guaranteed to make your spine tingle and your pulse pound. With them you'll enter into the exciting world of Harlequin Intrigue— where your life is on the line and so is your heart!

THAT'S INTRIGUE—
ROMANTIC SUSPENSE
AT ITS BEST!

HARLEQUIN®
Live the emotion™

HARLEQUIN®

Super Romance®

...there's more to the story!

Superromance.
A *big* satisfying read about unforgettable
characters. Each month we offer *six* very different
stories that range from family drama to adventure
and mystery, from highly emotional stories to
romantic comedies—and much more! Stories
about people you'll believe in and care about.
Stories too compelling to put down....

Our authors are among today's *best* romance
writers. You'll find familiar names and talented
newcomers. Many of them are award winners—
and you'll see why!

If you want the biggest and best
in romance fiction, you'll get it
from Superromance!

Exciting, Emotional, Unexpected...

HARLEQUIN®
Live the emotion™

HARLEQUIN®
Presents

The world's bestselling romance series...
The series that brings you your favorite authors,
month after month:

Helen Bianchin...Emma Darcy
Lynne Graham...Penny Jordan
Miranda Lee...Sandra Marton
Anne Mather...Carole Mortimer
Melanie Milburne...Michelle Reid

and many more talented authors!

Wealthy, powerful, gorgeous men...
Women who have feelings just like your own...
The stories you love, set in exotic, glamorous locations...

HARLEQUIN®
Presents

Seduction and Passion Guaranteed!

HPDIR08

www.eHarlequin.com

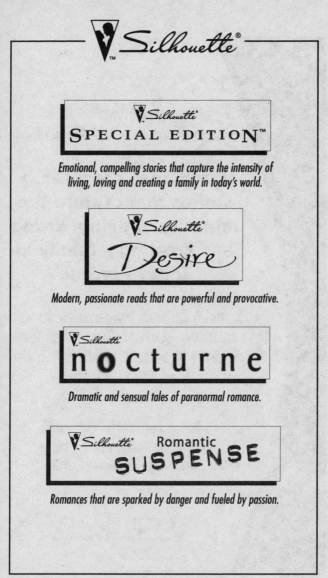

Silhouette®

SPECIAL EDITION™

Emotional, compelling stories that capture the intensity of living, loving and creating a family in today's world.

Silhouette® Desire

Modern, passionate reads that are powerful and provocative.

Silhouette® nocturne

Dramatic and sensual tales of paranormal romance.

Silhouette® Romantic SUSPENSE

Romances that are sparked by danger and fueled by passion.

SDIR07